THE WAY LIES NORTH

THE WAY LIES NORTH

JEAN RAE BAXTER

RONSDALE PRESS

THE WAY LIES NORTH
Copyright © 2007 Jean Rae Baxter

RONSDALE PRESS
3350 West 21st Avenue, Vancouver, B.C., Canada V6S 1G7
www.ronsdalepress.com

Typesetting: Julie Cochrane, in Minion 12 pt on 16
Front Cover Art: Ljuba Levstek
Cover Design: Julie Cochrane
Paper: Ancient Forest Friendly "Silva" — 100% post-consumer waste,
    totally chlorine-free and acid-free

Ronsdale Press wishes to thank the Canada Council for the Arts, the Government of Canada through the Book Publishing Industry Development Program (BPIDP), and the Province of British Columbia through the British Columbia Arts Council for their support of its publishing program.

Library and Archives Canada Cataloguing in Publication

Baxter, Jean Rae, 1932–
    The way lies north / Jean Rae Baxter.

ISBN 978-1-55380-048-4

    1. United Empire loyalists--Juvenile fiction. 2. Mohawk Indians--Juvenile fiction. I. Title.

PS8603.A935W39 2007   jC813'.6   C2007-902434-3

At Ronsdale Press we are committed to protecting the environment. To this end we are working with Markets Initiative (www.oldgrowthfree.com) and printers to phase out our use of paper produced from ancient forests. This book is one step towards that goal.

Printed in Canada by Marquis Printing, Quebec

For
Elizabeth and Peter
Alison and Marc
John and Anne

ACKNOWLEDGEMENTS

It was the late Dr. Shirley Spragge, then Chief Archivist of Queen's University, who introduced me to such historical figures as the Reverend John Stuart, Sir William Johnson and Molly Brant. With Shirley as guide and learned commentator, I visited the Mohawk Valley and saw the places where these people had lived, and which they lost in consequence of choosing the Loyalist side in the American War of Independence. If in this novel I have succeeded in creating a sense of place and time, I owe that to Shirley.

The fictitious characters in this book came into being when Ronsdale Press proposed an anthology, *Beginnings: Stories of Canada's Past* (2001) and invited submissions. I am grateful to Ronsdale Press for including my short story, "Farewell the Mohawk Valley," and to the editor, Ann Walsh, for her keen eye and helpful suggestions. "Farewell the Mohawk Valley" became, in an altered form, the opening chapter of *The Way Lies North*. I would also like to thank Ronald B. Hatch for his editing. Whenever I was the slightest bit unclear in my thinking or presentation, he helped me to clarify it. His literary sense and deft editorial touch kept me from countless errors of commission.

To Chris Pannell and the other members of Hamilton's New Writing Workshop, my heartfelt thanks. Special thanks also to Linda Helson, Barbara Ledger, and Debbie Welland of the Creative Writing Group of the Canadian Federation of University Women, Hamilton Branch, for their insightful suggestions. To Karen Baxter, Alison Baxter Lean and Janet Myers, who read the original manuscript of this novel with tough and generous criticism, my abiding gratitude.

Prologue

May 1777

The trees were coming into leaf, and from the valley a warm breeze wafted the scent of blossoms and wild honey. Charlotte and Nick sat side by side, yet not touching, under the sycamore tree at the edge of the ravine.

"We've had word from my brothers," Charlotte said. "They're all in the same battalion. Isaac writes——"

"Stop! Don't tell me about it. I hate this war." Nick was staring across the ravine to the hills on the far side. His jaw was clenched. He'd been moody like this for months. She wanted to reach out her hand to brush back the lock of blond hair that fell across his brow, but a sense of hard separateness prevented her.

"We have to fight for what we believe in," she said.

"Why?"

"Because duty matters. I would fight if I were a man."

"Thank God you're not."

A hopeless feeling came over her because Nick was a Whig and she was a Tory. He loved her, and she loved him, but that seemed to matter less and less.

And yet — God be thanked — Nick had not joined a Rebel regiment. She thought about it all the time: Nick in a blue uniform and her three brothers in red, bayonets drawn, advancing toward each other in battle lines. With every prayer for the safety of James, Charlie and Isaac, she also prayed that Nick would not take up arms on the Rebel side.

Nick spoke suddenly. "My father thinks I'm a coward. He said so when I told him that I don't believe in war. He said that if I were a real man, I'd want to fight." A bitter laugh. "That's what you think too, isn't it?"

"I never said so."

"You said that you would fight if you were a man."

"I said we have to fight for what we believe in."

"So you think I should kill another human being because I want to live in a republic and he doesn't? Charlotte, I don't think war is glorious or heroic. I cheered for those fellows who dumped the tea into Boston harbour. Yet I can't understand why your brothers are ready to kill or be killed for mad King George, who doesn't give two hoots for any of us even when he isn't stark out of his mind."

"My brothers aren't like you. To them, war is an adventure." For a moment Charlotte felt uncomfortable, almost ashamed.

"Some adventure! Neighbours burn each other out. Fathers and sons become enemies. Lovers are divided."

"Are you divided from me?" Birds were singing, but a silence fell upon her heart.

"That's how it feels."

They stood up at the same moment, staring at each other. This was the closest they had ever come to a quarrel. Nick looked away first. He placed his fingers upon the heart that he had carved one year ago in the smooth bark of the sycamore tree, with their initials C.H. and N.S. entwined.

"Remember this," he said.

When she saw the sadness in his eyes, she could not bear it.

"I must go," she said. Straightening her shoulders, she turned and walked away.

"I'll always love you, Charlotte." His voice followed her along the path. She did not look back.

Chapter one

"Why is your father galloping off down the road with supper almost ready?" Mama exclaimed as she turned from the window.

"He has to see Mr. Herkimer about something," Charlotte answered.

"He's trying to sell the livestock, isn't he?"

Charlotte looked away. "We have to leave, so he might as well try to get something for the animals."

"I told him I'm not leaving this house." Mama stood firm, her arms crossed. "Until Isaac comes home, this is where I stay." She looked determined, but her lower lip trembled just the same.

"Papa says the Rebels are going to drive us out."

"Not me."

Straightening her narrow shoulders, Mama marched from the window across the kitchen to the open fireplace, grasped the crank that rotated the roasting pig on the spit, and turned it. Dripping fat sizzled in the flames

"We'll wait supper till your father gets back," she said.

The platter of fresh bread was already on the table, and the pot of turnips ready to be mashed sat on the hob. Mama had the table set with three places. Papa's place was at the head, with Charlotte's on his left and Mama's on his right. The other end of the long wooden table looked empty without places set for Charlotte's brothers. The room, too, felt empty without them there, joking and whistling and shoving each other around.

"Papa won't be long. Maybe an hour." Charlotte figured that Mr. Herkimer wouldn't take more than a minute to refuse him. "While we wait, I'll let the cows into the barn."

She lifted the latch and hurried out the kitchen door. It was not yet dark, although the sun had set. Papa had five miles to ride, then five miles back. The moon would be up before he reached home. Charlotte smelled frost in the air.

In the barnyard, the ten cows stood in a huddle, steam rising from their warm flanks. Charlotte grabbed the collar of Daisy, the lead cow, and led her into the barn. Cowbells jangling, the others followed. Charlotte forked hay into their mangers before leaving the barn.

After closing the barn door, she glanced toward the house. Mama was standing at the window again. She looked as if she was marked off into little squares by the panes of window glass. With the light of the fire behind her, her hair was the colour of flame.

When Charlotte returned to the house, Mama was still watching out the window. Charlotte pulled off her boots — work boots that had belonged to her brother Charlie — and padded across the kitchen floor to the bottom of the staircase. She wanted to go up to her bedroom. There was still time, before Papa came home, to brush her hair and change her gown for one that didn't have cow dung on the skirt. As Charlotte set her foot on the first tread, Mama turned from the window.

"Charlotte?" Her voice was low, almost a whisper. "You do believe that Isaac is . . . alive?"

"Of course I do. They didn't find his body on the battle-field."

"But you don't think he'll come home, do you?"

"Oh, Mama!" Charlotte turned back and walked up to her mother. "He may have been captured. You heard the same report I did, how James and Charlie died at Saratoga, but there was no trace of Isaac. You heard how the Rebels marched their prisoners off to Boston. If Isaac was among them, he'll be there until the end of the war."

"But he may have escaped," Mama insisted. "We were told that those Indians who had been helping the British simply melted into the forest. Isaac could have escaped with them."

"Mama, that's what I hope too. But General Burgoyne surrendered a week ago, and it's only a three-day journey from Saratoga, even through the bush. Isaac would be here by now, if he were coming home."

"He might be hiding . . . or wounded." Tears brimmed in Mama's eyes.

Charlotte gathered her mother into her arms. There was nothing more she could say, so she said nothing. Mama might be right. This very night there might be a rap at the door, and Mama would rush to let him in, for she slept downstairs now, in constant readiness for Isaac's return.

"Mama, all we can do is pray."

Charlotte's mother pulled gently away. "I know that God will hear our prayer." She rubbed her eyes with the corner of her apron. "Now you go change your gown, while I mash the turnips."

What chance was there, Charlotte thought as she climbed the stairs, of Isaac returning before the family left their home? They had to leave, and soon. It was no longer safe for Loyalists to remain in the Mohawk Valley.

Charlotte put on her grey gown, the one with lace at the throat, and tied the strings of a clean white apron around her waist. She brushed her black, unruly hair and twisted it into a knot at the nape of her neck, and settled her white, ruffled cap onto her head. Over her shoulders she draped her deep red woollen shawl. Inspecting her reflection in the looking glass that hung above her washstand, Charlotte considered that she looked quite fetching, for a girl who had spent most of the day mucking out a barn.

Charlotte had a bedroom to herself because she was the only girl, although for the past year she had not lived a girl's life. With her brothers gone, she had to help bring in the hay, slaughter pigs and chop wood just like a man.

There was a framed hole in the floor of Charlotte's bedroom, as in all the bedrooms, to allow warmth to rise to the upper storey. Sound also rose, so nothing happening downstairs was secret from anyone upstairs.

She was still studying her reflection when she heard the snick of the door latch. Papa was home. As soon as the door closed, she heard her mother's voice.

"You sold Herkimer the livestock, didn't you?"

"I tried to." There was a long pause. "But he wasn't buying. Herkimer figures they'll soon be confiscated anyway. By waiting a bit, he can get our animals dirt cheap." Charlotte heard the thump of her father's boots on the floor, first one then the other, as he took them off.

"Martha, there's nothing we can do. We can't stay here any longer. The law won't protect us."

"Henry, I don't want to leave."

"I know, dearest, but we must."

"How will Isaac find us if we're gone when he comes back?"

"He'll find us. We'll go north to one of the British forts. Isaac will seek us there. He's a sensible young man. If we aren't with the refugees at one fort, he'll try another. Never fear."

"Henry, please. Can't we wait just a few more days?"

Papa hesitated. "We leave the day after tomorrow."

Charlotte listened as she walked slowly down the stairs. When she reached the bottom, she saw that her mother's face was turned away.

Papa hardly noticed Charlotte entering the room, though he usually looked at her with a smile when she appeared with her hair dressed, wearing a fresh gown. He did not like to see her skirts trailing in the mud or stained with barnyard manure. But when all three boys went off in the same week to join the New York Royal Rangers, it was Papa who had said, "Well, Charlotte, I reckon you'll have to put away your knitting and help me run the farm."

Charlotte had not complained. At fifteen, she knew her duty and was proud to do it. She was strong and tall — her father's child, with the same big frame, brown eyes and black, curly hair (though Henry's was grizzled now). Solid as a rock, people said.

In no point of appearance did Charlotte resemble her brothers. Most people found it difficult to tell one Hooper brother from another, though the three, taken together, with their flaming red hair and freckled skin, looked different from anyone else in the Mohawk Valley — except their mother. They had the same hair, the same lightly built frame. They were Martha's boys, flesh and bone, body and soul.

The boys were all fire and air — quick to ignite and fast to burn. They had taken the King's shilling before the ink was dry on the Declaration of Independence, never stopping to think how Papa would manage with all of them gone. But how dashing they had looked in their new uniforms! They had strutted about in their red jackets with the blue lapels and the black feather in their caps. Charlotte had hugged her handsome brothers and wondered whether she would ever see them again.

The boys had always been Charlotte's heroes. They had seemed so exciting when she was still a little girl. She remembered how they used to arrive home from the village schoolhouse, bold, boisterous and carefree, bursting in like a whirlwind — all fists and freckles, shouts and rude jokes — while she, too young for school, sat playing with her doll in the chimney corner. James and Charlie had paid her little attention, beyond a smile. But Isaac, the youngest, had taught her how to roll a hoop and play jacks.

As the family ate supper, Papa had more news to relate. "On my way to Herkimer's farm, I passed by the church in Fort Hunter. There was singing and shouting inside that did not sound like a joyful noise unto the Lord. I stopped my horse and went to the door. My dears, they have turned our church into a tavern. The scoundrels had a barrel of rum set upon the reading desk. I looked, then rode away."

"You were lucky they didn't stop you," said Charlotte. "There's no telling what they might have done."

"Reverend Stuart has angered every Whig in the valley," said Mama. "He preaches loyalty to the Crown and never omits prayers for the King. Now it seems that he has lost his church. I wonder what will happen to him and his family."

"They'll not come to harm," said Papa. "John Stuart is respected by people in high places. But plain folks like us are not safe. We should have left a year ago when Sir John Johnson asked us to join his group of Loyalists. We would all be in Montreal by now."

"Not the boys," said Mama.

"No. Not the boys. They were bound to go for soldiers. Not even you could have stopped them, Martha."

"I wouldn't have tried."

"What are we going to do?" Charlotte asked. "Will you try to sell the animals in town?"

"No, daughter. Forget about the animals. We'll put them out in the pasture and leave them there. While I was riding back from Herkimer's place, I thought it over. We must go while we can. But first I want you and your mother to do some sewing."

"Sewing?" Charlotte asked.

"Yes. Tomorrow, take whatever money we have in the house, and your rings and brooches, and any other small things that are valuable, and stitch them into your petticoats.

"I have a strongbox for our papers and our family Bible, and a piece of canvas to wrap the silver tea set my parents brought from England. I'll bury everything down by the rock pile the boys made when we cleared the back acre for potatoes. Anyone going by will think I'm just spading the last of the potatoes. After the war is over, Isaac and I will come back to dig up the box and the silver. Even if we lose the farm, we'll find a way to recover things buried in the earth."

The next day was blustery, with cold rain lashing the windows. Charlotte laid a fire in the parlour so that she and Mama would be warm while they sewed. After moving the big family Bible from the parlor table to clear some space, she pulled up two chairs.

Charlotte and her mother each took two petticoats and, placing one inside the other, quilted them together. Coins and pound notes, rings, brooches and buckles, silver spoons, Papa's gold watch and chain — all were stitched into place between the two layers of fabric. There was a silver locket too, which Nick had given her months ago, before "Tory" meant Loyalist and friend, and "Whig" meant Rebel and foe.

Through the long, rainy morning Charlotte and her mother sewed. From time to time Charlotte stood up and, holding the double petticoat by its waistband, tested the weight. Finally she said, "This is enough. I shan't be able to walk if my petticoats are weighted with one more thing."

Mama went to the window. She looked out over the orchard and the pasture, all the way to the dark forest beyond. She's thinking about Isaac, Charlotte supposed. She's wondering if he is out there in the bush, trying to make his way home.

Charlotte took her mother's arm and gently drew her away from the window. "He'll find us, Mama, wherever we go."

Mama shook her head. Without a word, she put her thimble, her pincushion and her spools of thread back into her sewing box.

While Charlotte and Mama were sewing, Papa had buried his strongbox and the silver. Then he came back to the house and changed his clothes.

"I'm going to call on Reverend Stuart," he said. "I hope he'll want to buy my horse."

Papa was gone the rest of the day. When he returned, he was on foot. He took a handful of coins from his pocket.

"Three guineas," he said. "That's a fair price. And see what else he gave me." From another pocket he drew out a folded sheet of paper. "A map."

Papa spread it on the table. It was crudely hand-drawn — more a sketch than a map. Charlotte and her mother stood beside him as he traced the route that they would follow. Here was their home. There, the Mohawk River with its western branch leading towards Oneida Lake. They must cross Oneida Lake and then follow the Oswego River to its mouth. He rested his finger on the spot where Lake Ontario flows into the St. Lawrence River. "Carleton Island lies here. It is well fortified, with a strong garrison and good provision for refugees. We shall stay the winter there."

"There are no towns along the way!" exclaimed Mama. "Only wilderness!"

"Martha, do you think it would be safer for us to go through towns? The Sons of Liberty are everywhere. You don't know the things they have done to Loyalists in the last few months. Men tarred and feathered. Women subjected to the most terrible, unspeakable insult."

Charlotte knew what that meant. In 1777 a Loyalist girl was fair game for any Liberty man. She didn't want to think about that. Yet if they had to make their way through the woods, there would be other problems. "How can Mama and I walk through the bush in long gowns?" she asked.

"We'll follow Indian trails," he said. "One of Reverend Stuart's Mohawk friends marked them on this map. When we reach Oneida Lake, Mohawk guides will meet us with a long canoe. They'll take us the rest of the way. It is all arranged."

Mama clasped her hands together. She looked up at Papa. "Henry, wait a little longer. Three or four days cannot make much difference. Isaac may still come home."

Charlotte wanted to cover her ears. She could not bear to hear those words one more time. They broke her heart.

We might as well go, she thought. Canada couldn't be

worse than this. Here we are prisoners in our own home, surrounded by enemies who only two years ago were our friends.

Papa took Mama's hands and held them in his own. "We're ready now. In ten days the Mohawks will be at Oneida Lake waiting for us. We must leave tomorrow."

When Charlotte woke the next morning, the room was still dark. She snuggled deep into the feather mattress and pulled the warm quilts over her head. How long would it be before she slept in a bed again? She thought about Nick and wondered how often he thought about her. Once there had been sweet kisses. She remembered the first time he had said, "I love you." That was the day he had carved their initials into the bark of the sycamore tree.

She could hear Mama already busy downstairs. The aroma of frying bacon rose through the framed hole in the floor. It was time to get up, time for the day of departure to begin.

When Charlotte came down the stairs, Papa had already settled himself to the table. Mama was serving up a feast. There was sweet corn mush, rashers of bacon, fried eggs, bread slathered with butter and strawberry jam.

Papa looked up from his plate. "Eat your fill, daughter. This is the last good meal we'll have for a long time."

After breakfast, as Papa pushed his chair away from the table, he said, "Charlotte, I want you to take the cattle out to the pasture. Don't fodder them. They'll manage on grass till somebody notices we've left them there."

With a willow switch in her hand, Charlotte drove the cows along the path through the orchard, between two rows of apple trees. The grass was wet, although the rain had stopped. Charlotte walked slowly, letting the cattle pick up windfalls on their way. She pushed open the pasture gate and then flicked Daisy's rump with her switch to get the herd moving inside.

At that instant, she heard the crack of a rifle from the direction of the ravine. She froze, the switch still raised in her hand. Who was there? A hunter? A soldier? A Liberty man? She looked back toward the house to see whether her father was coming. She waited, but he did not appear. Should she fetch him? Maybe Papa had not heard the shot. He was in the house packing his rucksack, with the windows closed, and his hearing was not keen.

Somebody had to investigate. If she went back to the house to ask Papa to go with her, Mama would think of Isaac and take alarm. I reckon I'd better go alone, Charlotte thought. It's up to me.

She passed the rock pile, where spade marks and boot marks were still visible in the soft soil. She climbed over the snake fence and struck into the woods, picking up the familiar path that led to the great sycamore on the crest of the ravine. When she reached it, she stood listening. She heard no sound of men in the forest below. The only noise was the screech of a jay.

On the sycamore tree was the heart that Nick had carved

in the grey bark, with their initials C.H. and N.S. entwined. Dearest Nick. She would never sit with him again under this tree, looking out over the lovely valley.

Below, down the steep slope, were cedars and hemlocks, white birches and dark pines. At the bottom of the ravine a little brown snake of a creek wound its way. Under the overcast sky, everything was shadowed and dim.

Then she saw the splash of red among the trees below. It looked like a daub of scarlet paint, brighter than blood.

Charlotte could not take her eyes from the red. Fear stopped her breath. She stood with her back braced against the sycamore, her open palms pressed against the smooth bark. Then, slowly, her legs began to move, and she scrambled down the steep slope faster and faster, grasping at roots, stems, branches.

Trees hid the red from her sight; then she saw it again. Near the bottom she ran and fell, then ran again. She pushed through bushes, brambles catching at her clothes and twigs at her hair. At the edge of the tree line she paused, too afraid for a moment to face what might lie ahead. She had to force herself to take the last few steps.

When she entered the clearing there was no sound, no motion — only the body of a soldier sprawled with one arm flung out on the carpet of pine needles and damp leaves. Above the scarlet coat was her brother's pale, freckled face, and on his face an expression of faint surprise. His hair was soaked with blood. Charlotte knelt beside him and touched his cheek. It was not yet cold. With her fingertips she separated the sticky strands of his matted hair and saw the small, round hole where the bullet had entered. Then she closed his eyes.

Anguish welled up inside her. She could not stop it, did not try to stop it. She took Isaac's limp hand in hers and sobbed. So close, she thought. Home was so close. Dear Isaac, you almost made it back.

What a fine target his red coat must have been for any Rebel skulking in these woods! A cold feeling ran through her. One of our neighbours killed him, she thought. Someone we know took Isaac's life. Tears of grief and despair and rage ran down her cheeks. Charlotte stood up. Still looking at Isaac, she slowly backed away and returned to the shelter of the trees. Once there, she looked around, half expecting to see a shadowy figure disappear behind a tree. But no evidence of the rifleman remained, apart from Isaac's body on the forest floor.

Her eyes were almost blinded with tears as she struggled up the hill. How could she tell Mama and Papa? What words could she say? She could think of none. Charlotte climbed over the snake fence and trudged across the fields to the farmhouse. She paused in front of the door, then pressed the latch and went in.

Mama turned pale when she saw Charlotte's face. "What happened to you?" Her voice trembled. Papa said nothing. His eyes met Charlotte's above Mama's head.

Charlotte opened her mouth. "Isaac," she said. "I found him." No further words would come, only the sobbing that she could not control.

Reaching out her arms, she ran to Mama and Papa from across the room. They clung to one another, all three weeping. Mama was shaking so hard that she might have fallen to the floor if Charlotte and Papa had not held her tightly.

They went together to the ravine. Papa carried Isaac home across his shoulders. He dug a grave for him in the orchard. Mama brought her best quilt to wrap his body. Charlotte nailed two sticks together to make a cross. Then they went back to the house.

"I'm ready to leave now," Mama said. "Isaac has come home."

Chapter two

⁂

Moonlight filtering through a veil of cloud transformed the forest, making it strange and hostile.
Overhead, bare branches tossed in the wind. On a night like
this, it was easy to imagine a man with a gun hiding behind
every tree.

"I'm not afraid," Charlotte told herself again and again.

But there was plenty to fear. The Sons of Liberty could be
anywhere: coming after them on the path, lurking in the
undergrowth, waiting in ambush around the next bend.

Papa led the way. On his back was the rucksack contain-
ing their supplies, with the camp kettle tied on top. Mama
came next, then Charlotte.

They had been walking for hours — Charlotte had no idea how long — and her whole body felt heavy with tiredness. Her very clothes weighed her down: her thick wool shawl under her cloak, two gowns, three petticoats (including the two that held her share of the family's portable wealth), three chemises, three pairs of underdrawers and three of stockings. On her feet were Charlie's old boots. With every step an ache came up through the earth into the heel of her foot.

Gradually the eastern sky lightened. Bushes took on definite shapes, shadows retreated from between the trees, and through rising mist Charlotte saw the gleam of water.

Papa halted and pulled out the map that Reverend Stuart had given him. He held it close to his eyes to study it in the dim light. "There should be a duck blind around here. It might be a good place to stop for a rest."

Charlotte stood on the riverbank and peered around. In the lea of a bend, the water had spread to form a pool. At the edge was a palisade of poles. "I think it's just ahead," she said.

The duck blind was a fence of roughly trimmed saplings with their ends buried in the earth. As soon as they reached the blind, Charlotte sank gratefully to the ground. When she leaned back, the poles felt bumpy but solid. "Ah!" she sighed, glad to have something to rest against.

"We can't stay long," said Papa. "Duck hunters may come along. We don't want men with guns to find us here." He took the canteen from his belt, undid the stopper, and passed it to Mama. "Just a sip of brandy to revive you."

"Not for me." She gave it back.

Papa handed the canteen to Charlotte.

She sniffed the fumes. Sweet and fiery, they tickled her nose. If brandy tasted as good as it smelled, she certainly would like to try it. Charlotte tilted the canteen. But before she had tasted a drop, Mama's protest reached her ears.

"Henry! She's too young."

"A nip does no harm on a cold night."

"No!"

Charlotte frowned as she gave back the canteen. Too young — when for a year she'd been doing a woman's work, and a man's work too!

Papa took a sip, stoppered the canteen and put it back on his belt.

A blue jay screamed, breaking the silence. Nothing remained of the shadows of the night. The jay called again. Then there was another sound. From far behind them on the trail came men's voices.

"Listen," Charlotte whispered.

"I hear nothing," said Papa.

Mama turned her head in the direction of the sound. "I do."

After a moment, Papa heard them. "Damnation!" he muttered. "We've stayed too long." He stood up and hoisted his rucksack onto his back.

As Charlotte scrambled to her feet, a branch stub on one of the poles hooked the hem of her gown where it hung below her cloak. With a tug, she jerked it free and followed her parents back to the trail.

They headed west, away from the river, pushing their way through heavy brush along an overgrown track. Wild grape vines festooned the trees, their withered leaves rattling in the wind. Gnarled roots crossed the path. Charlotte stepped carefully, holding her skirts in a bundle against her stomach to keep them from catching on the bushes that crowded in upon the trail. Soon she could no longer hear the men's voices.

At a fork in the path, Papa pulled out the map. He pointed to the right. "In a mile or so we'll come to a hut that Iroquois hunters use for shelter. We can rest there."

A hut in this dense forest? A bear's den or wolf's lair was more likely. But the map was right. About one mile further on, the trees parted and there it was: a bark-covered hut beside a stream. The bark was weathered, green with moss and scabbed with lichen. All around were the tumbled remains of other huts, decaying slabs of bark and broken poles sticking up through the grass.

"Long ago, this was a Huron village," said Papa, "or so I was told."

"I wonder why this hut didn't fall down like the others," said Charlotte.

"I reckon it's worth the hunters' efforts to keep it in repair."

Mama hung back. "Henry, it will be full of spiders."

Charlotte expected this. Mama's fear of spiders was well

known. "If it is, I'll get rid of them." Stooping, she entered the hut and looked around.

Despite the smell of humus and slow decay, the hut was in good shape — better than appeared from the outside. The roof was tight, its bark slabs lashed to a framework of poles.

Mama was right about the spiders. They were everywhere. Stretched between the poles, their webs looked like fine lace in the morning light that poured through the open entry. Charlotte swatted down the webs with her hands and stamped on the fleeing spiders. As she wiped the spider silk from her cheeks and pulled it from her hair, she called out, "It's safe now."

Papa led Mama into the hut, took off his greatcoat and spread it on the ground. He gently took her arm and helped her to lie down. With a sigh, Mama closed her eyes. Freed from her bonnet, her hair fanned out like tongues of flame upon the dark wool. How delicate she looked! The translucence of her skin, the blue veins traced upon her temples, the dark shadows under her eyes — all were exposed in the morning light. Mama breathed softly. She was soon asleep.

Charlotte pulled out her shawl from inside her cloak, folded it to make a pillow, and lay down. The ground was hard. Worse still, all those spoons and things quilted into her petticoats made it impossible to get comfortable. Whichever way she turned, something lumpy was underneath. After lying in various positions, she found that flat on her back was best. Fortunately, a thick layer of New York pound notes in the back of her petticoats provided a bit of padding between her bottom and the ground.

Even after she had made herself relatively comfortable, sleep did not come easily. When she closed her eyes, she saw Isaac's body on the forest floor. There was a hot, sore lump in Charlotte's throat when she fell asleep. And then she dreamed.

She was back in the farmhouse kitchen. Charlie and James were playing cards at the long table in front of the fire. They wore work clothes, as if they had just come in from the fields. There was no sound as they slapped the cards down. Their mouths laughed noiselessly.

Suddenly Isaac was there too, wearing the scarlet coat of his regiment. Where had he come from? Not through the door. How had he got into the room? Isaac stood watching his brothers, who played on as if he were not there. Charlotte called out voicelessly to warn Isaac of danger. He looked straight at her, his shoulders thrown back, his eyes furious. His mouth opened and his lips moved in a silent shout. What had she done to anger him so? What was the word that his lips hurled at her? He shouted again, and this time she heard the word, "Traitor!"

"Traitor!"

That wasn't Isaac's voice. Charlotte opened her eyes. A man was standing over Papa with his musket pointed at Papa's chest.

"Trapped like rats in a barrel! Three loyal subjects of the King."

"Be damned!" said Papa.

The hut was crowded with men. One was staring at Charlotte. He was a young man, heavy set, with sloping shoulders and a bull neck. From his fingers dangled a scrap of dark blue ribbon.

"Here's the lady we been looking for." His voice was harsh and too high for a man. "Madam, we found something of yours. Reckon you'd like to have it back." With a laugh he tossed the scrap of ribbon onto her face.

Yes, it was hers: a bit of trim that must have torn off when she snagged her gown in the duck blind.

"Get up!" The man hauled her to her feet.

Papa shouted, "Keep your hands off my daughter!" Charlotte heard a thud. Mama screamed.

The bull-necked man dragged Charlotte from the hut and threw her to the ground. For a few moments he stood prodding her with his foot, as if uncertain what to do next. Two young men came from the hut and joined him. One was tall and scrawny with a sparse beard that gave his cheeks and chin the look of a badly plucked chicken. The other was short and square.

"Look what I got here," said the bull-necked man.

"A nice bit of sport," said the tall one. The short man laughed but said nothing.

She knew that she had seen them before. But where?

After a moment, she remembered. It was in Johnstown on market days, where they used to hang around in front of the tavern, whistling at women and making lewd remarks.

Charlotte's stomach twisted with fear, but she refused to show it. She sat up and smoothed her skirt over her knees. "You'll pay for this," she said, ignoring their stupid grins. "You have no right to abuse loyal citizens."

"Who's going to stop us?" the tall man sneered. "Will Georgie Porgie send his redcoats to shoot us?"

The short man stopped laughing. "Boys," he said, "you know who this is? She's Nick Schyler's sweetheart."

"Why, so she is," said the tall man. "Nick's Tory sweetheart! Well then, I reckon she wants to send him a kiss." He held out his arms, puckered his lips, and noisily kissed the air. "I'll see that he gets it."

"No!" She jumped to her feet. "Don't you dare touch me!"

As he reached for her, she turned her head away. But then he gripped her face with both hands and pressed his mouth against hers. Charlotte clamped her lips together.

"That's not much of a kiss. You can do better. Nick told us you're a right handy kisser. Didn't he, boys?"

"Nick sure did," sniggered the bull-necked man. "Let me have a turn."

"Ben, I never thought you'd kiss a Tory wench."

"Never did before. Most are too ugly. But this one's not bad." He grabbed her by the shoulders. "Come on! Give me a kiss." He had a fleshy mouth and little blue eyes like a pig's. When he pulled her to him, she spat in his face.

"Damn you," he snarled.

The tall man snorted. "I reckon she's too wild for you to handle."

"I like them wild." Ben thrust his knee hard between Charlotte's legs and toppled her backwards. Then he was sitting on her, a leg on each side. He had her shoulders pinned to the ground.

Now what? Her feet were free, but she didn't dare to kick. If she kicked, these Liberty men would see her petticoats and notice their strange, lumpy appearance. All she could do was beat her fists on the ground and scream.

The short man called out, "Boys, leave her alone."

"Not till I get that kiss."

"If Nick hears about this, he'll kill us."

"He won't care," the tall man laughed. "Nick wants nothing more to do with this girl."

Ben's face came closer. Piggy eyes. Sour breath. Bristly hairs in his wide nostrils. Charlotte was ready. At the touch of his lips, she bit with all her strength.

With a grunt, he let her go. Crouching on the ground, Ben held one hand over his mouth. Blood ran from between his fingers. "You cursed witch!"

Charlotte sat up. With shaking hands, she pulled her skirts right around her ankles. Thank God no one had noticed the petticoats!

An older man wearing a broad-brimmed hat emerged from the hut. "What's going on here?" His eyes narrowed. "Ben Warren," he said, "I want none of this."

Ben spat a mouthful of blood and picked himself up from the ground. The last two men came from the hut, the first with Papa's rifle, the other with his canteen.

"They got no money," said the one with the rifle. "This gun is the only thing worth taking."

"Before we leave," said the other, "we may as well finish the brandy." He took a swig, then passed Papa's canteen to the next man. The last to drink threw it into a bush.

"Wait," said Ben, who was still mopping blood from his chin, "Let's truss up this she-devil. Stick her in the hut with the others and make a bonfire of the lot."

"No," said the older man. "We've had too much swamp law already."

"Let them go," said the man holding Papa's rifle. "Good riddance. If they want to freeze in the snow up in Canada, why should we stop them?"

"When your Pa wakes up, tell him the Sons of Liberty thank him for the brandy," said the one who had taken the canteen. He turned to his friends. "Maybe we still got time to shoot some ducks."

Their boots crashed through the undergrowth as they left.

Charlotte pulled herself to her feet and entered the hut. Mama lay on her side, with her wrists tied behind her back and her ankles bound. Papa was sitting up, holding the side of his head. He looked up at Charlotte.

"Did they hurt you, my dear? Did those scoundrels do you harm?"

"Only a few bruises. I was lucky they didn't notice my petticoats."

She knelt down by Papa to inspect his wound. "There's some swelling, and a bit of blood."

He shook his head. "Fortunately, I have a thick skull."

"Thank God they did no worse," said Mama.

"Do you still have your knife?" Charlotte asked Papa.

He drew the knife from its sheath. "I'm surprised they left it. My hand axe too."

Charlotte cut the cords that tied Mama's wrists and ankles. Mama sat up and rubbed the red marks on her skin. "How can men act like that?" she said. "They called themselves Patriots and bragged about their crimes. Houses fired. Barns burned. Crops destroyed. Every evil committed under the sacred name of liberty!"

"Do you know who they were?" Papa asked. "I got knocked on the head before I recognized anybody."

"One was called Ben Warren. He was the worst. If the others had let him, he would have burned down the hut with us inside."

"Who were the others?"

"I've seen a few of them in Johnstown. Ben Warren was the only name I heard."

"Ben Warren," Papa repeated. "I'd like to get hold of him when I have a horsewhip in my hands."

"So would I," said Charlotte. "Just give me a chance."

Papa's rucksack was empty. Biscuits, apple slices, cakes of sugar, bowls, cups and spoons were scattered on the ground.

The big ham that would have to last all the way to Oneida Lake lay outside the hut's entrance. Mama picked it up.

"I'm glad the Sons of Liberty weren't hungry," she said as she brushed off leaves and twigs. "But I wish they had spared our tea. Those scoundrels dumped it out, looking for money in the bottom of the tin."

Tiny flakes of tea lay scattered on the hut's earth floor. "I'll see what I can do," Charlotte said. Crawling on hands and knees, she gathered the fragments into a bowl. When she had found all she could, she took the bowl outside where the light was better. Using her fingertips as pincers, she picked out bits of bark, twigs and leaves, wisps of web, and dozens of spider legs, heads and abdomens. "The tea may taste odd," she admitted.

Papa had already found his flint, steel and flax tinder, and he had a good fire blazing. When the water reached the boil in the camp kettle, Charlotte tossed in the tea.

"Our first day," she said as she waited for it to steep. "I hope the rest won't be like this."

"No guarantees," said Papa gruffly.

Charlotte poured the tea into the family's three tin cups.

Mama's eyes widened as she sipped. She peered into the cup. With a small shudder, she set it down and did not lift it to her lips again.

"The taste is unusual," said Papa, "but refreshing." He finished his.

Charlotte finished hers as well. Not to drink it would feel like defeat.

Chapter three

⁓

Charlotte ached all over. Her ribs, her shoulders, her neck, even her mouth felt sore. But nothing hurt more than the taunts of those Liberty men. "Nick told us you were a right handy kisser." "Nick won't care." "He wants nothing more to do with this girl." All lies. Nick would never say such things. So why did she feel so miserable when they couldn't be true?

I'll always love you, Charlotte, was the last thing he had said when they parted. She knew that he meant it. There was no falseness in Nick.

Since that day five months ago she had told herself a hundred times what she should have done. She should have run back and thrown her arms around him. She should have vowed to love him despite everything. If only she could live that day over again, that's what she would do.

Yet what difference would it make? Her brothers would still be dead. The British would still be losing. And she would still be on this long trail, a refugee heading north on a dark October day.

The forest felt dead and sodden. Rain was falling. It had been falling steadily for hours. Rain dripped from the trees. Drop. Drop. Drop. By late afternoon the trail was slick with mud.

They were walking down a slope when Papa fell. A sudden skid, and there he was — on his hands and knees, or rather on his hands and his left knee, for his right leg was stretched out behind him. Something had caught his foot.

"Damnation!" he muttered.

Charlotte knelt on the muddy path. She saw what had happened: when Papa slid, his foot had wedged under a tree root that snaked across the path.

"Don't try to move," she said. "I can get it out." Grasping Papa's boot, she pulled it backwards until it came free.

Papa got to his feet, took a step forward, and then sank to one knee. "My ankle," he grunted. "It can't bear my weight."

Mama took both of Papa's hands, and they looked at each other in that special, close way they had when everything was going wrong. Charlotte didn't say a thing. If Papa's ankle was broken, they might as well sit down and wait for the Rebels to find them. She and Mama would never be able to carry a two-hundred-pound man sixty miles through the bush to Oneida Lake.

"Let's get you over to that tree where there's a bit of shelter," said Mama, turning her head in the direction of a big maple a few yards off the trail.

Charlotte and Mama helped him to stand up. With his arms across their shoulders, Papa hobbled to the tree. When he was settled with his back against the trunk, Mama pulled off his boot. "Does this hurt?" she asked while she kneaded his foot and ankle.

"Not much."

Charlotte saw him wince.

Mama looked up. "Henry, your ankle is sprained. You'll have to keep off it for a few days. We must find somewhere to stay."

Charlotte looked around. Nothing except trees and rain. Even the shabbiest old bark hut would be a palace.

"We're a mile from Canajoharie," said Papa. "Half the folks there would risk their lives to help us; the other half would hand us over to the Sons of Liberty."

"Well," said Mama, "we can't spend the next three days under a tree."

"I'll go to Canajoharie to look for a safe house," said Charlotte.

Papa grimaced. "How would you know it if you've found one?"

Charlotte thought hard. Obviously, she couldn't just walk

up to someone's door and ask. But there had to be a way. "I can look in people's windows for signs."

"What sort of signs?" Papa asked.

"Things like flags and pictures. If I see the King's portrait on a wall, I'll knock and ask for help."

"You'd probably get caught for a Peeping Tom. And even if you didn't, there isn't much chance of seeing anything like that. It's a bad gamble. I can't allow you to go."

The rain changed to an icy drizzle. Charlotte walked around to keep warm. Papa was being unreasonable! If he wouldn't let her go to Canajoharie, what plan did he suggest? They couldn't stay out here. By the time Papa's ankle got better, they'd all be sick with an ague. Or captured by Rebels. Or both.

"Papa," she pleaded, "I want to try."

He glanced towards Mama, who sat huddled in her wet cloak. "The risk——"

"Let her go, Henry," said Mama in a tired voice. "We don't have a choice."

"I still don't like it." But he pulled out the map. While he unfolded it, rain dripped on the paper and the ink started to run. "Here's the path to Canajoharie. It's just ahead, on your right."

Mama took the map from him. "Godspeed," she said as she folded it again.

Mud and wet leaves made the path as slippery as if it had been greased. Charlotte walked with her head bent and the hood of her cloak pulled up. At first the only sound she heard was the splatter of rain, but before long it was joined by the gurgle of swirling water. The Mohawk River. Canajoharie was just ahead.

She must have quickened her step without knowing it, because that was when it happened. Her heel skidded on a pad of wet leaves; her feet flew up from under her, and there she lay — flat on her back in mud as thick as chocolate pudding. High above her, the trees waved their naked branches. For a moment she did not move. The back of her head felt numb, but when she moved her limbs, testing first her arms and then her legs, nothing hurt.

Charlotte picked herself up. This was a bad beginning. First Papa and now her. If they couldn't even stay on their feet, how were they ever going to get to Oneida Lake?

"More haste, less speed," she muttered. After a time she was able to make out the shape of a house. And after a few more steps, she saw another. Two frame houses, both white clapboard with green shutters. At least they looked green, but daylight was fading so fast that all colours were starting to look the same.

A row of pine trees divided the space between the two houses, running all the way from the forest to the river road. The trunks weren't quite thick enough to hide her completely. But with the rain and the fading light to veil her, she probably would not be seen.

Picking up her skirts she dashed for the nearest tree. From behind its trunk, she peered about, and then scurried to the next. Once again, she looked about. No one was in sight. Darting from tree to tree, Charlotte moved closer. Halfway down the row, she came level with the two houses.

A pink light glowed in a downstairs window of the house on her left. That glow must be from the fireplace. Good. It would give enough light for her to see what was in that room. But what if people were there? She did not see anyone. Maybe they were all in some other room, having supper. Better wait for a few minutes. But then they might come back. Better not wait. Besides, it was cold outside, and she was soaked to the skin. Oh, what should she do?

Charlotte made up her mind. Nothing hazarded; nothing gained. She raced across the side yard. With her body pressed against the window shutters, she peered inside.

The room she saw was a parlour, and it was almost a vision of home: upholstered chairs, a sofa, a big family Bible on a round table, a clavichord standing in one corner. There were pictures on the walls. Some were landscapes, some portraits. She screwed up her eyes, trying to see a recognizable face. There was only one. From a heavy, ornate frame George Washington's stern eyes stared right at her.

She would find no help here. Charlotte shrank back, edged along the wall, and then in a crouching run headed back to the row of trees.

The house next door had a shed, a backhouse, half a dozen apple trees, and a garden that already had been spaded over for winter. Set into the stone foundation was a root cellar door. Maybe this house would be the one.

Charlotte made a dash to the nearest window and peeked in. The room was a kitchen. A banked fire glowed in the fireplace, a braided rug lay on the plank floor, and in the middle stood a trestle table with wooden chairs ranged along its sides. But she saw no portraits and no flags.

Better try a different room. The parlour was a likelier place. It would be at the front of the house. She drew back and took one step — just one — when something hard struck her in the back and a voice cried out, "Halt! Or I'll drive this pitchfork through your kidneys."

Charlotte stood still. It was a young voice, that of a boy on the verge of manhood. She did not dare to turn her head.

"Put your hands up. Walk around to the front!" He gave her a jab with what certainly felt like a pitchfork. She obeyed.

When they got to the front door, the voice said, "Knock good and loud." Charlotte raised her fist and banged on the door. A minute passed. "Knock again."

She was starting to think no one would ever come, when finally she heard a bolt being drawn. The door opened, and in the doorway stood a very pregnant woman wearing a white nightgown and a frilled mobcap.

"Elijah, what in heaven's name are you up to now?" the woman exclaimed as Charlotte stumbled into the room.

"Ma, I caught a spy looking in our window."

The woman's eyes widened. "That's the dirtiest spy I ever seen."

"I'm not a spy!" Taking her chances, she turned around.

The boy with the pitchfork looked about thirteen. Though nearly as tall as Charlotte, he was skinny as a fence rail.

"I was coming from the backhouse," he said, "when I seen her prowling around next door. Then she snuck over here and looked into our kitchen. I got a pitchfork from the shed and came up behind her."

"Huh!" said the woman. "Likely she was figuring what to steal."

"I am not a thief."

"You're a damn Rebel. It amounts to the same."

The tines were aimed at Charlotte's chest, but the boy's hands shook so hard and the pitchfork wobbled so wildly that she wasn't sure what part of her body would be hit if he attacked.

"I'm not a Rebel, either. Please put that down and let me explain."

"Put it down, Elijah. Whatever she is, she can't hurt us."

Elijah lowered the pitchfork. He licked his lips. "What'll we do with her, Ma?"

"We'll start by hearing what she has to say."

Charlotte relaxed. These people were Loyalists. They would help.

"My name is Charlotte Hooper," she began.

As the woman listened, she pursed her lips and frowned. The longer she listened, the more worried she looked. When Charlotte had finished, she shook her head.

"I believe you. But suppose I let you stay here and the

Sons of Liberty find out. Do you know what they'll do? They'll hang Elijah and burn down the house."

"Her folks can hide in the root cellar," said Elijah. "If they get caught, we'll say we didn't know they was there."

"You think Liberty men will swallow that? In a pig's eye!" She turned to Charlotte. "Still, I reckon we're obliged to help you. Go get your ma and pa. I'll unlock the root cellar so you can slide right in. Once you get in there, don't come out till you're ready to leave. Don't say good-bye. Just go."

Charlotte felt like hugging the woman. "Thank you, Mrs. . . ."

"Cobman. Sadie Cobman. My husband and my eldest son are in the west with Butler's Rangers. This is my middle boy, Elijah. My youngest is asleep in his bed. He's nine years old, but he won't be the youngest for long." She laid her hand on her ample belly. "God willing."

"Ma, shall I go along to lend a hand?"

"Do you need a hand?" asked Mrs. Cobman.

"It would help. My father is a big man, and he can't walk."

"All right. Elijah can go with you."

"I'll get my musket."

"Hold your horses!" She turned to Charlotte. "How far away are your folks?"

"About a mile."

"No gun, then. One shot would rouse the village. Be quiet and be quick." She looked out the window. "This rain's a blessing. Nobody will stir outdoors that doesn't have to."

"I'll put the pitchfork in the shed," said Elijah, "and catch up to you."

Charlotte hardly noticed the cold and the rain as she started up the path. Her gamble had worked. Next time Papa would pay more heed to what she said.

The Cobmans' root cellar smelled like apples and earth. By the light of a candle set in a tin cup, Charlotte saw open barrels of apples and winter vegetables ranged along the rough stone walls. Three quilts lay folded on an unpainted board shelf.

"Looks like Ma has got things ready," said Elijah. "There's apples and carrots to eat — turnips and potatoes too, if you don't mind them raw. As for the calls of nature, our backhouse is in the yard. Just go at night." He started up the steps, then turned, "I'll check in the morning to see how you are."

After Elijah had gone, Mama found a stack of hemp sacks in a corner. "There, that's not too bad," she said as she spread them on the earth floor. "Better than outdoors, at any rate."

"Our clothes aren't going to dry down here," Charlotte said.

"No, but they won't get any wetter."

Charlotte draped her muddy cloak over a barrel. She took an apple, wrapped herself in one of the quilts, and sat down. She was warm enough, although uncomfortable in her soggy clothes. Overhead she heard voices and footsteps. So the plank ceiling of the root cellar must be the floor of the room above.

As she munched the apple, Charlotte remembered another time long ago when she had hidden in a root cellar with mud all over her clothes. She must have been six years old, because it was the year before she started school. After days of rain, the sun had come out, and she was racing down the lane to meet her brothers coming home from school. Just before she reached them, her feet had flown out from under her, and she landed on her backside. James and Charlie had burst out laughing: "You'll catch it now!"

But Isaac pulled her to her feet. "Go hide in the root cellar," he had told her. "I'll fetch you a clean gown."

For some reason it had been important not to get dirty. Probably company was coming. The only thing Charlotte clearly remembered was Isaac bringing her a fresh gown, concealed under his jacket so Mama wouldn't know. He had helped Charlotte to change. "Don't worry about the muddy gown," he said. "I'll take care of it." And he did. Isaac washed it in the horse trough and hung it in the barn to dry. Mama never knew; or if she did, said nothing.

Charlotte took another apple from the basket. What good apples! Crisp, juicy and sweet. She passed one to Papa, who was sitting with his legs stretched out in front of him. Mama, who was holding her hands over the candle flame for a bit of warmth, turned toward Charlotte.

"It's only for a few days," she said. "We'll make the best of it and get some rest." She took a blanket and settled down beside Papa.

The candle flame guttered and went out. Now the darkness in the root cellar was complete. Was this how it felt to be buried alive?

Chapter four

"You married me because I was afraid of spiders?"
That was Mama's voice.

"I grant that you had other charms, but it was your fear of spiders that won my heart."

Their voices had wakened Charlotte. In the pitch-dark root cellar she felt as if she were floating in a void, with her parents' voices her only lifeline to the real world. She needed to feel their nearness. But what in the world were they talking about?

"Spiders, of all things! Henry, be sensible."

"I am always sensible. Other men face wolves and bears to impress the woman they love. But I could be a hero to the prettiest woman in the Valley by killing a spider."

"And that was why you married me?" Mama sounded amused.

"Partly. But I had a practical motive too. I was thirty-five years old and tired of the bachelor life. I longed for regular meals, clean-swept floors and bright curtains. I wanted better company than the mice that shared my daily bread. With Martha Riley keeping my house, there'd be no mice, ants, earwigs, spiders——"

"That's enough, darling." Mama started to laugh, but her laugh ended in a cough.

"If you want to change the subject, we can talk about your other charms."

"Ah, yes." She cleared her throat. "You admit that I had other charms."

"Yes indeed. Your ivory skin, your emerald eyes, your beautiful red hair. Dearest Martha, I knew from the day we met that you were the only woman for me."

"And there I was, thirty years old and past my prime."

"Nonsense."

"After taking care of my parents all those years until God called them home, I expected to end my days as a lonely old maid. You rescued me from that."

"You rescued me from being a lonely old bachelor."

This time it was Charlotte who coughed. If her parents were going to talk about love, she didn't want to hear it.

"Hush!" Mama whispered. "We've disturbed Charlotte."

Now that all was quiet, the feeling of loneliness returned, tinged with envy. Mama and Papa had each other. All Charlotte had was a silver locket and a ring of braided hair to remind her of earlier hopes.

She had made the ring more than a year ago from Nick's hair and hers, light and dark strands twisted together, something of him and something of her. "This will do for the present," he had said when she showed it to him.

Now she was almost sixteen. Though there was still no gold band upon her finger, the braided ring was safe in her locket and her locket safe in her petticoat. Where exactly was it? She ran her fingers up and down her skirts, searching. Surely she hadn't left it behind? No. She was certain she hadn't.

At last she found the locket where she had quilted it into her petticoat, slightly above her left knee. As her fingers pressed the oval shape, she felt a little less lonely, and a little closer to Nick.

A thin line of light under the root-cellar door was the only visible sign of dawn. Outside, a rooster crowed. Charlotte heard footsteps overhead. She could distinguish three sets. The slow footsteps must be Mrs. Cobman's, the clunky ones Elijah's, and the scampering ones the little brother's. From the scraping of chair legs on the floorboards, she concluded that the kitchen was above the root cellar and that it was breakfast time.

Doors slammed. The scampering footsteps and the clunky footsteps ceased. Overhead, Mrs. Cobman plodded back and forth. Likely she was clearing the table.

In a few moments the root-cellar door swung open, and there stood Elijah at the top of the steps with a large basket over his arm. "I can't stay," he said as he came down the steps. From the basket he took out an oblong box. "Here's some extra candles. Ma says for Charlotte to put her cloak in the basket so she can dry it by the fire."

"That's kind of her," said Charlotte as she folded the muddy cloak.

"There's something else. Ma says I have to put the padlock on the door."

"You mean lock us in?" Papa asked.

"Just for the daytime."

"Is it necessary?"

"Ma thinks so." Elijah shuffled his feet, obviously uncomfortable to have to deliver this message. "Moses don't know you folks are here. He ain't allowed to take apples from the root cellar, but he sometimes sneaks one if the door ain't locked. Ma don't trust Moses to keep a secret. He's only nine."

"Isn't he at school all day?" said Mama.

"He is. But after school he might try to snitch one. Ma's worried about the neighbours too. No telling who might come snooping around."

Elijah picked up the basket and mounted the stairs. When he opened the door, Charlotte caught a glimpse of grey sky. Then the door shut, the latch clicked, and the padlock closed with a snap.

"This is a fine pickle," said Mama. "I don't fancy being locked up."

"Neither do I," said Papa. "But Mrs. Cobman makes the rules."

Charlotte shivered. Being locked in gave her a prickly feeling, as if ants were crawling over her skin.

There was nothing to do but eat and sleep. No one had thought about providing water, but the juicy apples held enough moisture to stave off thirst. When the line of light under the door disappeared, Charlotte knew that it was dark outside. There was more scraping of chairs overhead; the three sets of footsteps were heard again.

Late in the evening, when Elijah returned to take the padlock off the door, he brought back Charlotte's cloak, dry and brushed.

"I'll be back in the morning to lock you in if you're still here."

"We will be. I wish we could leave tonight," said Papa. "But my ankle needs one more day."

"Then I'll see you in the morning." Elijah closed the door behind him.

The next morning Elijah seemed nervous. He shifted his weight from one foot to the other and appeared to be listening for something.

"We'll leave tonight," Papa told him.

"That's good," said Elijah. "I don't like the way some of our neighbours eye the house. Ma is scared out of her wits. Today I've got a job cutting wood, and I hate to leave her alone."

After he left, Charlotte got out a carrot. She was tired of apples. There was food in the rucksack, but Mama said it had to be kept for the journey. Charlotte sat down, rested her head against a barrel of turnips, and munched the carrot. After she had finished it she decided to take a nap. Not that she was tired, but what else was there to do?

Mrs. Cobman's footsteps padded across the kitchen floor. Poor woman! The last thing she needed was Loyalists hiding in her root cellar. In her condition, with her husband and eldest son away, she must already be in a terrible state of nerves.

Now there was a new sound — not overhead, but outside in the yard. Carts rattled. Wagons creaked. Horses' hooves stamped. There was shouting, and then banging at the door.

Mrs. Cobman's footsteps thudded in the direction of the noise. Her voice cried out, "Be off with you!"

"Open up! Open up!" There was a crash.

"What?" Mama gasped.

"Hush!" Papa whispered.

"Villains!" Mrs. Cobman screamed. A second crash. Then loud scraping and bumping that sounded like furniture being dragged across the floor. There were shouts, smashing glass, the pounding of many boots, and a woman's sobs.

When the noise overhead died down, more shouting arose outside. It sounded as if men were loading wagons right outside the root-cellar door. "Give me a hand with this wardrobe," someone shouted.

"Next they'll come for us," Papa whispered.

Charlotte grabbed up the blankets and hemp sacks and shoved them into a corner. Mama blew out the candle. All three crouched behind barrels. No escape was possible. Their only hope was not to be seen. Charlotte's heart thudded as she waited for the axe blow that would smash the padlock, break down the door.

Horses whinnied. Wagons rumbled away. Then silence.

"They've gone," Charlotte whispered.

"They didn't know we were here," said Papa. "I can't believe it."

"What have they done to Mrs. Cobman?" Mama asked.

"God knows," said Papa.

"Henry," said Mama, "we must help her."

"We'll wait ten minutes. Let the scoundrels go on their way. If they saw us breaking out, matters would be worse for her."

They waited. Charlotte strained to hear some sound from above. Even weeping would be better than total silence.

"I smell smoke," said Mama. Charlotte smelled it too.

"Damnation!" Papa was on his feet. "They've fired the house."

He stumbled up the steps to the root-cellar door. Charlotte heard his hand axe clash upon the hinges, striking blow after blow. When the upper hinge gave way, he flung his weight against the door, smashed it open and lunged through. Charlotte followed; Mama, dragging the rucksack, was right behind.

"Which way?" Papa asked.

Charlotte pointed toward the back of the house. Racing past the kitchen window, she saw nothing through the glass except dense smoke as thick as raw wool. It poured out when Papa opened the back door. He and Charlotte plunged inside.

Shutting her eyes against the stinging smoke, she dropped to her hands and knees and felt her way across the floor. Where was Mrs. Cobman? Charlotte groped for a foot, a hand, or fabric of a gown. Her lungs were about to burst. She had to get out. Her hand made one last sweep of the floor — ahead, to the left, to the right — and her fingers touched an arm.

"I've got her!" Charlotte grabbed the limp arm. With the intake of breath, smoke filled her lungs. Through half-closed eyes she located the tall rectangle of light that was the doorway, and then squeezed her eyes shut again. Choking and gasping, she dragged the motionless body across the floor.

But the door was too far away. Charlotte's ears pounded and a burning mist swirled through her head. Her knees collapsed under her. She felt the plank floor against her cheek as a great tide of blackness swept her away.

"Breathe!" Mama's voice came from far away. "Take a big breath. Good. Now let it out!"

Charlotte's breath wheezed in the air passages to her lungs. She opened her eyes. There was Mama bending over her. Charlotte pushed herself up on one elbow and looked around. A little way off, Papa, kneeling on the ground, held Mrs. Cobman by the shoulders as she too struggled for breath. Behind them, flames shot from every window of the Cobmans' house.

"Can you walk?" asked Mama.

Charlotte nodded. But as soon as she got to her feet, her knees buckled.

"Lean on me. We can't stay out in the open."

"Where shall we go?"

"Back to the forest."

"What about Mrs. Cobman?"

"She has to come with us. We can't leave her alone."

Mrs. Cobman's eyes were fixed upon the burning house. Her lips fluttered, but no sound emerged.

Papa, still holding her shoulders, spoke quietly, "You are safe. Your sons are safe. That's more important than a house."

Mrs. Cobman seemed not to hear. Shudders passed through her body.

"You're coming with us," Papa said. Wincing as he stood up, he held out his hand to help her to her feet, but she jerked away.

"No. You folks go your ways."

"We can't leave you here," said Papa. "We're going back to the woods. When your sons join us, you can decide what you want to do."

"If I'm in the woods, they won't know where I am. They'll think I'm in there," and she pointed to the burning house.

"I'll wait here," said Charlotte. "When your boys get here, I'll bring them to you."

Looking back over her shoulder at the flames, Mrs. Cobman let Papa lead her away. With every step she leaned more heavily on Papa's arm.

Mama picked up the rucksack and followed.

What Charlotte needed was a place to hide and rest. To the side of the house stood a honeysuckle thicket. Somewhat unsteadily, she made her way to it and sat down on the ground. No one would notice her here as long as she stayed still.

Through the tangle of branches she had a view of the river road and of the passers-by who stopped to watch the fire. Some were on foot, some on horseback, and some in buggies. No one looked excited to see the house in flames.

A loaded barge moved slowly down the Mohawk River. In another day or two, it would go right by Fort Hunter. If she were on that barge, she could tell the bargemen: "Let me off at Chrysler's Grist Mill. I can walk home from there in half an hour." Charlotte felt a big sore lump in her throat as she watched the barge disappear around a river bend.

The fire burned on. The Cobmans' roof fell in, shooting a firestorm of sparks higher than the trees. Then the walls and floors collapsed. By mid-afternoon, all that remained were the stone chimney and a great hole filled with smoldering timbers.

Elijah ran toward the pillar of smoke with his head up, as if unable to take his eyes away. He ran until he reached the front gate, and there he stopped. Clutching the top rail, he stood motionless for several minutes. Then he opened the gate, walked slowly to the edge of the smoldering pit, and covered his face with his hands.

"Elijah!" Charlotte called. She saw how his shoulders shook. "Elijah!" When he still did not move, she left her hiding place and ran to him. Grasping his hands, she pulled them away from his face. His eyes were red, and tears streamed down his cheeks.

"Ma's dead." He choked on the words.

"No! We got her out. My parents took her to that big maple up the path. We'll go there as soon as your brother gets back from school."

"She's safe?" he said, not quite believing.

Charlotte nodded. Should she hug him? No. He was too

grown-up. She felt her own eyes fill with tears as she watched him rub his eyes with his knuckles.

At last he raised his head and pointed up the river road. "See that steeple? That's the church. The school is next to it."

"When does school let out?"

"Any minute now."

They stood awkwardly side by side, watching the road. Charlotte said, "Until Moses gets here, I'm going back to that thicket where I've been hiding."

"I'll start up the road to meet Moses. I want to tell him Ma's safe before he gets too scared." Elijah looked embarrassed. "Like I did."

From her hiding place Charlotte watched Elijah walk quickly and purposefully up the road, as if he knew exactly what to do.

She felt guilty, although she knew it wasn't her fault that the Cobmans had lost their home. The people who plundered and burned it didn't know that Charlotte and her parents were hiding there. They would have attacked it anyway. In the eyes of the Rebels of Canajoharie, the Cobman family stood already condemned.

Mrs. Cobman, wearing Papa's woollen shirt and holding a bundle wrapped in Mama's shawl, lay in the cleft between two great roots of the maple tree. Her face was pale with exhaustion. When she saw Elijah and Moses, she smiled weakly.

"I have something to show you," she said as she pulled back a corner of the shawl. "Your sister."

Elijah did not smile. He looked dismayed as he stared at the tiny wrinkled face. "Well, Ma," he said after a few moments, "you got what you wanted."

Got what she wanted? No doubt Elijah meant it kindly, but at his words, tears came to Mrs. Cobman's eyes.

Moses gaped; his blue eyes were wide with wonder. He laid one grimy finger upon the baby's cheek. "What's her name?"

"She don't have one yet."

"Why not?"

"I ain't had time to think about it."

Moses looked perplexed. "She got to have a name."

"It don't matter that much," said Elijah, "at least not for a while."

The baby lay still as a doll. With so slender a hold on life, how could she survive in this wilderness? Born too soon. No cradle. No home. Baby animals had at least a den or a stall in the barn. A name would be of no use to this poor mite.

"It does too matter," said Moses. "Everybody needs a name."

"Well," said Mrs. Cobman wearily, "what's a good name for a girl?"

"I don't know."

"Betty? Joan?"

"She don't look like those names."

"What name does she look like?" Mrs. Cobman asked.

"Hope," said Mama, right out of the blue.

Mrs. Cobman smiled. A real smile.

"Ma," said Moses, "can we call her that?"

"It sounds good, all things considered."

"Hope." Charlotte repeated under her breath. Tiny Hope. Faint Hope. But Hope nevertheless. It was either the perfect name, or a cruel joke.

"What do you want to do?" Papa asked Mrs. Cobman in the morning. "Have you relatives or friends to stay with?"

She snuggled the baby to her breast. "I'll get no help from family. They broke with me when my husband and Silas went off with Butler's Rangers. As for friends, they got troubles of their own."

"You're welcome to come with us to Carleton Island."

"That's a mighty long walk."

"We don't have to walk the whole distance — just sixty miles to Oneida Lake. Mohawk warriors will meet us there with a long canoe for the rest of the journey."

"Sixty miles! Lord! I ain't got the strength."

"Ma, we got to," said Elijah. "At Carleton Island you'll be safe — you and the baby."

Mrs. Cobman said thoughtfully, "I ain't felt safe in a long time."

"Then you're coming with us," said Papa firmly.

"I can do a mile or two. Then we'll see."

"We'll take it easy. My ankle won't be good for more than a few miles."

Mama checked the rucksack. "If we're careful, we have enough food for five days."

"How long will the Indians wait for us?" Charlotte asked.

"Until we get there," said Papa. "When Mohawks make a promise, they keep it."

Charlotte gulped. They had already lost three days because of Papa's sprain. How could he be so sure that the Mohawks wouldn't get tired of waiting? To be abandoned in the wilderness with winter coming meant certain death.

Chapter five

The trail led up from the river into pine-crested hills. Here the walking was easier than it had been through the dense brush on low ground. Charlotte could see everything in the valley below: houses, mills, churches, silos, barns, and fields that looked like brown corduroy where fall ploughing had furrowed the earth.

Although Papa and Mrs. Cobman needed frequent stops for rest, progress was better than expected. When they halted at sunset and Papa checked the map, he said cheerfully, "We covered eight miles today."

Charlotte did a bit of mental arithmetic. Eight miles today. That meant they would have to average thirteen miles each day for the next four in order to reach Oneida Lake before the food ran out.

Mama got ham, biscuits and dried apple slices from the rucksack. She cut the ham as thin as she could. "One piece of meat, one biscuit, and two apple slices for each person, but Mrs. Cobman gets an extra biscuit as Hope's share."

Charlotte chewed each bite twenty times to make it last longer. Then she folded her shawl for a pillow and lay down. Pine needles, thick on the ground, made a softer bed than the earth floor of the Cobmans' root cellar, and she was warm inside her cloak. Overhead, stars filled the sky. She looked for the Big Dipper and the North Star; and there they were, shining in their proper place, even though Charlotte's little world had turned upside down.

At daybreak Charlotte woke in a panic, her nose twitching at the smell of smoke. She jumped up to look around. In the wooded hills she saw no trace of fire. But from the valley below smoke rose in a dozen drifting columns.

She crept to the tree line for a better look. Mama and Papa were already there, watching flames shoot from farmhouses and barns. Silos blazed like pillars of fire. At the bottom of the hill, directly below them, men were carrying tables, wardrobes, beds and dressers from a farmhouse and loading them into hay wagons. Shouts and laughter rose on the breeze, along with smoke from the burning barn.

"The Sons of Liberty," Papa said bitterly.

"Those aren't Liberty men," said Mama. "Those are neighbours helping themselves to the furniture."

"And to the livestock," said Charlotte, for in the farm lane two men were driving a herd of cattle towards the river road.

"They might as well take the animals," said Papa. "The scoundrels have already fired the barn and silo. Without fodder, a man can't feed his stock through the winter."

Charlotte saw Papa's face tighten. Maybe he was thinking about their own cows, now lodged in someone else's barn.

"Neighbours!" said Mama. "Imagine!"

"It's the same everywhere," said Papa. "All these farms destroyed! If their owners ever return, they'll have to start over again."

"Henry, they'll never come back. How could they? It doesn't matter which side wins. Imagine meeting these people at the store, sitting beside them in church, going to quilting bees and barn raisings with neighbours who stole everything they could carry off and burned the rest!"

"I'd go back," said Papa angrily. "I could face them."

"So could I," said Charlotte. But she knew that this was empty talk. If there was any future for Loyalists, it lay far from here.

The next day their trail led down from the hills and back to the river valley. They were in deep wilderness now. Elijah pointed out a pile of black, tarry lumps beside the path.

"Bear scat," said Papa. His brow creased in a worried frown. "Today is the first of November. I thought they'd be hibernating by now."

"I wish you still had your rifle," said Charlotte.

"We have other weapons."

"A knife and a hand axe! I wouldn't want to fight off a bear with those."

"The best defence is the camp kettle," said Papa. "Just bang it with a metal spoon."

"What if the bear mistakes the noise for a dinner bell?"

Papa gave a wry smile. "It won't if you stand your ground. Remember: never run from a bear."

Late in the afternoon they came to a fork in the river. Papa unfolded the map.

"Look here," he said. "So far, we've been following the Mohawk River northwards. But to reach Oneida Lake, we have to turn west along this branch. And so . . ." He paused while he returned the map to his pocket. "We say farewell to the Mohawk Valley."

Mama looked back the way they had come. "We shall never see our home again."

"Martha, we'll get some land, build a house, plant crops. We can buy a cow and some chickens."

"Who sells cows and chickens in the middle of the wilderness?"

"We may have to go to Quebec to buy them. But cows can walk. With someone to lead her, a heifer can find a new home in the Upper Country, just as we can. As for chickens, they can be shipped by bateau up the St. Lawrence. In a few years, when you have your house, your cow and your chickens, you'll feel right at home."

A look of grief crossed her face. "It will never feel like home without my boys."

Papa put his arms around Mama. As he held her, his eyes stared straight ahead. He's afraid that Mama will never be happy again, Charlotte thought. A desolate feeling swept over her that this was likely true.

That night they ate biscuits and the last scraps of ham that Mama could whittle from the bone.

"Are there any more apple slices?" asked Charlotte.

"No," said Mama. "We finished them last night."

"How much food is left?" Papa asked.

Mama rummaged deep in the rucksack. "Six biscuits. Five cakes of pressed sugar that I've saved for emergencies. There's the hambone too; I can make broth if we ever get to a place where it's safe to light a cooking fire."

"Tomorrow," Papa promised. "By then we'll be past the furthest settlements."

Fog rolled in during the night. The air was white and dripping. Charlotte hugged herself for warmth. Even her thick woollen cloak was no barrier to dampness. It seeped through her clothes so that she could not stop shivering.

Nearby an owl hooted. Wolves howled from hill to hill. A

fox barked in the undergrowth. Something snarled. Something screamed. These were the usual noises of the night, though muffled in the fog. Despite the cold, Charlotte began to doze. She was drifting on the verge of sleep when a piping voice jolted her awake.

"Mammy, I'm cold."

"Hush! Hush!" a woman replied. "Just settle down and be quiet or the Liberty men will get you."

Then another woman's voice. "Nelly, don't frighten the poor child."

This was no dream. The voices meant only one thing: Loyalist women hiding with a child. Where were they from? What were they doing in the forest, miles from any town?

Charlotte sat up. She wanted to call out to let them know that they were not alone. But what if they had a gun? They might panic to hear a strange voice come out of the fog. They might shoot. I'll wait for daylight, she thought, and for the fog to lift.

A third woman spoke: "The Lord will not abandon us to our foes."

The second woman again: "Praise the Lord."

"Mammy, I want to go home!" This time the child's cry set off a chorus of wails that sounded like a dozen children crying, and their misery broke Charlotte's heart. She took a chance.

"Hello! I'm a friend." Silence. She called again. "I'm from Fort Hunter. I'm a Loyalist too."

This time they must have believed her. "God be thanked," said a trembling voice.

"God save the King," said another.

Through the wall of mist Charlotte felt her way towards them, her fingers brushing the wet tips of branches. She bumped into a tree, groped her way around it and then found herself abruptly in their midst. Shadowy shapes surrounded her, reaching out with cold hands. On their lips was a single question: "Do you have any food?"

In the morning, while Mama cut up the six biscuits and five cakes of sugar, the newcomers watched so intently that they appeared ready to fall upon the food like wolves and snatch it from her hands.

"Manna from Heaven," said one woman. She was tall and thin, with silvery-blond hair, a long face and grey eyes.

"Amen," said a second, who looked like her twin.

"Humph!" a stocky, brown-haired woman grunted. "Don't expect there'll be more of the same lying on the grass tomorrow morning."

"Nelly, the Lord will provide." The first speaker cast a reproachful look at the scoffer.

Charlotte hoped that this woman was right. There were sixteen newcomers, three women and thirteen children. And the hambone was the only food left. If ever they needed a miracle, it was now.

After they had finished eating — which took only a

minute, since each person's share was the size of a walnut — the women told their story. All three were soldiers' wives. The stocky, brown-haired woman was Nelly Platto. She had small, dark eyes, a wide mouth and a resolute chin. With her were her three small boys and a ten-year-old girl called Polly, who looked like a pocket version of her mother.

The other two women, Mercy Weegar and Prudence Vankleek, were indeed sisters. Between them, they had nine grey-eyed children, all with pale hair, long faces and runny noses. Charlotte could not tell which child belonged to which sister. All were so alike that each appeared to have two mothers, rather than a mother and an aunt.

"We lived near Fort Stanwix," said Mrs. Platto. "The Rebels burned us out two days ago."

"The day before yesterday we were in the hills above that region," said Papa.

"Then you saw the burning," said Mrs. Platto. "We lost everything."

"Everything," Mrs. Weegar said quietly. "I told my sister Prudence that we might as well trek up to Canada, for there was naught to keep us here. We were walking through the bush when we heard Nelly Platto's voice. She and her young ones were in the same plight as us. We joined up together and headed north. After one day, we were lost."

"You're lucky we found you," said Papa.

"It was a miracle," said Mrs. Weegar. "Surely the Lord sent you to help us."

"Amen," said Mrs. Vankleek.

Papa looked skeptical, but did not disagree. "Our destination is Oneida Lake, where Mohawks will meet us with a long canoe to take us to Carleton Island. They expect three people, not twenty-three. But if you want to come with us, I'm sure that they'll find a way."

"Aren't we still a fair distance from Oneida Lake?" asked Mrs. Platto.

"Two days," said Papa.

"The Lord has brought us this far," said Mrs. Weegar. "I trust Him to take us the rest of the way."

"Amen," said Mrs. Vankleek.

"There's enough of us to have a parade," Elijah said as the straggly procession set off.

Charlotte smiled. "For that we need a fife and drum."

"Oh, no! Nothing that makes noise. This is Oneida territory."

She glanced warily through the trees that edged the trail and imagined black, glittering eyes peering from the bushes. "From Liberty men to Oneida warriors. That's a leap from the fry pan into the fire."

"Don't speak of fry pans. You make me think about food."

"Tighten your belt," she said.

"I know that trick. I've tightened it two holes, and my stomach still grumbles."

Charlotte had no other suggestions. Before starting today's march, she had pulled in the laces of her petticoats,
not just to suppress hunger pangs but also to prevent her
double petticoat with its precious load from slithering over
her hips and landing in a tangle around her ankles.

They walked all day and then, shortly before sunset, Papa
called a halt. "We can have a fire tonight."

"You hear that, Polly?" said Mrs. Platto. "You get those
little ones busy gathering wood."

"Yes, Mama." Within minutes Polly had her little brothers
and all the Weegar and Vankleek children lined up ready to
go. Then she noticed Moses loitering by. "You too," she
ordered.

Moses ignored her.

Polly turned red and stamped her foot. "Mama, that boy
won't do as I say!"

Mrs. Cobman, sitting under a tree nursing the baby,
looked up and saw her younger son with his bottom lip
thrust out, scowling ferociously.

"Moses," she called, "I want no trouble from you. Do like
Polly says."

"I ain't taking orders from a girl." Moses stomped off
into the woods. He was gone half an hour. When he returned, his arms were loaded with brush. But his mood had
not changed.

Later, while the campfire blazed and the ham broth boiled
in the camp kettle, Moses sat alone and glowering on the

opposite side of the fire from Polly. Charlotte felt sorry for him. To be under Polly Platto's command would be a trial and tribulation for anyone.

The broth was delicious, with little bits of fat and shreds of meat floating in the hot liquid. They drank it in shifts, passing the Hoopers' cups, bowls and spoons from hand to hand. When the last drop had been drunk, Mama packed away the hambone to use again.

Before long, the smallest children piled themselves into a heap like a litter of sleepy puppies.

"At first I worried about travelling with so many children," said Mama. "But these little ones made hardly a peep all day."

"They were too hungry," said Mrs. Weegar.

"And frightened," Mrs. Platto spoke up. "My young ones are deathly afraid of the Rebels. Last week the Sons of Liberty hanged a man on an oak tree fifty feet from our front door. His crime was to bring me a letter from my husband. Some Rebel neighbour must have noticed the man come up our lane, because first thing I knew, those Liberty men were on our doorstep. I shooed the children inside, but they knew what was going on."

"The Lord will punish evil-doers for their wickedness," said Mrs. Weegar.

Mrs. Vankleek added, "Amen."

"Soon we'll put all that behind us," said Papa. "If we make an early start, we can reach Oneida Lake tomorrow before dark."

Charlotte lay down close to the fire's warmth. As the flames sank, the burning wood popped and hissed. That night she scarcely noticed the hardness of the ground.

At dawn Charlotte woke up before anyone else. Smoke was still rising from last night's fire. She put on more wood to start it blazing again, and then set water to heat in the camp kettle. Using Papa's hand-axe, she cracked the hambone and tossed it in. Even without much flavour, a hot drink would give everyone a good start for the day's march.

A dreamy feeling came over her as she gazed into the fire. It was lovely to have a few minutes alone. She tried to see Nick's face in the glowing embers. But though she could summon up individual features — his blond hair with the lock that tumbled over his forehead, his blue eyes with the dark ring around the iris that made them bluer still, his slightly bumpy nose — she could not fit the parts together. Did this mean that she was forgetting him? The thought frightened her, because if she forgot him, he was just as likely to forget her.

The possibility plunged her into gloom. It was foolish to have all her dreams focused on this one boy. Yet she could not imagine sharing her life with anyone else. If she could not be with Nick, she would rather die an old maid.

Charlotte had just about decided that her life was ruined when Elijah joined her beside the fire.

"You're looking glum," he said as he sat down.

"I have a lot on my mind. I was thinking about my future."

"You mean, when we get to Carleton Island?"

"No. Years and years further off than that. When we get to Carleton Island, we'll likely just sit there until the war is over."

"Not me. The King's Own Regiment, the Royal Greens, is garrisoned there. I'm going to enlist."

"What about your mother? Don't you have to look after her and Moses? And now there's your sister."

"Ma won't need me after we get to Carleton Island. She'll have plenty of company. As for Moses, he's going to enlist too."

"He's only nine years old!"

"That's old enough to be a fifer or a drummer boy."

"Will your mother let him go?"

Elijah laughed. "Ma can't stop him. Moses always does what he wants to do."

Charlotte shook her head. Even Moses, that skinny little boy who should be rolling a hoop down the Canajoharie boardwalk — even Moses wanted to be a soldier. Like his father and brothers. Like Charlotte's brothers. Of all the men and boys she knew, Nick was the only one who hated war.

Hunger gnawed at her insides. For a time she tried chewing a twig to ease the pangs, but all that did was leave a bitter taste.

All morning they kept on walking. Nobody said much. Apart from Hope's whimpering, there was scarcely a human sound. The chickadees in the bushes along the trail were the only reminder that the forest was alive.

The path was broad and clear — the easiest they had travelled so far. A small stream ran beside it.

"That stream is called Wood Creek," Papa said when they stopped to rest, "and this trail is the Oneida Carry. It's a portage that traders and Indians use between the Mohawk River and Oneida Lake." He took out the map. "See where it ends at the eastern shore. There are two landmarks, a pink granite boulder and a fallen ash tree, to show where the Mohawks will meet us."

"Are you so sure they will?" Mrs. Cobman asked.

"I don't doubt it. They have given their word."

He stood up and slung the rucksack onto his shoulders with one hand. That's how light it was. "Come on!" he said. "We'll be there for supper."

Supper! What sort of supper? It would not be like Mama's home cooking — roast pork and potatoes, apple pie. What did Mohawks eat? Corn bread. Dried deer meat. Maple sugar. Those would be fine. Her mouth watered at the thought of food.

As they neared Oneida Lake, the trail descended to low-lying land covered with heavy brush. The loamy smell of damp earth and rotting leaves filled her nostrils. Then the deep woods' odour gave way to something swampy as the trail ended at the shore. The rays of the setting sun, so low in the west that it seemed to rest on the water, gave the surface of Oneida Lake a leaden sheen.

"Here we are," said Papa. "There's the fallen tree, and there's the granite boulder."

But where were the Indians? Along the empty shore Charlotte saw no sign of another human being. Maybe the Mohawks had already left. Maybe they had never been here at all.

Papa must have seen the fear in everyone's eyes. "Don't worry," he said. "When we've lit our fire, they'll know that we've arrived."

Charlotte stood at his elbow and looked out over the water. The only sign of life was a flock of mergansers fifty feet offshore.

"If we could catch those ducks, we could eat them."

"Fish ducks," said Papa. "No good to eat."

"I'm willing to try."

"Oneida Lake holds better things. It's full of salmon and whitefish. Eels too. Your friend Nick would like those. Smoked eel. Isn't that a favourite with Dutch people?"

Charlotte stiffened. A year had passed since Papa last mentioned Nick's name. Why do it now?

"I reckon he might. But I never asked him."

Papa got out his flint and steel. As he knelt to strike a spark, he said, "I suppose you haven't seen Nick for a long time."

"Five months." She knelt beside her father and puffed at the red glow in the flax tinder.

"I reckon love and war don't mix," Papa said gently.

"Especially when your sweetheart is on the wrong side."
She fed a wisp of grass to the tiny flame.

She felt Papa's hand upon her shoulder. "I'm sorry," he
said.

As the water heated in the camp kettle, Mama tossed in
the ham bone. Steam rose, but this time there was no smell
of broth.

They sat around the fire and talked about food.

"When my husband's regiment was on a march from
Montreal to Lake Champlain," said Mrs. Platto, "the men
ate their boots and leather cartridge cases to keep from
starving. They had already eaten their mascot. It was a New-
foundland retriever. Some men swore they'd never eat the
flesh of their own dog. But they all did, after it was cooked."

The poor dog! Charlotte thought. The poor soldiers!

A long silence followed Mrs. Platto's story. Then Hope
began to cry. "Eh-eh-eh." It was not a wail, merely a fretful
whimper that went on and on. Mrs. Cobman put the baby
to her breast. For half a minute there was silence, then the
crying began again.

"She's starving," said Mrs. Cobman. "I think we've come
to the end. I ain't got strength to go on. And even if I did,
there's nowhere to go."

"The Lord is our refuge and our strength," said Mrs.
Weegar.

Mrs. Platto spoke sharply. "I'd sure like to see some sign
of that."

Chapter six

E xactly when did the Mohawks arrive? One minute they were not there, and the next they were — eight dark shapes moving from the trees into the light of the fire.

They were dressed in leather — breechcloth, leggings, shirt and moccasins. Their heads were shaved except for a crest of hair into which feathers were fastened. For a moment they stood watching, then turned to one another and spoke in their own language. One spoke, then another, until each had had a turn. Finally they nodded their heads in unison, and one man stepped forward.

He looked older than the others, between thirty-five and forty years of age. His bearing was dignified, his expression quietly alert.

"My name is Axe Carrier," he said. "White men know me as Nathaniel Smart."

Papa held out his hand. "I am Henry Hooper. How am I to address you?"

"As Axe Carrier, while we're on Indian land." He looked about. "John Stuart told me that Henry Hooper had one wife and one daughter. But I see many women and children."

"All are Loyalists from the Mohawk Valley. They joined us as we went along. The Rebels burned their homes."

Axe Carrier nodded. "It happens everywhere."

Steam rose from the camp kettle, though there was not the faintest whiff of cooking. Axe Carrier glanced into the kettle, where the lonely hambone bobbed up and down in the boiling water.

"Okwaho!" he called to a young warrior. Charlotte didn't like the look of this one. His cheeks were painted with jagged yellow streaks like bolts of lightning, and there was a cruel glitter in his dark eyes.

The young warrior peered into the kettle, grunted and walked away into the dark.

"I hope he's gone to get food," said Charlotte to Mama.

After a few minutes he re-appeared, carrying a covered basket the size of a milking pail. After removing the lid, he tilted the basket over the kettle. A stream of fine white meal poured into the boiling water. Instantly the broth bubbled into a milky froth, splashed down the sides of the kettle, and hissed in the fire.

"Praise the Lord!" exclaimed Mrs. Weegar.

"Amen," said Mrs. Vankleek.

"Humph!" said Mrs. Platto as she picked up a stick from the ground to stir the mixture. "Better give credit where it's due."

What a sweet smell! It made Charlotte's mouth water and brought back memories of home, when corn meal mush bubbled in the pot over the kitchen fire.

Mrs. Platto's stick moved more slowly as the mush thickened. She lifted the kettle from the fire and gave one last stir while Charlotte fetched the family's cups, bowls and spoons from the rucksack.

Four shifts were needed to get everyone fed. When the kettle was empty, the children swarmed upon it to wipe the inside clean with their fingers, then licked their sticky hands.

The Indians sat apart, not sharing the meal but talking quietly among themselves while the others ate. Then Axe Carrier approached the fire.

"My warriors want to leave tonight. We have camped nearby for five days, with nothing to do but eat and sleep. Now we're short of food. The sooner we leave, the sooner we reach Carleton Island."

"How many people will your canoe carry?"

Axe Carrier shrugged. "Half of you."

"Only half?"

"Unless we tie you up in bales like beaver pelts."

"There might be objections to that," said Papa. "It sounds as if two trips are needed."

"Yes. Some must wait for the canoe to return."

"For how long?"

"About two weeks, depending on the weather."

Papa turned to the others. "You heard that. Who wants to go tonight?"

From the shouts of "I do!" it sounded as if everyone wanted to.

"Well," said Papa, "we may have to draw lots."

"Just a moment," said Mrs. Cobman. "Provided there's shelter and food, I'd as lief stay and get some rest."

"If she stays, I'll stay," said Mrs. Platto. "Let Mrs. Weegar and Mrs. Vankleek go together. With their little ones, they'll fill the canoe."

"Okwaho and I will stay," said Axe Carrier. "Six paddlers are enough."

"Fine," said Papa. "Two women and nine children go tonight, leaving twelve and a babe in arms for the next trip."

While Mrs. Weegar and Mrs. Vankleek alternately praised the Lord and called their children together, the warriors who were leaving retrieved the canoe from its hiding place further along the shore.

Elijah turned to Charlotte with a look of disgust. "Looks like we're stuck here."

"Two more weeks out in the cold," Charlotte sighed.

"It ain't fair," said Moses. "I don't want to stay if Polly Platto's going to be here."

"Pay her no heed," said Elijah. "You stick with me. Maybe we'll go hunting."

"Do you mean it?" Moses smiled.

The long canoe emerged like a ghost from the darkness as the paddlers brought it in close to shore.

"That's a big canoe," said Charlotte to Papa. "I never saw anything that size on the Mohawk River."

"It's a freight canoe, made for the fur trade by Ojibwas up north. That one looks about thirty feet long."

"Is it strong enough to hold all those people?"

"It's built for heavy loads. The Ojibwas line them with cedar. The birchbark is just a skin."

While the warriors held the long canoe steady in the shallows, Axe Carrier and Okwaho removed their moccasins and undid the thongs that attached their leggings to their belts. Wading barelegged into the frigid water, they carried Mrs. Weegar and Mrs. Vankleek to the canoe, and then the nine children, one by one.

Paddles swished, and the long canoe moved away from shore. The passengers looked like a row of dark bumps along the gunwales. Above them knelt the paddlers, two near the stern, two near the bow, and two in the middle, silhouetted against the rising moon. The soft plash of paddles was the only sound. Then from across the water a woman's voice rang out:

"Praise the Lord!"

And a second voice responded, "Amen!"

Charlotte giggled.

"Now, now!" said Mama. "Those are religious women. We must respect them."

"Humph!" said Mrs. Platto. "My religion teaches that the Lord helps those that help themselves. And I never saw Mrs. Weegar or Mrs. Vankleek lift a finger. Maybe the Lord doesn't need our help, but we should offer!"

Charlotte agreed, but not out loud. She had noticed recently that people were of two types: those who worked and those who let others work for them. She also suspected that her own fate was to be one of the workers, whether she liked it or not.

Axe Carrier and Okwaho carried their moccasins and leggings back to the fire. Neither gave any sign of noticing the cold. When dry, they dressed themselves again.

The next morning, Axe Carrier and Okwaho showed the others how to build shelters. For each, they made a framework of long flexible poles set in a circle, with the two ends of the poles planted in the ground on opposite sides. They covered the poles with slabs of bark. To Charlotte the shelters looked like upside-down mixing bowls, or perhaps toadstools with no stem. They were small, no more than eight feet in diameter and four feet high. "They're what we use as sweat houses," Axe Carrier said.

In the Hoopers' shelter there was barely room for all three to lie down. It would be like sleeping in a doghouse, Charlotte thought. Still, that was better than the open air.

"Now we'll set snares for small game and put out lines for fish," said Axe Carrier when the shelters were complete. "Okwaho and I will teach you to live off the land."

"There must be plenty of deer," said Papa. "I see you have a rifle."

"No guns. This is Oneida territory. We don't want to attract attention." Axe Carrier paused. "Okwaho has his bow with him. He'll get us a deer."

Later, after Charlotte and her parents had crowded into their little hut and settled for the night, she had a question to ask.

"Why are the Mohawks helping us? They waited five extra days for us to arrive. They fed us. We would have died without their help. I don't understand why they would do so much for strangers, especially of a different race."

Papa answered. "There's a long history behind it, daughter. It began with self-interest on both sides. The Hurons and the Iroquois were ancient enemies, evenly matched until France established a foothold in the New World. French explorers hired Hurons as guides, paying them with trade goods, including guns that they could use against the Iroquois."

"So the Iroquois wanted guns too?"

"Understandably. That was the original reason they formed an alliance with the English. During the French and Indian Wars, the Hurons helped the French, while the Iroquois helped the English. But with the fall of Quebec, the French and Indian Wars came to an end."

"The Battle of the Plains of Abraham!" Charlotte exclaimed. "Wolfe and Montcalm."

"That's right. And for more than twenty years, Mohawks and colonists shared the Mohawk Valley in peace. Then all that fuss began about the Stamp Act and No Taxation without Representation. The Iroquois didn't know what to make of English colonists fighting each other. Both sides wanted the Iroquois nations as allies. The Oneidas chose to help the Rebels. That decision upset the Mohawks a great deal."

"Why did the Mohawks stay loyal?"

"They figured that England had treated them fairly and would continue to do so."

Mama spoke up. "Don't forget about Molly Brant."

"I was getting to that, Martha. It was after his first wife's death that Sir William Johnson married Molly Brant. Molly and her brother Joseph were royalty among their own people. It was their influence that settled the question of loyalty. From then on, we weren't just convenient allies to the Mohawks. We were friends. Friendship has high value among them, a sacred value. A Mohawk will go a long way to help a friend."

"I hope that some day we shall be able to repay them," Charlotte said.

She fell asleep feeling safer than she had for weeks, knowing that a man like Axe Carrier regarded her as a friend.

The Loyalist women liked Axe Carrier. "If he'd just grow his hair and put on some decent clothes," said Mrs. Platto, "he'd almost pass for a white man."

But they did not like Okwaho. There was a wildness to

him that no change of clothing could have altered, and it went deeper than the lightning bolts painted on his face. Okwaho had dark copper skin and high cheekbones. His eyes were black, with a menacing glitter, and the trophy feathers attached to his scalp lock waggled as he strutted about the camp.

Charlotte thought that Okwaho's scalp lock looked like a black shoe brush glued to the top of a shiny bald head, for he had plucked out every unwanted hair and rubbed his scalp with bear grease until it gleamed. Charlotte stayed out of Okwaho's way. There was nothing about him that she liked at all.

Yet the young warrior had one devoted admirer. To Elijah, Okwaho was a hero.

"His name means the Wolf," Elijah told Charlotte one evening as they relaxed by the fire. "He earned that name."

"It suits him. He looks fierce enough."

"Oh, he's plenty fierce. He's only nineteen, but he's been in dozens of battles and he's taken ten scalps."

"Has he really?" said Charlotte. The hair on the top of her head prickled.

"He even showed me how to do it."

"Good heavens!" She laughed nervously. "Don't practise on me."

"I don't plan to scalp nobody. But it's useful to know how."

"I can't imagine why."

"Anyway, that's just one thing he's taught me. I'm learning how to throw a tomahawk, strike with a war club, and hunt with the bow and arrow. He's teaching me his language too." Elijah leaned toward Charlotte and lowered his voice. "I've changed my mind about soldiering. With the things he's teaching me, I can become an interpreter or a guide or even a fur trader. Lots of white men go off to live with the Indians."

"I reckon they like the freedom."

"That's the truth. It's a hard life, but it's free."

Elijah stood up. "I promised to show Moses how to set a snare. He's jealous because I spend so much time with Okwaho. Ma makes Moses gather nuts with the little ones. He can't abide Polly Platto. He says he's going to run away. But Moses always says that when he's angry, so we pay no heed."

Axe Carrier squatted on the ground, plastering a dead pheasant with moist clay. The pheasant had not been plucked, although the long tail and wing feathers had been pulled out and the body cavity cleaned.

When he saw Charlotte watching, he leaned back and said to her, "You should learn to do this."

"What are you doing?" Charlotte thought it looked like child's play — something like mud pies.

"I'm going to bake it in clay. That's the best way to cook a pheasant."

"What about the feathers?"

"They come off when you crack open the clay. Inside you'll find the juiciest meat you ever tasted. You should try it."

"I will, someday."

"Mohawk cooking is very good. My eldest daughter could teach you."

"You have a daughter?" She had never thought about Axe Carrier having a family.

"Four daughters and three sons. My oldest daughter is fourteen. Her name is Drooping Flower. She can cook, tan leather, do beadwork — all the things that a woman must know how to do. Last year she had her ceremony of maidenhood. I think she'll be married soon."

"Does she have a sweetheart?" This was interesting. Charlotte sat down beside Axe Carrier.

"Oh, yes. I suspect she has already chosen the man she wants to marry."

"Really? Is a Mohawk girl allowed to choose her husband?"

"Most of the time, they choose each other."

"Anyone they want?"

"It must be someone from a different clan. My family is Turtle clan, so Drooping Flower must marry a Wolf or some other clansperson. When she makes up her mind, she will tell her mother."

"And then?"

"My wife will pay a visit to the young man's mother. The mothers will talk it over. If they agree, Drooping Flower will cook a basket of double ball biscuit loaves and hang them outside her sweetheart's lodge. If he eats one, he must marry her."

"Hmm," said Charlotte. "Perhaps that's what Drooping Flower should teach me. What did you call them?"

"Double ball biscuit loaves." He looked amused.

Moses ran away. The next day, when Polly Platto led her band of nut gatherers back to camp, he was not among them. Polly, red-faced with rage, blubbered, "I told him to sort the nuts, because I didn't want butternuts mixed up with hickory, and he said I was just a girl and he didn't have to do what I told him. Then he threw nuts all over the ground and ran off into the bush."

"Someone should tan his hide," said Mrs. Cobman. "If his Pa was here, that boy would sure catch a licking."

Polly wiped her eyes. "Maybe a bear ate Moses. That would serve him right!"

She looked pleased at the idea, until Mrs. Cobman burst into tears and Mrs. Platto smacked the side of her head and exclaimed, "What a wicked thing to say!"

"I didn't mean it!" Polly wailed.

Axe Carrier ignored the commotion, but his face looked grim. "I'll go after him. He can't have gone far."

He left immediately, and returned within minutes with Moses trudging at his side. "I found the boy up in a cedar tree," he said.

"I climbed there to get away from Polly," Moses explained defiantly.

"Don't you dare do that again!" shouted Mrs. Cobman.

Axe Carrier laid his hands on Moses' shoulders. "Child, listen to me. The forest is full of dangers. You might have an accident, or meet a hungry animal, or be captured by an enemy. Until you are much older, never go into the bush alone."

Moses hung his head. "It's not fair," he grumbled. "Elijah goes off with Okwaho, but I have to gather nuts with girls and babies."

At the edge of camp, hanging by a thong from a high branch of a jack pine, a dead squirrel swung back and forth in the breeze. Okwaho was giving Elijah a shooting lesson with the bow and arrow. The squirrel was the target.

Charlotte, Mrs. Platto and Mrs. Cobman, who sat cracking hickory nuts on a flat rock, watched the lesson with half an eye.

"Doesn't it bother you," said Mrs. Platto to Mrs. Cobman, "to see your boy spending his time with that wild Indian?"

"Bother me? Yes, indeed. That young man is a savage through and through." She lifted the stone she held in her fist and with a sharp blow cracked the nut that lay in front of her. "It galls me to see Elijah copy everything Okwaho does. I'm properly grateful to these Mohawks, but I'll be mighty glad when we get to Carleton Island and Elijah's red friend goes back to wherever he came from."

Charlotte, half listening to the women, paid more attention to the lesson than to the nuts she was supposed to be cracking. She felt sorry for Elijah, who had launched a dozen arrows and never once came near hitting the squirrel.

When the quiver was empty, Elijah went off to search for the arrows. Okwaho leaned against the tree as he waited. Half a dozen times his piercing eyes glanced at Charlotte. She pretended not to notice.

The lesson resumed when Elijah had retrieved the arrows. This time it was Okwaho who held the bow. He fitted an arrow to the cord and pulled it back. The cord twanged. The arrow whizzed like a whip lashing the air. The squirrel came to life, leapt like a dancer, then fell back to dangle on its thong, doubly dead.

"Show-off!" muttered Mrs. Cobman.

Okwaho handed the bow to Elijah. The boy grinned, shrugged, and got out another arrow. Okwaho stood behind him, reaching over his shoulders to correct the angle of shaft to bow and to adjust his grip. The arrow flew again, sailed past the target again, but this time barely missed. Okwaho stepped back.

Elijah tried again. His arrow flew, and the dead squirrel danced.

"Look!" Charlotte shouted. "Bravo!"

With a proud smile, Elijah bowed.

"Well, that was pretty good," Mrs. Cobman had to admit.

Late the same afternoon, Okwaho and Elijah headed off into the bush. Elijah carried Okwaho's bow and wore his quiver. When they returned, they were dragging the carcass of a doe. Each held onto one hind leg, while the doe's head bounced on the dry grass.

"We'll have a feast!" Elijah's face was flushed with pride. "Plenty of meat for everybody."

"Did you kill the deer?" Charlotte asked.

"I surely did," said Elijah. "Okwaho took me to a place along the shore where deer come down to drink. When this doe raised her head, I got her right in the throat."

Okwaho skinned the doe and peeled off most of the meat in sheets. Charlotte watched curiously. This was nothing like the way Papa butchered a hog.

"How are we supposed to eat it?" Charlotte asked.

"On sticks," Elijah said. "We spear strips of meat, wrap them around the stick, and grill it over the fire. That's what Okwaho said to do."

The feast went on for hours. When it was over, when every strip of deer meat had been eaten and the children had been taken into the shelters to sleep, Elijah and Charlotte sat side by side on a log near the fire. Elijah stretched out his legs so that Charlotte would be sure to notice the moccasins he was wearing.

"Look what Okwaho gave me. He said I'd never be a mighty hunter until I stopped cracking branches under my boots."

She leaned forward for a better look.

"Want to see them?" Elijah pulled off one moccasin and handed it to her.

The moccasin had been cut from a single piece of smoked buckskin, with its top turned down in a sort of collar. She held it up to examine the beadwork — green, black and white beads in a complicated geometric pattern.

"It's beautiful," she said as she gave it back to him. Charlotte looked down at her own battered boots. "I wish I had moccasins."

"Okwaho says his mother always packs him lots of spares. Maybe he'll give you a pair. I think he likes you."

She looked across the fire to where Okwaho sat glaring at her. Charlotte flinched at the fierceness of his gaze.

"Oh, no! I'm quite certain Okwaho doesn't like me at all."

Chapter seven

O n the evening after the feast they were sitting by the
fire — Axe Carrier, Papa, Charlotte and Elijah — talking about the differences between the life of the Indians
and the life of the colonists. Everyone else except Okwaho
had returned to the shelters for the night. Okwaho, sitting
cross-legged on the opposite side of the fire, stared into the
flames. For once, to Charlotte's relief, he was not staring at
her.

Charlotte's attention had drifted away from the conversation until one statement by Axe Carrier brought it
quickly back.

"I was eighteen years old when I started school."

Eighteen when he started! Everyone Charlotte knew finished school at thirteen. From the corner of her eye she glanced at Elijah. His expression showed that he was just as surprised as she was.

"At that age, I had been a warrior for five years." Axe Carrier took a long pull at his pipe. "I fought in my first battle when I was thirteen. It was at Lake George in the time of the French Wars. We beat the French. Thayendanegea, the man you call Joseph Brant, fought by my side. It was his first battle too. Our commander was Sir William Johnson, Sir John's father."

Elijah spoke up. "If you were already a warrior, why did you want to go to school?" Elijah looked as if he couldn't believe such folly.

"Yes," said Papa. "How did it happen?"

"Thayendanegea talked me into it." Axe Carrier puffed on his pipe as he collected his thoughts. "Thayendanegea's older sister, Konwatsi'tsiaiénni, married Sir William Johnson after his first wife died."

"We call Joseph's sister Molly Brant," said Papa.

Axe Carrier nodded. "Most white people do, or Miss Molly." He took another puff at his pipe. "After his sister married Sir William, Thayendanegea spent a fair amount of time at Johnson Hall. Sir William liked him, and couldn't help noticing that he was clever and ambitious. So when Thayendanegea said that he wanted to learn to read and write, Sir William decided to send him away to school. As he thought about the advantages, the idea kept getting bigger. Sir William ended up sending five of us to the Moor School in Lebanon, Connecticut. So there we were — five Mohawk warriors sitting at desks making scratches on paper."

"Was that when you got the name Nathaniel Smart?" Papa asked.

"Yes. We were all given names to use in the white man's world. You would be calling me Mr. Smart if I had become a clerk in the Indian Agency. But that life did not interest me. Thayendanegea was different. He wanted to live in both worlds. Do you know what his name means?"

"No," said Papa.

"He Who Places Two Bets."

Papa laughed. "You double your chances when you place two bets."

"Yes," said Axe Carrier. "And he won both. The Iroquois respect him as a warrior, and the English as a statesman. When he was in England to negotiate with the King's ministers, he was treated like a prince."

"What about you?" asked Papa. "Why didn't you place two bets?"

Axe Carrier raised his arm in a sweeping gesture that included forest, lake and sky. "This is my world. When I grow too old to paddle a canoe, I'll probably work in the Indian Agency. But not yet. I am not a tree, rooted in one place."

"In that way," said Papa, "you and I are different. I reckon that I am a tree — a tree that was pulled up by the roots. My dream is to own some land, plant crops, and sink my roots into the soil again."

Axe Carrier knocked out his pipe into the fire. "There's good land in the Upper Country."

"If you know of a likely place, please tell me."

"Half a day's journey from Carleton Island, there's some land that's partly cleared."

"Where might that be?"

"The old French fort at Cataraqui."

Papa looked surprised. "Fort Frontenac? Hasn't the forest swallowed that up?"

"Not quite. It takes longer than twenty-five years for land to return to wilderness."

"I'll think about it. That would be very convenient." Papa stood up. "Right now, I'm going to get some sleep."

"Me too," said Elijah.

As the fire burned low, Charlotte thought about Axe Carrier's suggestion. Cataraqui would be perfect. Nick could easily find her there . . . if he tried.

On the far side of the fire, Okwaho suddenly jumped up. He looked straight at Charlotte as he strode around the fire with his eyes fixed upon her. In one hand he carried a pair of moccasins.

When he reached her, he thrust the moccasins at her.

"Ho!" he said. "*Atatawi.*"

She saw that the moccasins were new, and very like the ones he had given to Elijah, although the beadwork on this pair was red, green and white.

Okwaho pointed at her boots. "Too old. Too bad."

Charlotte did not know what to do. That her boots were "too old" and "too bad" was obvious. This must be Elijah's doing. Elijah meant well, but he shouldn't have asked Okwaho to give her a pair of moccasins. She could not accept such a gift.

Okwaho's eyes were black points, and his face was a rigid mask.

"No, no!" she exclaimed, pushing away the moccasins.

Axe Carrier was watching. "Take them," he commanded. '*Atatawi*' means gift. You must accept them."

"But I can't."

"You will insult him if you don't."

Okwaho remained motionless, staring at Charlotte with his glittering eyes.

"Thank you," she said faintly, and took the moccasins from him.

Okwaho stalked away.

"He's angry," Charlotte said.

"No. He doesn't know how to talk to a white woman."

"Please advise me. Tell me what to do."

Axe Carrier looked at her gravely. "Okwaho is young and needs a wife. In you he sees a beautiful maiden, strong and tall. I fear that he has an impossible dream."

Charlotte gulped. Okwaho, of all people! She thought he hated her.

"I advise you to tell him that you are already pledged to marry a man of your own people. Or it may be easier if I tell him for you. That will save his pride. Then, for the sake of your honour, you must give him a present. With us, one gift calls for another."

Axe Carrier paused for a moment and then said, "I have been to your school. Now you must go to mine. We Mohawk have customs of great antiquity, and you must learn them. I wish I could send you for lessons to a wise woman like my wife. Then you could be She Who Places Two Bets — at home in your world and in ours."

"One world is enough for me."

Axe Carrier shook his head. "Be ready. For many years to come, the lives of Loyalists and Mohawks will be entwined."

The next afternoon, while all were gathered around the campfire, Charlotte heard a faint noise, a peculiar clanking that sounded both familiar and strange.

"Listen!" she said. "What's that?"

Mama raised her head. "I don't know. It sounds a bit like someone hammering metal or banging on a tin. Could it be soldiers?"

The others shifted uneasily, exchanging nervous glances. Strange noises meant danger. The sound was coming closer. The youngest Platto started to cry.

"Shush!" Polly smacked him.

"It couldn't be soldiers," said Papa. "We're too far north for Rebel troops and too far south for any of ours."

Clank, clank, clank.

"Maybe we should hide in the woods," Mrs. Cobman murmured, snuggling Hope to her bosom.

"If it's Oneidas, we'd walk right into them," Charlotte said.

"It can't be Oneidas," Papa said. "If they attacked, they wouldn't make any noise, and certainly not a noise like that."

Clank, clank, clank. It was coming closer.

Mrs. Platto, who continued stirring the kettle of mush over the fire, said, "If we weren't sixty miles into the bush, I'd say it was a cowbell."

And before anyone could offer a different suggestion, a brown cow walked out of the woods. The cow's udder was so full that her teats nearly touched the ground. Following the cow was a short, bow-legged man wearing patched trousers and a coonskin hat. He had a pack on his back and a switch in his hand.

"I'm Tom Snelgrove," he announced. "This is Bessie. I smelled your cooking a mile off. I'm tired of milk. I'll trade you a whole pail of it for one hot meal."

"Where's your pail?" asked Mrs. Platto.

"That's just a manner of speaking. You'll get your milk, even if it ain't in a pail." He squatted on the ground next to the cow's flanks. "Watch this." He grasped one teat, squeezed, and a stream of milk shot through the air into his open mouth.

Then he turned to the wide-eyed children. "Anybody else want a drink?"

The younger Plattos did, though Polly stood aloof. Snelgrove squirted the milk into the children's open mouths with an aim so accurate that scarcely a drop splashed on their clothes or on the ground.

Charlotte laughed. "I wish I could do that."

"Open your mouth," said Snelgrove.

"No! No!" She backed away. "It was your aim that I admired."

"Dinner is ready," announced Mrs. Platto in a stop-your-fooling voice. "When we've cleaned out the kettle, Mr. Snelgrove can fill it with milk, and we'll drink some in a civilized manner."

After dinner, Snelgrove told his story.

"Me and Bessie been walking for seven days," he said, "all the way from Cherry Valley. The Rebels burned me out. I didn't lose much, because I never had much to start with. Just Bessie. I wasn't going to leave her for those damn Rebels."

"Where are you heading?" asked Papa.

"Carleton Island."

"How do you plan to get there?"

"By way of the Black River, I'll follow it north. The

mouth ain't far from Carleton Island."

"There's a channel to cross. How will you manage that? You can't swim your cow over at this time of year."

"I haven't got that part figured out. We'll make it some-how."

In the morning Snelgrove traded another kettle of milk for a packet of cold corn mush.

"Time to be off," he said, and picked up his switch.

"First, a word of advice," said Papa. "Take off that cow-bell and stuff it in your pack. Otherwise, the Oneidas will hear you a mile away."

Snelgrove scratched his chin. "I reckon you're right. Bessie won't be happy without her bell, but it's for her own good." He took off the bell and crammed it into his pack. "We'll see you at Carleton Island before Christmas!"

Bessie lowed softly as she plodded beside him into the forest.

It was an hour later that Mrs. Cobman, Hope in her arms, rushed up to the others. "I can't find Moses," she said. "Have you seen him?"

"No, I haven't," said Charlotte.

"Wasn't he with the other children when they said good-bye to Snelgrove and the cow?" Mama asked.

"No." Mrs. Platto shook her head. "Moses wasn't there."

Mrs. Cobman turned to the children huddled near the campfire. "Did you young 'uns see Moses?"

Polly's arm shot up as if this were a classroom quiz.

"I saw him!"

"When? Where?" Mrs. Cobman's voice rose. She clutched the baby to her chest.

"When Bessie left, Moses went the other way."

"Which other way?"

"Bessie went that way." Polly pointed east. "And Moses went the other way." She pointed west with a smug smile. Yes, Moses was in trouble again.

Mrs. Cobman bit her lower lip. She looked angry, but also afraid. "If that boy went off alone, after everything we told him——"

"Don't worry, Ma. He must be checking our snares," said Elijah. "We set some for rabbits last night."

Polly smirked. "Or maybe he climbed another tree."

The adults stood in a circle, looking at each other's faces but avoiding each other's eyes.

"We'd better go after him," said Papa.

"No search party," said Axe Carrier. "He's had an hour's head start. Okwaho and I can track him faster if we go alone. There's an Oneida fishing village at the west end of the lake, and that's the direction he has gone. Unless we hurry, they'll find him before we do."

After the two warriors left, a feeling of dread settled in. All conversation stopped. Mrs. Cobman gazed bleakly into the fire. When Elijah sat down beside her, she turned her back to him.

"Ma," said Elijah, "they'll find Moses. He always turns up."

At midday Mrs. Platto cooked a kettleful of cornmeal mush. No one ate much. Mrs. Cobman did not pick up her spoon.

"Sadie, you must eat," said Mrs. Platto firmly. "You got Hope to think about too."

"Yes." Mrs. Cobman's voice sounded hollow. At the reminder, she began to eat. She ate mechanically, as if clockwork raised and lowered her hand.

When a cold drizzle started to fall, Mrs. Cobman took Hope into her shelter. The others remained standing about the fire. Polly Platto was in tears.

Time passed slowly. Minutes stretched into hours. Nothing happened. Water was trickling down Charlotte's neck. What was the point of staying out in the rain? Charlotte looked westward one last time, and then went into the shelter. Mama joined her. Papa remained outside, tending the fire.

The rain had changed to sleet, and darkness was falling by the time the searchers returned. Moses was not with them.

"We followed his tracks all morning," said Axe Carrier. "Around midday we came to a leaf pile beside the trail. Some leaves were scattered about, some pressed down as if someone had been lying in them. From that point on, the boy was no longer alone. Beyond the leaf pile, there were moccasin prints as well as boot marks in the earth."

"Moccasin prints," Mrs. Cobman said in a low voice. "Where did they lead?"

"We don't know. The trail went cold."

"What do you mean?"

"We lost the trail." He spoke slowly. "Oneida warriors move like wolves in the forest. They double back on their tracks over and over, each time heading off in a different direction so nobody can tell which way they've really gone. I know their tricks."

"Where do you think they've gone?" Papa asked.

"Most likely to their fishing village at the far end of the lake."

Mrs. Cobman looked as if she had been turned to stone. Her voice shook, "Won't you go after them?" All eyes turned to her. No one moved or spoke.

Axe Carrier broke the silence. "There's no use. If the boy is there, we have no way to rescue him."

Mrs. Cobman's eyes shifted from Axe Carrier's face to Papa's. "Do something!" Her voice rose. "You can't let those heathen savages kill my child."

Axe Carrier flinched but said nothing.

Hope wailed. Mrs. Cobman tightened her grip. There was a tiny squawk, then silence.

The baby can't breathe, Charlotte thought. Somebody has to get her away from Mrs. Cobman before she suffocates. Charlotte reached out her arms. "Let me take her."

"No! Don't nobody touch my baby!" She twisted away and ran, stumbling through fallen leaves, toward the forest. Okwaho blocked her path. At the sight of him, she screamed, "You're the cause. Elijah took good care of his brother before you lured him away."

Okwaho took a step backwards. His hand strayed to the handle of his knife, though he didn't look as if he planned to use it.

"Ma!" said Elijah. "It ain't Okwaho's fault."

Not a sound came from the baby. Charlotte watched in horror. Didn't Mrs. Cobman know that she was crushing her own child?

Suddenly Mrs. Platto grabbed Mrs. Cobman by both shoulders. "Sadie! Pull yourself together! You'll kill that baby if you don't stop." She shook her hard enough to loosen her bones. "You must bear this like a soldier's wife."

Mrs. Cobman seemed to hear, and her frenzy passed. She made no further resistance as Mrs. Platto took the baby and gave her to Mama. Then Mrs. Platto gently took Mrs. Cobman's arm. "Come out of the rain, Sadie. In a few minutes, you can have your baby back."

"They won't kill your son," Axe Carrier said calmly.

She wiped her eyes. "What will they do with him?"

"They'll keep him as a hostage or they'll adopt him. Either way, he is safe."

After Mrs. Platto had led the tearful woman away, Papa asked, "Is that true?"

"If there had been signs of struggle, I'd fear for him. But there were none. The tracks showed that all three were walking at an ordinary pace — a boy in boots and two men in moccasins. The warriors used no force."

That night Charlotte lay inside the hut listening to sleet strike the bark roof over her head. Where was Moses now? He might be out in the rain, cold and wet on a wilderness trail. Or he might be snug and dry inside an Oneida lodge, sleeping on a pile of warm pelts. Was he lonely? Was he frightened? Or did he think it a fine adventure to be captured by Indians? She wondered whether she would ever see him again.

Chapter eight

Squinting into the setting sun, Charlotte and Elijah watched the long canoe approach over the green lake.

"It's two days early," said Charlotte."

"I reckon we'll leave tomorrow," Elijah said glumly.

"If the weather holds."

"I keep hoping that Moses will come back. But if he does, there won't be anybody here. I wish we could stay a while longer."

"We can't," she said regretfully, not adding that it would do no good anyway.

Others joined them as they watched. There were no shouts of welcome. As soon as the canoe was hauled up on land, Axe Carrier spoke in Mohawk to the paddlers. They nodded from time to time, adding comments of their own. Then Axe Carrier addressed the Loyalists.

"The warriors tell me that twelve nights ago, when they paddled by the Oneida fishing village at the west end of the lake, smoke was rising from the fires, the drying racks were covered with fish, and many canoes were pulled up on the shore. This morning before dawn, they passed by again. The village looked deserted. No fires. No fish. No canoes. What did it mean? It was too early to break up fishing camp. My warriors knew something must have happened. Now they understand. They believe that the Oneidas have taken the boy away to their main village, many miles to the west."

The Mohawks unloaded blankets for everyone — rough, woollen army blankets from Fort Haldimand's commissary — and a barrel of flour from which Mrs. Platto mixed up bannock dough to bake over the fire. That night Axe Carrier and Okwaho ate their meal with the other warriors, sitting apart from the white people.

Charlotte feared that Mrs. Cobman would become hysterical again when the time came to leave, but she took her place in the canoe meekly and sat on a folded blanket with Hope in her arms.

"Well, here we go," Charlotte said as she climbed in. Though she had seen hundreds of canoes on the Mohawk River, she had never been in one before. She gripped the gunwale as it moved away from shore. The shifting motion made her nervous. She worried what would happen if the canoe tipped over, or if an enemy shot at it from the shore. One bullet piercing the birchbark skin would sink them all in the deep, icy water of Oneida Lake. And so their journey would come to a disastrous end.

There was little to see when she peered over the side: a sunken log, some rocks, a few perch. It was better to keep her head up, she decided, and watch the trees along the shore. Solid ground. That was where she would rather be.

With ten paddlers — Papa and Elijah had each taken a paddle — the canoe ploughed steadily forward.

After a while, Charlotte's nervousness disappeared, leaving her bored. Squatting in the bottom of the canoe was tedious and uncomfortable. Tomorrow she would ask Axe Carrier if she might paddle too.

A breeze rose late in the afternoon. It was a stiff wind by the time the long canoe was pulled up on shore at the Oneida fishing village. Charlotte climbed out of the canoe, stretched, and looked around. Wind whistled among the deserted huts and shook the empty drying racks that stood over the ashes of dead fires. At the edge of the camp, Elijah was poking around in the bushes. Charlotte joined him out of curiosity.

"I think I've found something," he said as he knelt by a fallen log.

Even before he rolled it over, Charlotte half knew what lay under the log. In a shallow cavity were Moses' coat, shirt, breeches, dirty socks and battered boots, lined up in a row.

"Well," she said, "this proves that Moses was here."

"And that he's alive."

"What do you mean?"

"It's simple. If you were the Oneidas, and you'd captured a white boy, and you planned to keep him, you'd dress him so he wouldn't stand out, and then you'd get rid of his old clothes."

"I reckon so." She wasn't sure that Elijah had proved his case, but it sounded likely.

Elijah picked up one of Moses' boots, brushed off the earth, and turned it upside down. When he shook it, a black beetle fell out. For a moment Elijah cradled the boot in his hands, then replaced it exactly as he had found it. When he rolled the log back, there was no sign anything had been disturbed.

"We'd better keep this to ourselves," said Elijah.

"Shouldn't we tell your mother?"

He shook his head. "She'd only run crazy again."

Elijah was right, but Charlotte felt guilty all the same.

"Let me take a paddle," Charlotte requested the next morning.

Axe Carrier shook his head. "Paddling is harder than you may think. When we reach white water, your paddle would flail about and get in the way. Now, if you were a Mohawk girl—"

"You're about to tell me that Drooping Flower can handle a canoe," Charlotte said with a smile.

"She can shoot the worst rapids on any river."

Charlotte sighed. There might be advantages in becoming a woman of two worlds.

From Oneida Lake to Lake Ontario was downriver all the way. Over long, smooth stretches of the Oswego River, the canoe seemed to fly with invisible wings. Then a sudden change would bring it close to jutting rocks where the water foamed white.

The first run through rapids took Charlotte's breath away. She clutched the gunwale, waiting for a smash. But the warriors leaned into their paddles and laughed, their faces flushed with triumph at each danger overcome. Soon she caught the excitement and began to enjoy the noise and swirl of the leaping water.

On the next day, the sky clouded over in the afternoon and rain began to fall. It had soaked through Charlotte's cloak by the time the paddlers stopped for the night. After unloading the canoe, they turned it over and propped up one side with paddles to make a shelter to keep off the rain.

Late into the night, Charlotte, Papa and Axe Carrier stayed awake to tend the fire. They sat so close to its warmth that their clothes steamed. Charlotte's woollen blanket smelled like a wet sheep.

In the shelter of the canoe, Mrs. Cobman curled like a mother cat around her baby.

"I pity that woman," said Axe Carrier. "It is great sorrow to lose a child."

"What can be done to get the boy back?" asked Papa.

"Nothing. When you get to Fort Haldimand, you should report what happened. But the Commander can't order out the regiment to search for one child. If the Oneida plan to use him as a hostage, they will start the bargaining. But if they adopt him, they won't give him up.

"It troubles me that I cannot go to the Oneidas and ask for the boy. In the past, I could have walked into their camp and said, 'Brothers, you have the son of my cousin with you. My cousin is full of sorrow. I bring you presents and ask you to return the boy.' It would have been as easy as that. But now the Oneidas are the friends of our foes."

Axe Carrier stared into the fire. "The breaking of nations is a terrible thing. Long ago we were the Five Nations: Mohawk, Seneca, Cayuga, Onondaga and Oneida. Then the Tuscaroras joined our Confederacy and we became the Six Nations. We were *Aganuschioni* — United People. But today we are no longer united. We have lost our brothers, the Oneidas and the Tuscaroras. We have lost our lands."

"You share our story," said Papa. "You are Loyalists too."

By the fourth day the rapids were behind them, and the long canoe moved silently over grey water reflecting a grey sky. On both sides lay wetlands full of sere, yellow rushes and cattails with bent stems. Marshes stretched for miles.

The river widened and widened until it was no longer a

river but an unending vista of waves. Charlotte had never seen so much water. So this was Lake Ontario; no wonder they called it a Great Lake.

The long canoe trembled as the first breaker hit. As if this were a signal, all the men rose onto their knees, leaned over the gunwales, and thrust their paddles into the swell. The bow shot up as the canoe crested each wave, then smacked with a crash into the trough.

The canoe was rocking and bouncing and plunging. With every tilt Charlotte's stomach lurched. She squeezed her eyes shut, trying to block out the waves crashing all about her. But even when she could not see, she still felt the canoe pitch and toss. She tasted vomit. She had to hold it down, keep it in. This is the worst, she thought. I'm going to be seasick in a canoe.

Abruptly, the rocking stopped. When Charlotte opened her eyes, she saw that the canoe had entered a sheltered bay where the biggest wave was a ripple. She took a long, slow breath, and the heaving of her stomach stopped.

The canoe glided onto the beach and came to rest. Two warriors jumped out and pulled it further up on the soft sand. Somewhat shakily, everyone climbed out — everyone but Charlotte. When she tried to rise, she found that one leg, bent under her, had gone to sleep. Her foot tingled. Pins and needles ran up and down her nerves. She was reaching out her hands to unbend her knee, when someone grasped her arm.

"Papa, my leg has . . ." But before she could finish the sentence, she knew that it wasn't Papa. Okwaho was the man helping her out of the canoe. It was Okwaho's firm hand that steadied her as she stood on the sand, Okwaho's shoulder that she leaned against. For a moment she did not move, did not want to move. She wished that the moment could last. But no, that must not happen. As soon as normal sensation returned to her leg, she gently pulled away.

"Thank you." She could not bring herself to meet his gaze.

All that evening Charlotte was silent. She was, in fact, afraid — not of Okwaho but of the feelings he stirred in her. She had liked the touch of his hand. It had been a long time since a young man had taken her arm. I must not be foolish, she told herself. I am not a Mohawk maiden. I have no idea how to conduct myself with a Mohawk man. We can barely talk to each other. Besides, I already have a sweetheart.

The thought of Nick brought a pang. Feelings of guilt and anger came over her. She stared into the fire and cursed the war. She cursed Nick for being a Whig, and she cursed herself for having walked away when he said, "I'll always love you."

She did not curse Okwaho, although his presence threw her feelings into confusion. His dark eyes no longer looked cruel; now she saw nobility in the high curve of his cheekbones and warmth in the burnished copper of his skin.

Through the long evening he sat only a few feet from her, staring into the fire just as she was doing. What was he thinking about? Was he sorry or glad that they would part the next day?

She wished that she had not been so cold and hostile. Why hadn't she followed Axe Carrier's advice and given him a present? "With us, one gift calls for another," Axe Carrier had told her. Her behaviour had been ignorant and rude. Yet it was not too late to make amends. Right now, tonight, she could give him something, and then he would remember her as a friend.

Charlotte knew just the thing. Sewn into her petticoats was a brooch that she had bought on a family visit to Albany when she was thirteen. The brooch was silver, set with a large gemstone that looked like yellow sunshine trapped in clear water. Mama had called it a cairngorm.

Where exactly had she sewn it? Charlotte ran her hands over the skirt of her gown, trying to feel its shape. There it was, quilted into her double petticoat just above the hem. Good. She could easily get it out.

Charlotte felt nervous as she approached Okwaho and knelt beside him. He turned his grim face towards her. A bit of her old fear returned when she pointed to the scalping knife he wore in his belt.

"Please. Give me your knife."

He looked puzzled as he pulled it from his belt and handed it to her. She remembered Elijah's words, "He's taken ten scalps." This very knife with its razor-sharp blade had sliced hair and skin from the heads of ten human beings. Forcing herself not to think about that, she freed the brooch with one slash.

"*Atatawi*," she said, and held it upon her open palm. The gemstone glowed in the firelight. When she put the brooch into his hand, she did not allow her fingers to touch his.

"Good present," he said. "*Nya weh*. Okwaho thanks his friend."

The fire flared up, and the light fell not only upon her face but also upon his, so that they saw each other clearly despite the darkness all around.

The next morning Charlotte settled herself upon her folded blanket in the bottom of the long canoe and looked about. A scattering of islands interrupted the vastness of the lake as they neared its eastern end. Some were large and forested, some not much bigger than a rock surmounted by a single stunted tree.

One of the larger islands was their destination. Charlotte peered into the distance, watching for the British flag. Just after midday she saw it — red, white and blue against the grey sky — and her heart gave a lift. Carleton Island at last!

A tower came next into view, and then the top of a block-house peeping over ramparts. As the long canoe came closer, she saw a score of bark-covered huts outside the fort's walls, and birchbark canoes pulled up along the water's edge.

There was a shipyard, too, with a half-built ship lying in the slips. How strange to build a ship on an island in the wilderness!

A broad limestone shelf at the water's edge served as a dock. As the canoe came alongside, two warriors jumped out and held it steady for the passengers to disembark.

"Well, here we are," said Papa as he helped Mama and then Charlotte out of the canoe. Charlotte stamped her feet and stretched her arms to get rid of her stiffness from sitting so long. What now? she wondered.

Axe Carrier stood with Mama and Papa near the bow while the other warriors unloaded the canoe.

"Am I now to address you as Mr. Smart," Papa was asking, "since we are entering an English fort?"

The corners of Axe Carrier's mouth turned up, though his eyes remained grave.

"That name has no power for me. Let me be Axe Carrier until the day you see me sitting at a desk with a pen in my hand."

He walked with them through the open stockade gate. Inside the fort, he pointed out the blockhouse, the soldiers' barracks, officers' quarters, infirmary, gunpowder magazine, even the latrines. Beyond lay the parade square, and beyond that the Loyalist refugee camp, where dozens of white tents stood in rows.

"That's where you'll live."

"In a tent!" Mama gasped.

"It will be fine, Martha," said Papa. "We shall manage."

At the blockhouse door Axe Carrier left them. "You register here," he said. "I shall join the other warriors. We'll spend the night on Carleton Island, then leave at dawn."

"Where will your travels take you next?" asked Papa.

"To Lachine to spend the winter with my family." His eyes brightened. "I haven't seen my wife and children since April. I left Lachine when the ice broke up."

"I hope you'll find them well." Papa held out his hand. "Thank you for bringing us safely here."

"*Nya weh*," said Charlotte. "Thank you."

Axe Carrier looked at her hard. "*Nya weh*? Ho! Young woman of two worlds. You learn fast, and you will travel far."

Chapter nine

Papa pulled open the heavy plank door, and the Hooper family entered a large, square room. A wide wooden counter ran the length of one wall. Behind the counter a red-coated soldier with a long, melancholy face was scooping flour onto the pan of a set of scales. In front of the counter waited a queue of ragged men and women. Mrs. Cobman and Mrs. Platto, with their children, were already standing in the line.

Across the room, an officer sat at a table with a record book open in front of him. "Over here!" he called. "New arrivals must register."

Mama leaned wearily on Papa's arm as they walked across the room. Papa told the officer their names.

"Where was your home?"

"Fort Hunter."

"Where were you born?"

"Fort Hunter."

"All of you?"

"Yes."

"How old is your daughter?"

"Fifteen."

Papa spoke for the whole family, although Charlotte could perfectly well have spoken for herself. When the officer had written everything down, he sent them over to the counter, where they joined the line-up waiting for supplies.

The melancholy soldier was giving out flour, dried peas and salt pork. Charlotte overheard several complaints about the lack of rice and corn meal. At each complaint the soldier sighed, "There should be some on the next bateau." He looked so mournful that even his moustache drooped.

When Charlotte and her parents reached the head of the line, he introduced himself. "I am Sergeant Major Clark, clerk and naval storekeeper. You'll draw your rations every week. Bring back your bags to be refilled. We don't have extra."

He issued them a canvas army tent, a small sack of flour, a bag of split peas and a chunk of salt pork.

Mama took charge of the rations, while Charlotte and Papa carried the tent to the Loyalist encampment. When they had it set up, Papa held open the flap for Mama and Charlotte to step inside. Charlotte looked around. There was no window, but the white canvas admitted enough light for her to see clearly. "It's not a bad tent," she said cheerfully. "It will keep out the wind and rain. And there's plenty of room."

"This is a six-man tent," Papa said. "We're lucky to have it to ourselves. I was afraid they'd stick us in with another family." He shrugged the rucksack from his back and set it on the ground. "Since there's no floor, I can dig a hole to bury those valuables you two have been dragging around in your petticoats." He spoke with enthusiasm, as if the lack of a floor were a real advantage.

"We can bury our paper money in the tea tin," said Mama. She sounded optimistic, but Charlotte wondered what she really thought.

Papa built a cooking fire outside the tent and made a tripod of stout, green sticks from which to hang the camp kettle. While Mama rested, Charlotte stewed up a mash of salt pork and split peas. It was a good supper, considering that she hadn't had time to soak the peas.

Next morning Charlotte woke up early. Without waking Mama and Papa, she opened the tent flap and stepped outside. The Loyalists' tents were so white in the dim light that they made her think of ghosts — an army of giant ghosts standing row on row.

If she hurried, she thought, she would be in time to say goodbye to the Mohawks. Looking between the rows of tents, she saw Elijah ahead of her, walking toward the stockade gate.

"Wait for me!" she called.

He waited. But when she caught up to him and saw his glum face, she realized that he was not eager for company. Without talking, they walked side by side down to the shore.

When they reached the long canoe, the warriors were loading bales of furs. Okwaho saw them, put his bale into the canoe, and joined them. A shadow passed over the young warrior's face when he saw Elijah's scowl.

"Little brother," he said, "do not look at Okwaho with angry eyes."

He took from his own neck a tiny bag suspended on a leather thong and lowered it over Elijah's head. The bag was brightly painted with many signs. Curiosity broke through Elijah's cloud of gloom.

"What is it?" When Elijah lifted the bag to inspect it, a look of awe crossed his face, as if he understood that something wondrous had been bestowed.

"It is medicine bag. In it is powerful medicine. There is a stone the colour of blood and a dust made from the skin of a rattlesnake and the beak of an eagle. Make you good hunter. Make you strong in war." He looked intently at the boy. "Never open medicine bag. If you open, power turn against you. Bring bad luck."

"I swear not to open it. I'll never take it off."

Okwaho put his hands on Elijah's shoulders. "Your hair is colour of the beaver and your eyes are colour of the sky, but you are my brother."

"Then take me with you. If we are brothers, we should stay together."

Okwaho looked hard at the boy, and then shook his head. "My path not good path for you." He dropped his hands from Elijah's shoulders. "*Ska-noh!*" he said. And then in English, "Be strong!"

"*Ska-noh,*" said Elijah.

Now the long canoe was afloat, and the other Mohawks were calling. Okwaho turned towards Charlotte.

"*Ska-noh!*" she said.

Okwaho's stern face relaxed into a smile. He touched her cheek with his fingertips. "*Ska-noh.*" Then he raced to the water's edge, placed his hands on the gunwale and vaulted into the canoe.

As the canoe entered the channel and began its journey, Charlotte hoped that Okwaho would find a Mohawk girl to love, one who could bake him double ball biscuit loaves. And she hoped that someday their paths would cross again.

*　*　*

Laundry day. Charlotte had no washtub, no scrubbing board, no soap. But she did have hot water in the camp kettle and a washerwoman's pummel that Papa had whittled from a basswood sapling.

She felt like singing as she pounded out the dirt. Chemises, underdrawers, stockings — the kettle wouldn't hold much, but at least it was a start. Thump! Thump! Thump!

She pummeled the clothes until the wash water turned grey, then forked them out with a stick, wrung them, and carried them into the tent.

Charlotte was draping the wet clothes over a rope strung between two tent poles when she heard someone shout: "Bateau! Bateau coming up the channel!"

Pushing open the tent flap, she saw men, women and children streaming towards the fort gate. She pulled her cloak about her shoulders and joined the rush.

Hurry was unnecessary, as Charlotte knew as soon as she caught sight of the bateau creeping up the channel from the east. It had a mast with a crossbar intended for a square sail, but the mast was empty. Driven by manpower alone — six oarsmen along the sides and two men with poles at the stern — the bateau lurched like a crippled turtle toward the landing.

When the bateau finally bumped up against the limestone shelf at the water's edge, the Fort Haldimand regiment helped to unload the cargo, soldiers and bateau men hoisting it onto the shore. The soldiers worked silently, but the bateau men never stopped laughing and talking. What were they saying? It was all in French. The only word Charlotte recognized was *rhum*.

Well, she thought, there was plenty of *rhum* on board — dozens of barrels, each so large it took two men to roll it up the hill into the fort. There were also casks of brandy, hogsheads of salt pork, and innumerable sacks with their contents stamped in red letters: flour, peas, beans, rice.

Four soldiers struggled with a four-poster bed, complete with rods for bed curtains. That must be for an officer. Following the bed came two soldiers carrying a bathtub — a tin hipbath like the one Papa used to set up Saturday nights in front of the kitchen fire. What luxury — a real bath!

The bateau's single passenger, an English officer, was hardly out of the boat before the crowd began to question him about the trip.

"It took twelve days," he said. "Worse for the men than for me. When we were ascending the rapids, half of them stayed on board and pushed with poles, whilst the others had to get out and tow with ropes. They waded in water up to their thighs."

"Mighty cold, this time of year," said a by-stander.

"That's why there won't be another boat until spring. Tonight the men will have a party. Tomorrow they'll be gone. They say they'll be back in Montreal in three days."

"Twelve to get here and three to go back?"

"Apparently that's normal," the officer said as he excused himself to report to the Commander.

The bateau men spent most of the night singing, dancing and drinking rum. Charlotte was happy to be kept awake, for the sound of fiddle music coming from the barracks reminded her of jigs and reels at country-dances back home.

"Are they going to keep it up all night?" Mama groaned.

"Only until they pass out," Papa said.

Charlotte did not know when the party ended. She was groggy with sleep when Papa roused her in the morning.

"Wake up!" he said. "You're missing the excitement."

Charlotte half opened her eyes. "I heard enough excitement last night."

"I don't mean *that* excitement. On the midnight watch, a sentry spotted a campfire on the south shore. Half a dozen people are over there, waiting to come across. There's a cow with them."

Charlotte opened her eyes the rest of the way. "Bessie!"

"That's right. I recognized Snelgrove and the cow. He's a lucky man. If he'd arrived two days later, the bateau would be halfway to Montreal, and there'd be no way he could ferry his cow across the channel."

"Has the bateau gone to get them?"

"Not yet. The bateau men are moving mighty slow this morning."

"I want to see this." Charlotte threw off her blanket and stood up.

"Not I," said Mama. "Tell me about it later. I'm going back to sleep." As Charlotte closed the tent flap, she heard her mother cough.

When Charlotte and Papa reached the shore, six groggy-looking bateau men were climbing into the boat. Slowly it lurched towards the opposite shore, where a cluster of people and a brown cow stood watching.

"Now we'll see how they get Bessie on board," said Papa.

As soon as they landed, the bateau men hauled a plank out of the boat and set it up as a gangway. But the cow must have guessed what was up and wanted no part of it. She allowed Snelgrove to lead her right up to the base of the plank, but that was as far as she was willing to go. Planting her forelegs, Bessie lowered her head and bellowed.

Charlotte laughed. "She's behaving more like a mule than a cow."

Now the bateau men joined forces with Snelgrove. They tied a cable around her body. Snelgrove pulled; they pushed — seven men against one cow.

Bessie surrendered with style. Tossing her head nonchalantly, she ambled up the gangway. For a moment she hesitated at the top. After that, Charlotte was not sure whether she jumped or she was pushed. At any rate, Bessie landed in the boat. With a few prods, the men positioned her near the centre. Raising her head regally, the cow gazed about and then, lifting her tail away from her body, released a flood of dung.

The human passengers went aboard, giving the cow a wide berth.

The bateau was halfway back when Papa exclaimed, "Well, I'll be blasted! Do you see who else is on that boat?"

Charlotte, who had not been paying attention to the human beings on board, took a good look. "Aren't those the Vroomans?"

"The very same. I never expected to see them again. Peter swore he'd never give up his farm."

But there he was, the Hoopers' friend from half a mile down the road, a beefy-looking man with a red face, standing at the bow. At his side, her elbows resting on the gunwale, was his wife Louisa. Flanking them were two little girls and two little boys.

"I'm glad to see them," Charlotte said. "They'll have news." It was hard to hide her excitement. Yet Papa probably guessed. He knew as well as she that the Vroomans' farm was right next to the Schylers' place. They would surely have news about Nick.

When the bateau reached shore, Peter Vrooman climbed out and then helped his wife and his daughters over the side. By the time the girls were out, the two boys had already scrambled over the gunwale and were inspecting the Indian canoes that lay along the shore.

Louisa gazed about. She was a pretty, plump woman, matronly although still in her twenties. That's what came of having four children before she was twenty-two. But she always appeared cheerful, even now as she stood on the Carleton Island shore, her bonnet tied with ribbons that looked as if they hadn't been pressed for weeks.

"Louisa!" Charlotte called.

Louisa's eyes opened wide. "Charlotte Hooper!" She rushed forward, holding out both hands. "We knew your family had left Fort Hunter, but nobody had any idea where you'd gone."

"Papa thought we'd be safest if we came north to an English fort."

"After what happened to us, I reckon he was right."

"What do you mean?"

"Well, when Peter finally admitted that we had to leave, we decided to head for New York. It sounded safe, with all the English troops stationed there. We planned to rent a house, live there till the war was over, then go back to our farm."

Louisa made a wry face. "The Sons of Liberty wrecked that plan. We'd loaded up the wagon with our best furniture and started off. But we hadn't travelled half a day before the Sons of Liberty stopped us. They smashed the furniture and threw everything about. Then they took off with our horses and wagon and left us standing beside the road.

"After that, Peter said we should forget about New York and go up to Canada. We took to the woods because we didn't want meet those Liberty men again. After a couple of days, we came upon that man and his cow. They saved our lives."

Charlotte looked at the round, pink faces of the two little girls who clung to Louisa's hands. They appeared healthy, considering what the family had been through.

"We met them too," said Charlotte. "Snelgrove and Bessie were heading for the Black River when they spent a night at our camp on the shore of Oneida Lake."

"Snelgrove figures he'll make his fortune at Fort Haldimand," said Louisa. "As long as that cow produces, there'll be milk, cream and butter to sell to the officers. It's an ill wind that blows nobody any good."

As Louisa spoke, Charlotte noticed that a crowd of children had gathered around Bessie. Snelgrove was again demonstrating his marksmanship, shooting streams of milk into their open mouths.

Later that day, while Papa and Charlotte were helping Peter to set up his tent, he told them what he could about life in the Mohawk Valley after the Hoopers had fled.

"We left a fortnight after you did," Peter said. "During those two weeks, things got worse every day. You never knew who was going to attack you, or when. They'd smash windows. Throw fire into your house. Even your minister, Reverend Stuart, had his property plundered."

"Rebels were using his church as a tavern before we left," said Papa.

"Now they've turned it into a stable — not that he has much need for a church any longer. Only three families are left of his whole congregation. There's talk about trying him for treason."

"Treason!" Papa exclaimed. "On what grounds?"

"Befriending Mohawks. Helping Loyalists. Some people think he's a spy. Both his brothers have turned against him."

"I'd heard that," said Papa.

"It's the same everywhere. Brother against brother. Neighbour against neighbour. Father against son. Like the Schylers."

Charlotte caught her breath. The Schylers. Nick and his father. What about them?

"Like the Schylers?" Papa asked. "What happened?"

"Oh, of course you haven't heard. It happened a week after you folks left. I learned about it from Schyler's brother. He's a Tory, as you likely know. The two brothers haven't been on speaking terms for three years — one being a Tory and the other a Whig. Anyway, Nick showed up at his uncle's door with his clothes tied in a bundle. He said his father had thrown him out because he changed sides."

"Nick changed sides!" Papa said. "Well, I'm glad he saw the light. What reason did he give?"

"He told his uncle that he had seen some ugly sights. The violence of the Sons of Liberty bothered him most of all. But he refused to talk about it."

"So the lad is living with his uncle."

"Not any longer. He stayed there a couple of days. Then a press gang showed up to recruit him for the Rebel army. They got off their horses, walked up to the front door and asked for Nick Schyler. Nick was in the next room, listening. He tiptoed out the back way, sneaked around to the front of the house, jumped on the best horse and galloped away. That's the last of him anyone has seen or heard."

Charlotte could scarcely take it in. Nick had changed sides. Nick was gone.

For the rest of the day, Charlotte never stopped thinking about what she had heard. When night came, vivid dreams disturbed her sleep: Nick on a horse galloping down the river road, Nick calling to her from under the sycamore tree, Nick lying on the ground covered with blood. She woke up sweating, afraid to sleep lest she dream again.

Until dawn she lay awake wondering what to make of it all. Nick had changed sides, so politics no longer divided them. But wherever he was, his life was in danger. Traitor. Horse thief. He'd hang if the Rebels caught him.

Ever since she fell in love with Nick, fear had not been far away. Papa had warned her from the beginning. She would never forget that evening or that warning.

There had been a barn-raising at a nearby farm, followed by a dance in the upper space that would become the hayloft as soon as the early hay was ready to mow. But for this one night, there would be jigs and reels for as long as the fiddler played.

After helping to raise the barn, Papa said he was too tired to go. Mama, who had a quilt to finish, was content to stay home. And so it was Charlotte and her brothers who set off in the wagon, since the Hoopers' buggy was not big enough to carry four people. James drove. Charlotte sat up on the high board seat beside him, taking care that her new yellow gown not be soiled or crushed. Isaac and Charlie rode in the back, where hay or market produce was the usual load.

When the dancing began, each of her brothers in turn was her partner, before going off to ask other girls. Left standing with the wallflowers, Charlotte wondered if she would ever be asked to dance by a boy who was not her brother. When no one had claimed her for the next two dances, she decided no one ever would. And that was when Nick Schyler stepped up to her.

"May I have the honour?" he asked.

She glanced around quickly, thinking that he meant this invitation for some other girl. Handsome, lanky, blue-eyed Nick was seventeen years old, a farmer's son who lived a mile down the road from the Hoopers. Until this moment, he had never paid any attention to Charlotte. But there he was, offering his arm. With a smile she placed her hand in the crook of his elbow, and they were off.

It was just as well that they danced every jig and reel, for she was too shy, at fourteen, to have carried on a conversation.

At the end of the evening, James beckoned from across the room, signalling that it was time to return home.

"I have to go now," she said, reluctantly pulling her hand from Nick's, where it most certainly belonged.

"May I call on you tomorrow?" Nick asked. "After church?"

Charlotte felt herself blushing and was barely able to meet his eyes.

"Yes, I reckon that will be all right."

In the morning she told Mama and Papa that Nick had asked to call.

"He's a fine lad from a good family," Mama said, "though I'm not sure you're old enough to have a young man calling on you."

Papa frowned. "The Schylers are Whigs. Best not mix with him too much."

"But may he call on me? Papa, please!"

"I would not close the door against him. But I see trouble ahead."

Plenty of trouble, as it turned out. Yet until the day her brothers joined the Loyalist regiment, she never could have guessed how bad.

Chapter ten

"Poor man's chicken feathers, my grandmother used to call them," said Mama. She was stuffing beech leaves into hemp sacks. Sergeant Major Clark had given them six empty sacks — enough to make three mattresses.

"Why did she call them that?" Charlotte asked.

"Because that's what poor people used, in the old days. They're not as soft as chicken feathers, but they'll block the cold that rises from the ground."

"What we need is a fire inside the tent. I see smoke rising from the Indians' huts. Papa, if they can have their cooking fires inside, why can't we?"

"Canvas burns a hundred times faster than bark. One spark, and whoosh! Fire's dangerous in a tent. What we need is a metal pail. If we had one, we could fill it with embers and hot ashes and bring it into the tent. That way, we could have warmth without danger."

Mama grasped the open end of the sack she was filling, and as she gave it a shake, she started coughing.

"I don't like the sound of that," said Papa.

"It's nothing." Mama caught her breath. "Just dust from the leaves." A moment later she coughed again.

The next day her cough was worse.

"A touch of ague," she said. "Nothing to worry about." She sat huddled in her blanket. Her teeth chattered, but her skin was hot.

"Martha, you have a fever," said Papa. "The doctor should see you."

"I'll ask him if he'll come," said Charlotte. She pulled her cloak tightly around her shoulders. When she opened the tent flap, snow swirled inside. Wind buffeted her as she crossed the parade square.

She found the regiment's doctor and his assistant in the outbuilding that housed the surgery and the infirmary. The doctor, a tall, thin man with greying hair, wore over his uniform a smock splashed with blood. A putrid smell filled the air. Lying on a narrow cot, a soldier moaned with pain as the assistant bandaged his feet.

"Gangrene," the doctor told Charlotte as he took off the smock. "The poor fellow has lost four toes from frostbite. His marching days are done."

The doctor listened attentively as Charlotte described

Mama's symptoms. He asked, "Has your mother a rash? Does she vomit? Are her bowels disturbed?"

"No. Just fever and a cough."

He put on his greatcoat and fur hat. "It doesn't sound infectious. Not like typhoid or small pox. I'll have a look at her."

In the icy tent, the doctor took off only his gloves while he tapped Mama's chest and back and listened to her breathing.

"She suffers from an asthma and water on the chest. I shall bleed her. Then you must burn sulphur to cleanse the air. I'll write a script for you to get it."

When the doctor had drawn off a pint of blood, Mama said that she felt better.

Papa took the doctor's script to the commissary and returned with a lump of yellow sulphur the size of a lemon. It burned with a blue flame, filling the tent with acrid fumes. Within seconds, all three were choking.

Mama gasped. "I can't breathe."

Papa opened the tent flap and kicked the burning sulphur into the snow. "Better freeze to death than be poisoned by those hellish fumes!"

"If we were back home," Mama whispered, "Dr. Ruttan would give me laudanum." Her eyes were red, and every breath wheezed in her chest.

Dear old Dr. Ruttan! Charlotte remembered how he used

to arrive in his high-wheeled buggy, for Mama was often ill. He would peer at her through his square-framed spectacles. "Give her port wine, half a glass every day." That was his favourite prescription. From his black bag he would take out a vial of laudanum to help her rest.

"Maybe the doctor has laudanum in his dispensary," Charlotte said.

"Ask him," said Papa. "It's worth a try."

Again Charlotte stepped out into the gale. Wind-driven grains of snow lashed her face as she made her way to the surgery. The doctor was not there.

Charlotte asked at the blockhouse.

"Try the officers' mess," said Sergeant Major Clark.

That was where she found him, playing cards at a table near the fire. The junior officer who opened the door looked out at the swirling snow and motioned her inside. As she stepped closer to the fire, her cheeks tingled from the warmth of the blaze. The scent of nutmeg rose from a steaming punchbowl on the sideboard.

Glancing up, the doctor recognized Charlotte. At the next break in the play, he got to his feet. "I'll be back," he told the others, "after I've seen to the young lass." He joined her by the fire. "Is your mother worse?"

"Yes. She needs laudanum."

"Oh? Are you telling me what to prescribe?"

Charlotte winced at the disdain in his voice. "Please, I didn't mean . . ." She knew that she ought to apologize, but the lump in her throat made speech impossible. No laudanum for Mama. She backed towards the door, trying to escape before she started to cry.

"Stop."

She paused, still not looking at him.

"Laudanum, you say?" The doctor cleared his throat. "Come along. I have it in my dispensary." He put on his greatcoat and fur hat. "No woman should have to spend the winter in a tent."

She tramped after him through the snow. When they reached the dispensary, Charlotte stamped the snow from her boots and waited inside the door while he took out his key and unlocked the dispensary cabinet. From a glass-stoppered bottle he filled a small vial.

"Twelve drops every night."

Charlotte held the vial under her cloak all the way back. When she entered the tent, Mama turned her head at the blast of frigid air.

"Is that Isaac?" Her voice sounded strained and weary.

"My dear, it's Charlotte," Papa said gently.

The wind shook the tent, making the canvas flap like a loose sail.

"Where is Isaac? Hasn't he come home?"

Charlotte looked at her mother's blank, unseeing eyes.

"Yes," she said. "Isaac came home. But he isn't here right this minute." She handed the vial to Papa. "Twelve drops every night."

"I'll give it to her now." He counted out the dose.

"When Isaac gets back, tell him . . . tell him . . ." Whatever the message, she never gave it. The laudanum took effect in moments, and Mama was asleep.

Charlotte too slept heavily that night, not waking until morning light filled the tent. The first thing she heard was Papa's deep voice.

"We'll have a brown cow. We can call her Daisy, after that cow we had back home."

Mama mumbled something.

"What's that, my dear?" said Papa. "Buttercup? Yes, we could call her Buttercup. Then she would have to be a yellow cow. Well, I'll find one for you."

When Charlotte sat up, she saw a smile on her mother's face.

"A dozen chickens," Papa continued, "and a rooster to keep them laying. The rooster will wake us every morning. Cock-a-doodle-doo!"

"Henry Hooper, I love you." Still smiling, Mama closed her eyes and slept again.

When she awoke, she was wet with sweat, but the fever and delirium were gone. Papa continued with the laudanum. Mama's chest cleared, and the fever did not return.

⋆   ⋆   ⋆

Christmas Eve. Sitting with Mama and Papa in the cold tent, Charlotte couldn't help thinking about the family's last Christmas. There had been plum pudding boiling in the pot, a turkey roasting on the spit, mulled cider in the punch bowl and evergreen wreaths in the windows. Mama had played carols on the clavichord while the rest of the family gathered around to sing. Nick had taken Charlotte for a sleigh ride. She remembered the sound of harness bells jingling. When he kissed her, his mouth had been warm although his cheeks were cold. That was only one year ago.

Outside the Hoopers' tent, people walked by calling out, "Merry Christmas." A drum began to beat, and a fife joined in. Charlotte stepped outside to see what was going on. Through softly falling snow, a drummer and a fifer were making the rounds of the Loyalist camp. The drummer shouted, "Come one! Come all! Sing carols at the block-house."

Louisa Vrooman walked by with her husband and children. When she saw Charlotte, she called out, "Come along with us."

Charlotte shook her head. It was fine for Louisa, surrounded by her family, to share the Christmas spirit. If James and Charlie and Isaac were alive, Charlotte might feel like singing carols too.

Louisa motioned the others to go on ahead. She stood outside the Hoopers' tent, arms folded, waiting. "I know how you feel," she said. "But next year won't be any better unless you try."

The music of the fife and drum was fainter and further away, yet Louisa did not budge.

Charlotte hesitated. Behind her, inside the tent, Mama was weeping while Papa held her in his arms and tried in vain to comfort her. What more could anyone do?

"You're right," Charlotte said to Louisa. "I'm coming."

Louisa linked her arm with Charlotte's. "If we hurry, we can catch up."

They stomped through the snow to join the others. When they reached the blockhouse, the singing had already begun. To her own surprise, Charlotte felt happy to be there, surrounded by people who still had the heart to sing,

Glad tidings of great joy I bring
To you and all mankind . . .

In the crowded blockhouse Charlotte stood between Louisa and a copper-skinned girl in a buckskin cape and listened to the Christmas story. The journey to Bethlehem. The angelic host. The shepherds. The Three Kings. Charlotte knew it all by heart. But the last part moved her, as it never had before:

Behold, an angel of the Lord appeareth to Joseph in a dream, saying, Arise and take the young child and his mother, and flee into Egypt, and be thou there until I tell thee: for Herod will seek the young child to destroy him.

And he arose and took the young child and his mother by night, and departed into Egypt.

Just like us, Charlotte thought. They couldn't go home. She met Louisa's eye. Louisa nodded. Yes, she saw it too.

Rations were cut back after Christmas. For each person, Sergeant Major Clark measured out half a pound of flour, six ounces of salt pork, four ounces of dried peas and six of rice. "I'm sorry it's so little," he said. "But it's the same as the soldiers get."

When Charlotte brought the rations back to the tent, Mama grumbled, "Hardly enough to keep body and soul together."

"I wish we were bears," said Charlotte. "We wouldn't notice hunger or cold if we slept all winter."

When anyone spoke, the words came out in white puffs of vapour.

"Well, we aren't bears," said Papa grumpily. "And a tent is no place for human beings to spend the winter. By this time next year, we'll have a house. I give you my word."

"At Cataraqui?" Charlotte asked.

"Yes. And if we're going to build it in the spring, it's time I had a look around."

"How will you get there?" Mama asked.

"Soon the channels will freeze. When the ice is strong enough, I'll walk. It's only a one-day journey there and back."

"I'll go with you," said Charlotte. "I'd like to see that old French fort."

Freeze-up came the following week, on a windless day so cold that Charlotte's nostrils stuck shut when she breathed through her nose. Mist veiled the water. It rose straight up, higher than a man's head, with wisps drifting above like threads of spider silk.

In the afternoon the mist disappeared, revealing an unbroken sheet of ice that stretched for miles. Now that the water had released its heat, the day seemed not so cold. Charlotte walked down to the shore, where a group of children had gathered to skim stones across the ice. Could she still do that? Hoping that no one was watching, she picked up a flat stone and hurled it underhand, across her body. Yes, she could. Her stone skidded a hundred feet over the ice.

"Good throw!"

Caught in the act, she whirled around. "Oh! Elijah! I didn't notice you there."

"See this!" He flung a stone that travelled twice as far as hers.

"I wasn't even trying," she protested. But she didn't try again. Feeling the tingle of frostnip, she drew her hands inside her cloak and tucked them under her armpits.

"I didn't expect to see you here. I heard that every man under sixty had been ordered into The King's Own Regiment."

"That's a fact. I start drilling tomorrow. In the spring, soon as that new warship, the *Ontario*, is fitted, The Royal Greens will be off to Fort Niagara."

She smiled. "So you're going to be a soldier after all. Will you still wear the medicine bag that Okwaho gave you?"

He laid his hand on his chest. "I vowed I'd never take it

off. Besides, if Ma got her hands on it, I'd never see it again. She hates all Indians since Moses ran away." He paused. "Sometimes she hates me too."

She looked directly at him, noticing for the first time, above the tight line of his lips, the sparse, coarse hairs that promised whiskers within a year.

"Your mother doesn't hate you. She just acts like that when she's feeling bad."

She felt sorry for Elijah, but not as sorry as she felt for Mrs. Cobman.

After two days of frigid weather, the ice could bear the weight of a man. Then came snow, followed by a thaw, then by more snow. The ice cracked explosively, opening fractures hundreds of feet long. At night the lake growled as massive ice plates rubbed together. Broken slabs a foot thick were driven onto the land. Along the shoreline, water mixed with crushed ice lapped with a tinkling, musical sound.

"There's just enough snow on the ice to give good footing," said Papa. "If the weather's not too cold, Charlotte and I will go to Cataraqui tomorrow."

"Wait a few days longer," said Mama.

"Martha, that ice could carry a team of oxen. If we delay and there's a heavy snowfall, we won't be able to walk without snowshoes. The right time is now."

Mama lowered her face. "Whenever you are out of my sight, I fear lest I never see you again."

Chapter eleven

The sheered sides of the ice slabs gleamed like green glass in the morning sunshine, and the snow on their tops looked like sugar frosting on a cake.

"They're beautiful," said Charlotte.

"Maybe so," said Papa, "but treacherous. Be careful how you walk. If you step on one that's tilted towards the water, you'll slide right in."

Papa went first. He jumped over the ring of water at the shoreline, and then held out his hand to help Charlotte cross onto the channel's solid ice.

"Thanks," she said. "Leaping across open water isn't easy if you're wearing a gown."

But once on the ice, Charlotte had no problem. Walking was pleasant over the light carpet of snow. In a few minutes she and Papa had crossed from the north shore of Carleton Island to Wolfe Island, its larger neighbour.

Here was a region of open woods where tufts of dry grass stuck up through the snow and brightly coloured winter birds flitted in the undergrowth — cardinals, evening gros-beaks, and redpolls. Charlotte and her father walked beneath tall trees whose bare branches cast black shadows on the white snow. A cottontail rabbit watching from the edge of a thicket twitched its nose as they passed by.

By midday they stood on Wolfe Island's north shore, looking out over two miles of snow-covered ice toward a dark line of trees.

"That's the mainland," said Papa. "Cataraqui."

Squinting into the glare of winter light, Charlotte saw a gap in the trees and, to the left of the gap, a slender column of smoke.

"Somebody has a fire over there."

"Where?" Papa raised one hand to shade his eyes. "Yes, I see it. If that gap is the mouth of the Cataraqui River, then the smoke is rising from Fort Frontenac. I thought it was deserted."

"Do you reckon somebody is living there?"

"We'll find out soon."

Once again there were ice slabs to climb over and water to jump across before they stood upon a level field of solid ice. Charlotte and Papa headed toward the column of smoke. When they were halfway across, she could see that the smoke was rising from a dome-shaped lodge. A little further, and she saw a man come out, walk a short distance, then stop.

"He's watching us," said Charlotte.

"Yes. We must be a curious sight — a man and a woman out on the ice, coming to visit in the middle of January."

They kept on walking, but the man did not move.

"He's wearing a red hat," said Charlotte.

As they neared the shore, the man came forward and held out his hand to help Charlotte over the clutter of broken ice.

"*Bonjour.*" His broad smile revealed a gap where front teeth ought to be. "*Je m'appelle Louis Tremblay.*"

Papa offered his hand. "Henry Hooper." Louis shook it vigorously.

When Charlotte introduced herself, he bowed.

"*Parlez-vous français?*" They shook their heads. "Then I speak English."

"Good," said Papa.

It took Louis a couple of minutes to find the words he needed, and when he spoke, he formed each phrase with care.

"Come at my house. It makes warm."

He led them to his bark lodge and lifted the frozen bear-skin that served as a door. The interior was smoky, with only a hole in the roof for a chimney. Overhead, dried fish hung from every spot that a rawhide cord could be attached — large fish suspended from lodge poles, small fish strung through the gills on lines from one side of the lodge to the other.

Louis fetched beaver pelts from a stack and spread them near the fire. "Sit yourselves. You have hunger?"

Without waiting for an answer, he pulled three small fish from a line overhead, handed one to Charlotte, one to Papa, and took one for himself. Following Louis' example, Charlotte peeled the skin from the flesh and took a bite. Smoked trout. It was delicious.

While eating, she regarded their host carefully. He had dark eyes and straight black hair — true Indian hair, but worn in a queue as a white man would wear it. His skin was light for an Indian's, and his features more sharply formed. He was dressed in buckskin, except for his red toque, which now lay on the ground by his side.

"From where come you?" Louis asked Papa.

"Our home was in the Mohawk Valley. But now we live in the English fort on Carleton Island."

"Why you are come to Cataraqui?"

"A friend told me there was cleared land here. I'm looking for a place to settle. We live in an army tent with no fire. My wife is not strong. She needs a warm house."

Louis looked around his lodge with evident pride. "A tent is good in summer. But in winter one has need of a house."

"This is a fine house," said Papa.

"I built it. I live at Cataraqui all my life."

"How do you live?" asked Papa.

"I hunt and fish. Every spring fur traders stop here. They trust me because my father was a *coureur de bois*. French, like them. They lend me all sorts of trade goods: blankets, beads, knives, hatchets. The Indians trust me because my mother was one of their people. In the fall the fur traders come back. I pay for everything with furs." He looked thoughtful. "It goes well. But it is not the life for a man like you. You want to plant the crops."

"Yes. I'm a farmer."

"There was land cleared at Cataraqui. Now it is grown over a little. But yes, this would be a good place." He tossed his fish bones into the fire. "If you like, I show you the fort."

"Yes." Charlotte stood up. "I want to see."

"Let's go, then," said Louis. He and Papa got to their feet. Louis jammed his toque onto his head and lifted the bearskin. They followed him outside.

Charlotte looked all about. So this was the fortress that had guarded the entrance to the Great Lakes for a century. Now there were gaps in the four curtain walls. The stone bastions at the corners and the fort's great central tower and the turret on the shore were all in ruins.

"Were you here when the English destroyed Fort Frontenac?" she asked.

Louis nodded. "I was twelve years old. I remember everything. We had one hundred and twenty French soldiers and forty Huron warriors to defend the fort. The English came in the night with three thousand men. When we woke in the morning, there were eleven cannons aimed at the walls. The old Commander, Monsieur de Noyan, was brave as a lion. He wanted to fight." Louis shrugged. "But what could he do?"

As Louis led them past a long, low wooden building with leaning walls and no door, Papa said, "Those look like barracks."

"Yes. The English did not bother to knock them down. Since twenty-five years they stand."

Barely, Charlotte thought. One good wind should finish them.

Papa stood at the entrance, looking in.

"Do not enter," Louis warned. "It is dangerous."

But Papa was already inside. From the threshold, Charlotte saw holes in the floor and bird droppings everywhere. And there was Papa, picking his way towards a heap of debris in one corner.

"Look!" He held up a battered tin pail. So that was it — the tin pail Papa wanted for holding hot ashes to warm the tent.

"May I take it?"

"*Bien sûr*. Who could object?"

They walked back with Louis to his lodge. "Come in," he said. "Warm yourselves before you go." Papa glanced at the sky. The sun had disappeared.

"I wish we could, but it looks like snow. If all goes well, we'll see you in the spring."

"*Au revoir*," Louis said.

Charlotte and Papa were halfway to Wolfe Island when a gusty wind sprang up, driving before it the first hard grains of new snow. Charlotte bent her head and drew her shawl about her face so that only her eyes were exposed.

The wind swept the snow into ridges, leaving patches of bare ice interrupted by drifts. As it swirled about, the wind seemed to push at her from every direction. Keep moving, she told herself. When she looked up, she caught glimpses of dark cedars between bursts of snow. The trees were getting closer. Soon she and Papa would reach Wolfe Island, where trees would break the force of the wind.

Then Papa had her by the arm to help her across the margin of dark water along the shore.

"The worst is over." He patted her shoulder reassuringly. His eyebrows and eyelashes were white with snow, and a watery drop hung from the end of his nose. "If we follow the footprints we made this morning, we won't get lost."

What footprints? Charlotte saw none. Snow had filled them. As she trudged at Papa's heels, fear seeped in. How could Papa be sure that they were walking in the right direction? Dogs and horses had a second sense for finding home, but people didn't. In a storm like this, lost travellers walked in circles until they lay down exhausted and waited for death.

Daylight faded, but darkness did not come. Snow filled the sky, whirled in the air and covered the ground. The only thing she could see as she plodded along was Papa, two paces ahead, his dark coat crusted with snow.

Abruptly, he stopped — halted so suddenly that she bumped into him. When she lifted her head she saw that the sky ahead was lit up with a rosy pink glow, softer and more magical than a sunset.

"Oh!" was all she could say as she looked up in wonder.

"That's the light from a hundred Loyalist cooking fires, reflected by falling snow."

Charlotte heard the relief in his voice. So they were headed in the right direction, and they were almost back.

One last channel to cross. The shore was white; the channel ice was white. The band of black water that lay between was easy to see and less than a yard wide. Papa had managed jumps just as broad many times before.

This time he missed.

Still on his feet, ankle-deep in icy water, he tossed the tin pail ahead of him onto the channel's solid ice and climbed out. He reached for Charlotte's hand to help her across.

"That was unlucky," he said, and picked up the pail.

"We'd better hurry." She did not need to say the word "frostbite." Papa knew as well as she did that wet feet could freeze in a quarter of an hour, and Fort Haldimand was still twenty minutes away.

They had covered half the distance when Papa stumbled. "I can't feel my feet. At first they were all pins and needles, but now they're numb."

She gave him her shoulder to lean on. With every step his

weight bore down more heavily. He stumbled when stepping from the channel ice to the Carleton Island shore and fell twice before they reached the fort gate.

Snow still whirled about them while they made their way across the parade square. The Loyalists' white tents were barely visible as they approached. But there was Mama, standing outside in her dark cloak, watching.

As soon as she saw them — they were barely twenty feet from her when she did — she ran forward and braced her shoulder under Papa's other arm.

"Quick! Get inside!"

"Wet feet," said Charlotte. "He slipped."

"I knew something like this would happen!" Mama wept as she helped him to sit down. She unlaced Papa's boots and pulled them off. The skin of his feet was hard, waxy and cold.

"Should we rub his feet?" Charlotte asked.

"That's the worst thing we could do. Frozen flesh needs gentle warmth. Body heat is best." Mama sat down facing him and drew his bare feet under her gown.

"How does that feel?"

"I can't feel anything."

"Then your skin is frozen."

Charlotte held out the pail that Papa had found in the barracks. "I'll put some hot ashes in this," she said.

Mama glanced at it, then at Papa's tense face. "So you got us a pail. Henry, I fear you paid too high a price."

Embers glowed and winked amongst the ashes when Charlotte brought the pail inside the tent. She held her hands over them to feel the rising warmth.

A few minutes later, Papa groaned. "I can feel my feet. They hurt like hell."

"That's a good sign," Mama said.

The next morning Papa's feet were blistered and red. "They feel as if I'd walked barefoot through fire," he said.

"I'll bandage them," said Mama. "We can't let the blisters break." She took some rags that once had been a petticoat and wound them all around Papa's feet, carefully separating his toes. Charlotte was surprised at how calm Mama was this morning, unlike last night. Or was she simply resigned to the worst?

Charlotte felt the pail of ashes. Stone cold.

"I'll bring in some hot ashes," she said.

"Thank you," said Mama. "And when you've done that, will you fetch our rations from the blockhouse?"

Carrying the tin pail, Charlotte stepped outside. During the night the wind had blown itself out. Snowflakes floated downwards in soft, feathery clumps. A blanket of snow a foot deep covered the ground.

Outside the tent, the cooking fire had been nearly extinguished by the blizzard, but there were enough embers and hot ashes at the centre to fill the pail. Before taking it into the tent, she added wood to the fire to start it blazing again.

When she entered the tent, Papa was sleeping. That must

mean that his pain had lessened. Snoring softly, he lay on his beech-leaf mattress, covered with Charlotte's blanket as well as his own for extra warmth.

"I'll get the rations now," she told Mama.

"Hurry back."

"I shall. And then I'll take a walk in the woods to gather firewood. Some dead branches must have come down in the storm."

As she trudged to the blockhouse, Charlotte wondered how soon they would know whether Papa's feet could be saved. Men lost fingers and toes from frostbite when frozen flesh thawed and could not heal. She had seen crippled men hobbling on crutches, no longer able to lift rocks, dig stumps or follow a plough. If that happened to Papa, he would never farm again. How would they manage then to keep body and soul together?

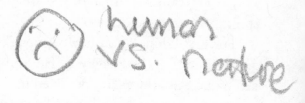

Chapter twelve

"Yesterday a man came looking for you. A courier."
Sergeant Major Clark was weighing out flour as he
spoke.

"For me? I don't know any couriers."

"He didn't say he knew you. He simply asked whether a
girl named Charlotte Hooper lived in the Loyalist camp. A
friend of his wants to find you." The Sergeant Major forked
a chunk of salt pork from a barrel and slapped it onto a
sheet of brown paper on the counter.

She caught her breath. "What's his friend's name?"

"He didn't say. I told him where to find your tent. Then
someone said you and your father had gone over to Catara-

qui and wouldn't be back all day." Clark wrapped the meat and pushed the package towards her.

"Has he left yet — the courier? Is he still here?"

"He's still here. He spent the night in the barracks, but he'll be off to Fort Niagara this morning."

Charlotte was halfway to the door when Clark called out, "You forgot your rations."

"Oh! I don't know what I was thinking." She glanced at the rations sitting on the commissary counter. "I'll come back for them."

He leaned across the counter. "Miss Charlotte, why don't you wait here? I'll send a soldier to the barracks to fetch him."

"Thank you." Her knees felt weak. She was glad to sit down.

The courier's friend must be Nick. Of course it was Nick. Who else could it be? She felt . . . Well, how did she feel? Frightened? Not exactly. But certainly taken by surprise. If only she had been warned! Yet even if she had been, there was little she could have done to make herself presentable. Charlotte looked down at her worn cloak. She was going to make a terrible impression. For a moment, she wanted to hide.

The blockhouse door opened, and the courier entered. He was a man of middle height. He wore high moccasins up to the thigh, a dark blue coat of some heavy material and a fur hat, which he took off and shook to get rid of the snow. His hair was brown with grey at the temples.

"Good day." She rose to speak to him. "I'm Charlotte Hooper."

He bowed. "Daniel Taylor at your service."

"I believe you are Nick Schyler's friend?"

"Friend and comrade. We both run dispatches."

So Nick had become a courier. That's what happened after he rode away on the recruiter's horse.

"How is he?"

"Very well last time I saw him, but desperate for news of you. He's had friends asking about you at every fort between Montreal and Detroit. He searched for you all over New York."

"Is Nick in New York?"

"He was there in December."

"Where is he now?"

"Sorry. I don't know. I haven't seen him for a month."

"When will you see him again?"

"Hard to say. I'm on my way to Fort Niagara. By next week I could be anywhere. When we meet again depends on where I'm sent and where he's sent. It's outside our control."

"If I write a letter, will you give it to him?"

He shrugged. "It may be a long time before he gets it. If I'm captured, he never will."

"Then you mean, no?"

"Oh, I'll carry your letter. But write it quickly, and don't mention anything that might be useful to the enemy."

"What sort of thing?"

"Nothing about that warship the British are building here. Or how many men are in the garrison. Better not mention Fort Haldimand at all. And don't use Nick's name. Start your letter, 'My dear one,' or something like that. Bring it to the barracks as soon as it's written. I'll be waiting."

He went back out into the snow.

Sergeant Major Clark coughed discreetly. "I believe you want to write a letter." Of course he had overheard every word.

"Yes." Her cheeks felt hot. Why did she blush so easily?

"Then you need writing materials. I'll bring them to you."

"Thank you."

While she waited, Charlotte thought about what to write. She hadn't seen Nick for eight months. Their last meeting had been awkward and painful. She needed time to think, but there was none.

The Sergeant Major brought her an ironstone jar of ink, a quill pen, a sand shaker, and a sheet of paper. She carried them to the far end of the counter, spread out the paper, opened the ink jar, and dipped her quill. *My dear one,* she began.

With those words, her pen stuttered and a splatter of black droplets fell across the page. Charlotte examined her pen; it was well trimmed. The awkwardness was hers. Again she dipped it into the writing fluid. How light the feather felt in her fingers! Half a year had gone by since she last held a pen.

I have heard such news about you, and I rejoice that the obstacles that once separated us have disappeared. Now it is only distance that keeps us apart. Every day I think about you and wonder where you are. For a long time I wondered whether you ever thought of me, but now I know you do, and that makes me so happy. I wear the locket you gave me next to my heart.

She paused. She wanted to tell Nick where she was, but that wasn't possible without mentioning Fort Haldimand. So Daniel Taylor would have to tell Nick where to find her.

Charlotte dipped her pen again: *Someday we shall find another sycamore tree and another green valley. God grant that it be so.*

She signed her name, and then drew a heart, shaping it like the one Nick had carved on the sycamore tree back home, but without the intertwined N.S and C.H. Maybe Nick will fill in our initials, she thought, when he reads my letter. Charlotte sprinkled the writing fluid with sand, and when it was dry, shook it off and folded the letter.

"Please don't tell anyone about this," she said to Sergeant Major Clark when she returned the sand shaker and writing fluid.

"I give you my word." He raised his mournful eyes to hers. "I know what it's like. I haven't seen my wife for two years."

"I didn't know you were married."

"Fidelia and I were married in Plymouth the day before my ship sailed. I don't know when we'll be together again." He smiled sadly. "But you must take your letter to the courier. He's anxious to be off."

Taylor was waiting inside the barrack door. As he placed the letter in his pack, he said, "No promises. But I'll do my best."

Charlotte returned to the blockhouse to pick up the rations. When she stepped outside again, she saw Daniel Taylor leaving through the stockade gate. "God speed," she murmured as she turned toward the Loyalist camp.

"Where were you all this time?" Mama asked as soon as Charlotte stepped into the tent.

"At the blockhouse."

"It doesn't take that long to walk two hundred yards and back."

"Martha," said Papa, "I told you not to worry." He lay on his mattress with his bandaged feet in front of him. The two furrows between his eyebrows had deepened. He must be in pain, Charlotte thought.

"But I do worry," said Mama. "I can't help it." Now she looked at the rations. "Is this all? No dried peas?" She set down the sack of flour and the package of salt pork. "Tell me how I'm to make pea soup without any peas?"

Charlotte's wanted to explain about the courier and Nick

and the letter, but this was altogether the wrong time. "I'll gather some firewood," she said. "We'll need it before night."

Every day Mama changed the dressings on Papa's feet. As the left foot healed, the dead skin peeled off. "We can stop bandaging that foot," Mama said. "But the other . . ."

". . . is not healing." Papa finished the sentence for her. "In fact, three toes have turned black, and they stink. If something isn't done, I'll lose the whole foot."

"Do you think you can walk as far as the surgery?" Charlotte asked.

"I don't think so."

"Then the doctor must come here."

As Charlotte left to summon the doctor, Mama's eyes darkened with fear.

The doctor knew what had to be done. As soon as Charlotte described the colour of the toes and the sweet, putrid smell, he assembled everything necessary — his black bag, a special leather case, and a wooden plank about four feet long. He gave Charlotte the plank to carry. Not a word was said as they walked side by side from the surgery to the Loyalist encampment, their feet crunching the snow.

Mama unwrapped the bandages. The doctor frowned while he examined Papa's right foot.

"That's a nasty business," he said. "Those toes should have come off days ago." He took a flask from his bag. "Young lady, do you have a cup I can use?"

Charlotte brought him a tin cup. As he filled it with rum, she waited for her mother to object, but Mama did not. "I did all I could," she said. Her eyes brimmed with tears.

Papa drank the rum in one draught. "I'm ready, doctor. Let's get on with it."

"We'll give that rum a minute to take effect." The doctor turned to Charlotte. "Find me two logs about the same size to set the plank on."

She went out to the woodpile and chose two logs. When she re-entered the tent, the doctor had taken off his coat and opened the leather case. In it was a set of half a dozen saws in various sizes, each neatly fitted into an exactly shaped hollow. He selected the smallest saw, not much bigger than a nail file. It had fine, sharp-looking teeth. Papa looked straight at it, but Mama turned her head away and started to weep.

"Mrs. Hooper," said the doctor, "I suggest you go for a walk."

"No," said Mama, "I'll stay with my husband."

"Martha," said Papa. "Go for a walk."

Mama left the tent, tears streaming down her cheeks. Charlotte was about to follow, but the doctor called her back.

"Not you, young lady. First, set up the plank on those two logs. Then I'll need you to hold the basin."

When the plank was in place and Papa's right foot was resting upon it, the doctor handed Charlotte a brass bowl about the size of a soup bowl, but twice as deep. Charlotte held it in both hands and tried not to tremble.

"Ready?" the doctor asked Papa.

"I'm ready." His chest rose as he took a deep breath.

What a sharp, fine little saw! The rasp of its teeth cutting through bone made Charlotte shudder. Papa's smallest toe dropped into the basin, and then the toe next to it, and then the middle toe.

The basin wobbled in Charlotte's hands. "Steady there!" said the doctor as he massaged Papa's foot, squeezing and kneading as pus and blood flowed into the basin. "The poisons must come out."

He finished by cauterizing the wounds with a glowing ember. That was when Papa fainted. Charlotte's stomach lurched. Life on the farm had hardened her to many gruesome sights, but no number of stuck pigs or beheaded chickens could have prepared her to see her father's toes in a basinful of blood.

Chapter thirteen

A month went by, and then one morning the round, yellow eyes of a great horned owl stared at Charlotte from an oak tree while she gathered wood. There was a hole in the tree trunk, and on the snow beneath were dozens of owl castings — the hair, bones and feathers of their prey. A good sign, she thought. When owls nested, spring was on its way.

In the woods snow still lay deep, but on open ground the thaw had begun. Rivulets of melt water trickled and spread. They flowed through the tents of the Loyalist camp, turning earth floors into muck.

The sun sucked the water from the ice slabs that still littered the shore, leaving their surfaces pitted. No longer gleaming like glass, the ice resembled a dirty sponge. The ring of water around Carleton Island widened to a moat.

"The river ice is rotten," Papa said. "It will go out soon. Two more weeks and the St. Lawrence will be open all the way to the Atlantic Ocean."

The Royal Greens were performing bayonet drill on the parade square. Passing by on her way to pick up rations, Charlotte stopped to watch. Peter Vrooman's beefy face was redder than ever as he charged and lunged. Elijah, looking every inch the soldier in his red coat, appeared to be enjoying himself. His rifle, bayonet affixed, was steady in his hands. What a difference from the boy with the trembling pitchfork who had surprised her outside his mother's kitchen window in Canajoharie six months ago!

Someday, she thought, these practice drills would become reality and Elijah would have to thrust his bayonet into the flesh of a man — perhaps a boy like himself, differing only in the colour of the uniform he wore. Elijah would do it if he had to, steeling himself just as she had steeled herself to help Papa slaughter pigs. Hogs died in terror. Did men in battle die like that? She turned away, banishing the thought.

Today she was later than usual when she reached the blockhouse. A long queue had formed at the commissary counter. Taking her place at the end, she regretted that she had stopped to watch the soldiers drill. The line moved slowly. Charlotte shifted her weight from leg to leg restlessly.

She felt as if she had been waiting for hours when the blockhouse door opened and a group of soldiers came in. Elijah was among them, wearing his Shako hat with the green badge and the plume that made him look six feet tall. When he saw Charlotte, he came over to speak to her.

"We'll be leaving soon," he said cheerfully. "The regiment is ready to go, and so is the ship. When Lake Ontario is clear of ice, we'll be off to Fort Niagara."

"It won't take long," she said. "I was down at the shore this morning. The ice is so thin you can see through it, and it's all in pieces like a jigsaw puzzle. One good wind will break it up."

"I can hardly wait to see some action."

When Charlotte reached the counter, Elijah rejoined his friends. His eagerness reminded her of her brothers. They too had marched off to war with shining eyes.

That night a brisk wind from the west stirred up Lake Ontario's currents. The ice pans that had collected at the foot of the lake were pressed eastward into the St. Lawrence River. During the night, they departed with a whispering sound. When the sun rose, all the ice was gone.

Even though her twenty-two guns had been secured in position, her sails attached to the rigging, and all supplies loaded on board, the warship *Ontario* still could not sail. For a week she stayed in the slips, waiting for a favourable wind from the east.

When the wind finally shifted, there was no time to be lost. Overnight it might shift again, and the *Ontario* lose her chance.

People streamed from the Loyalist tents and the Indian huts, all heading to the shipyard to watch the launch. Charlotte climbed atop a granite boulder to get a good view. From there she saw the captain, Commodore James Andrews, on the bridge, in his blue naval uniform with its bright brass buttons and gold braid.

A stiff breeze, funneling down the St. Lawrence, rattled the rigging lines against the masts. Then down the slope from the fort the regiment marched. Left. Right. Left. Right. The drum thumped the rhythm and the fife piped the tune. Private Elijah Cobman, in the outside column, passed within ten feet of Charlotte, his eyes straight ahead. How proud he looked, stepping along in his red coat! Who could tell that under it he wore a Mohawk medicine bag?

There was Peter Vrooman, grim faced as he marched by. Louisa, with her arms around the shoulders of her two little girls, smiled bravely.

Mrs. Cobman stood watching with Hope in her arms. The baby squealed with delight at the parade, but no smile brightened the woman's sorrowful face.

When all was ready, the crew pulled up the gangway. The

blocks holding the *Ontario* in the slips were removed, and with a rush she slid into the water. As her bow came up level, cheers echoed from ship and shore.

Someone began to sing:

> *God save great George our King,*
> *Long live our noble King . . .*

And all the rest joined in:

> *God save the King.*
> *Send him victorious,*
> *Happy and glorious,*
> *Long to reign over us,*
> *God save the King.*
>
> *O Lord, our God, arise,*
> *Scatter his enemies,*
> *And make them fall.*
> *Confound their politics,*
> *Frustrate their knavish tricks!*
> *On him our hearts are fix't,*
> *O save us all.*

The sails caught the wind, and the *Ontario*'s maiden voyage began. Charlotte tried to pick out Elijah amongst the rows of soldiers massed on the deck. But in their red uniforms, they all looked alike.

* * *

Papa's foot healed. With a crutch fashioned from a forked branch, he got about fairly well. Despite his accident, his hopes for the future remained undaunted. "I still have seven toes," he insisted. "Seven out of ten isn't bad. I can still build us a house. I can still plant crops."

When he talked like this, Mama seemed uneasy. Perhaps she did not share Papa's optimism or his dream. But then, perhaps she never had.

For weeks Papa talked about moving to Cataraqui. Then one morning he went for a walk without telling Charlotte or Mama where he was going. Charlotte suspected that he had gone to the blockhouse.

Charlotte and Mama were sitting outside the tent, rubbing the fuzz from sumac berries to ready them for making tea, when Papa came limping toward them between the rows of Loyalist tents. When he reached them, he sat down heavily on the log outside the entrance and slammed his crutch to the ground.

"Bad news," he said. "I've been talking with the officer in charge of refugees. I told him I wanted to move my family to Cataraqui, where we could build a house and plant crops. He said we were free to go, but he warned me that even if we built a house and planted crops, we would not get title to the land."

"Why not?" Mama asked. "By common law, we can get title by possession. Who else has a claim?"

"The King," Papa replied. "Since the land at Cataraqui

was part of LaSalle's Seigneury Number One in the French system, it belongs to the Crown. After the war, the government intends to have it resurveyed for disbanded soldiers."

Mama frowned. "So if we farmed at Cataraqui, we'd be ploughing another man's field. What would be the point?"

"No point at all. As soon as the titleholder claimed his land, we'd have to leave. For a second time, we'd be driven from our home." Papa paused. "However, the British government plans to grant one hundred acres to every Loyalist — not just to heads of families, but to every man, woman and child. Among the three of us, we'll receive three hundred acres, as well as tools and supplies."

"When is this going to happen?" Mama asked.

"After peace is declared."

"Henry, it might take years!"

"It will." Papa took Mama's hand and looked directly into her eyes. "Martha, my dear, forgive me for breaking my vow. I truly meant it when I swore that you would not spend another winter in this tent."

Charlotte heard in his voice the despair that he did not put into words. He knew — as she did too — that seven toes were not enough, and that he would be too old to start again.

Three months had passed since Charlotte wrote her letter to Nick. There was a good chance that he had it by now. Sooner or later — perhaps when least expected — his canoe would pull up to the shore. Since it might be sooner rather than later, she got up each morning, thinking: maybe today. And each night when she went to sleep, she thought: maybe tomorrow.

There was a tree trunk on the shore that had washed up from somewhere. It had been bleached silvery white by the sun and polished by the waves. This was a good place to sit and look out over the water, watching for Nick's canoe to appear on the horizon. If he came upriver from Montreal, his canoe would approach from the east. If he followed Lake Ontario's shore from Fort Niagara, his approach would be from the west. But the days passed, and he did not come from either direction.

In May a bateau arrived from Montreal. It lurched up the eastern channel with its square sail spread to catch the breeze. Near the bow were four redcoats and one woman. The woman wore a grey travelling cloak and matching deep-brimmed bonnet. She stood slightly apart from the others, leaning forward, her eyes searching the crowd gathered on the shore. Suddenly, she raised her arm and waved.

A soldier returned her wave, his right arm sweeping the air. Seeing him from the back, Charlotte did not know who he was. He rushed forward as the bateau bumped against the limestone shore. The woman raised her arms to him, and he lifted her over the side. When she raised her head, Charlotte saw a delicate, heart-shaped face under the bonnet's deep brim.

With one arm still holding her, the soldier turned half way around and pointed toward the fort. Now Charlotte saw his face — Sergeant Major Clark's long face, not melancholy but beaming with joy.

The boat that brought Fidelia Clark to her husband also brought news from the outside world. But it was nothing to cheer about. Molly Brant and her children had been driven from the Mohawk Valley. Rebel mobs were persecuting Quakers for their refusal to bear arms. The British had been forced to evacuate Philadelphia. There was a rumour that France would send a fleet to invade New York, where thousands of displaced Loyalists lived in overcrowded misery. And what was England doing? Almost nothing. Throughout the Thirteen Colonies, Loyalists felt betrayed by Britain's lack of effort. Didn't their Mother Country care what happened to them?

A week after Fidelia Clark's arrival, a canoe appeared in the distance. Charlotte, sitting on the sun-bleached log by the shore, felt the usual surge of excitement followed by the usual letdown, for once again the paddler was not Nick.

Yet something kept her eyes on him as he brought his canoe to shore and climbed out. He had the look of a courier — smooth shaven, not bearded like a fur trader. An uneasy feeling crept over her that this man brought bad news. Almost reluctantly, she joined the crowd of Loyalists that surrounded the newcomer.

He brushed past them all, refusing to answer questions.

"I can't talk to you now," he said.

There was urgency in the speed with which he hurried through the stockade gate.

Charlotte and the others followed him to the block-house. For an hour they stood around, waiting for him to emerge from the Commander's quarters. Surely, after making his report, he would answer their questions!

At last he came out.

"How are things in the Mohawk Valley?" someone asked.

"The Mohawk Valley? You wouldn't want to see it now. Some of those Loyalists who joined Butler's Rangers went back to burn their own homes rather than let Rebels live in them. There won't be a house or barn left standing by the time this war ends.

"But the Indians are getting the worst of it. George Washington is concentrating on driving them out. He put Major General John Sullivan in charge. Sullivan's troops are tracing every creek, looking for Iroquois settlements. So far they've burned forty towns — long houses, fields, store-houses. Complete destruction. Oneida towns as well as the others."

"That makes no sense," someone else said. "The Oneidas were helping the Rebels."

"Sullivan makes no distinction. An Indian is an Indian, as far as he's concerned."

"Do you have any good news for us?" another person asked.

The courier shrugged. "We've had some success disrupting enemy supply lines. But that's becoming more difficult because we no longer have enough couriers to carry messages. Last month we lost another, one of our best."

A courier lost. This was the news she dreaded. Charlotte held her breath.

"He was eating supper at a safe house when Rebel soldiers broke in. They saw him slip something into his mouth, so they gave him a dose of emetic tartar to fetch it back up. Sure enough, he'd swallowed a silver bullet with a message inside." He paused. "They hanged him. End of story."

For a moment there was silence. Charlotte waited for someone to ask the dead courier's name. Didn't anyone else want to know? Apparently not. The man had picked up his pack and the crowd was starting to drift away when Charlotte called out, "What was his name?"

She was trembling, and he must have heard the quaver in her voice. He turned his gaze toward her.

"Daniel Taylor."

"Oh. Thank God!" The words had passed her lips before she knew what she was saying.

Everyone stared at her. In their eyes she saw shock, disbelief and anger. No one understood. No one could possibly understand that her thanks were for Nick's life, not Daniel Taylor's death. With all her heart she grieved for Daniel Taylor. But how could she ever explain? She wished that a hole in the ground would open up before her so that she could jump in and never be seen again.

No hole opened up. All she could do was turn and run away. No one stopped her. Charlotte was out of the block-house before others could see the tears in her eyes.

Only half aware of where she was going, she headed toward the shore. As she passed through the stockade gate, she remembered her last sight of Daniel Taylor on that snowy day when he set out for Fort Niagara with her letter to Nick in his pack.

Her stomach clenched into a hard knot. Taylor had warned her that Rebels might capture him before he saw Nick again. Is that what had happened? And if so, what had become of her letter? She pictured Rebel soldiers passing it around, snickering over tender words meant for Nick's eyes alone.

When she reached the shore, she sat down on the sun-bleached log and sobbed. So this was how matters stood: Nick might have received her letter, or he might not. He might know where she was, or he might not. Once again she feared that she would never see him again.

Chapter fourteen

I t was burning hot, as hot as a July day could be — not a breath of air stirring. Charlotte felt dizzy and her head ached from the scorching sun. She had been picking raspberries all morning. Red and black raspberries filled the camp kettle.

The lake beckoned. Down at the shore there was cool, clear water to drink, to splash over her face and to bathe her feet. Through the tangle of wild raspberry canes she pushed her way to the shore. She sat down on a rock ledge to pull off her moccasins, the ones that Okwaho had given her; now that it was summer, she wore moccasins instead of boots.

The limestone ledges at the shoreline descended like broad, shallow steps into the water. Holding up her gown, she stepped down to the first submerged shelf. The water reached just above her ankles. One more step and it was up to her knees. Her skin tingled deliciously at the shock of cold.

Something tickled her toes. Glancing down, she saw a brown and yellow perch carefully inspecting them. It nudged her toes with its mouth, found them to be of no interest, and swam away.

If she had an island all to herself, Charlotte thought, she would strip off her clothes and swim sleek as a fish through that green underwater world. How far did it stretch? All the way from Carleton Island to Fort Niagara. At least two hundred miles. Squinting into the dazzling light over the lake, she saw blue water, green islands, gulls wheeling overhead, and in the furthest distance a black speck.

Charlotte studied the speck. A floating log. Or maybe a canoe. She raised a hand to shade her eyes. Definitely a canoe, and it was coming toward Carleton Island.

The canoe carried only one person, and it rode high in the water. So it wasn't a trader's canoe, laden with goods and furs. A courier, then? That was nothing to get excited about, since she had no reason to think it was Nick.

Whoever he was, the man paddled well, with a strong, steady rhythm. When she thought about it, there definitely was something about him — perhaps it was merely the set of his shoulders — that reminded her of Nick. But he could be anyone.

Charlotte waded back to shore and sat down at the edge with her feet still in the water. Everything was so quiet. The heat of the day had silenced the birds in the thickets behind her. The lake was still. The canoe seemed to be the only thing moving, and every minute it came nearer.

The paddler wore a wide-brimmed hat pulled down to shadow his face. If he would only take it off, she could see his face.

Now the canoe was passing the spot where she sat. It was about one hundred feet offshore, heading for the fort's landing place. In a minute it would be past her and the paddler would not hear her if she called. But of course she wasn't going to anyway. She would not make a fool of herself by shouting to a stranger.

And then he saw her. By chance, the man glanced shoreward. The paddle stopped in mid-stroke. He stared right at her, holding his paddle motionless in the air. The canoe glided on its momentum for a few yards until it stopped.

"Charlotte?" He did not sound as if he believed his eyes.

With one hand he tilted back his hat, and when she saw his face, she could not move. Her tongue felt stuck to the roof of her mouth, and she could not make a sound.

He called her name again, and this time her limbs unfroze. She jumped up and splashed toward him. Arms out from her shoulders for balance, she pushed through the deepening water. It was up to her chest when the canoe came alongside.

Nick dropped his paddle. Reaching for her, he leaned too far. Or did she pull him over? Whichever it was, the canoe capsized; and when Nick toppled out, he knocked Charlotte off her feet. She gulped air just in time.

With eyes wide open, they fell together through clear green water and a swirl of bubbles. Nick's hair floated upwards like undersea grass. Spluttering, they rose to the surface. His eyelashes were stuck together in points with water, and when he shook his head, shining drops flew off in all directions.

The canoe, upside down, bumped against Charlotte's back. Nick's paddles, rucksack and blanket roll drifted aimlessly about.

"We'd better rescue your gear," she said, laughing helplessly.

Nick took apart his rifle and laid the parts on a warm rock to dry. Charlotte helped him to spread out his blankets and the contents of his rucksack. She did this in a daze, vaguely grateful to have something to do that would steady her while she was bringing her life into focus again.

Not until they were sitting side by side on a patch of brown grass only slightly softer than the limestone shore, did Charlotte entirely believe that Nick was actually there, looking just the same. Well, not quite the same. His jaw was firmer, his cheekbones more pronounced. He had a man's face now, not a boy's.

Nick's kisses were the same as the kisses she remembered — but deeper in a way that stirred her mysteriously, invoking waves of feeling that curled and spread deliciously through every part of her body. After twenty or thirty of these kisses, Charlotte's mouth felt bruised and warm. She ran her tongue over her lips. Yes, they were swollen and probably red. She hoped that Mama would not notice.

"This is what I dreamed about when I was hiding in the mountains," he said.

"In the mountains?"

"Yes. The Adirondacks."

"I know nothing about your life for the past year."

"I'll tell you how it was." He lay down beside her with his arms folded under his head, and he seemed to be speaking to the sky, to the gulls wheeling overhead. "In April I had to carry a message from New York to Cherry Valley. There was supposed to be a safe house at a place called Harrietstown. When I reached it, the house was gone, burned to the ground. Woodcutters spotted me and spread an alarm. I went up Whiteface Mountain looking for somewhere to hide. I found a bear cave."

"A bear cave." She turned the picture over in her mind.

"It smelled like pig manure mixed with wet dog. For three days I was in that cave, and I read your letter so many times the paper was starting to——"

"My letter! When did you receive it?"

"In January."

"But January was when I wrote it."

"I received it five days later. By chance I was at Fort Niagara when Dan Taylor arrived."

"Oh." A chill ran through her. "When I heard how he was captured, I thought he likely never had a chance to give it to you."

"They captured him in February."

"I was told that he carried a message hidden in a silver bullet." She hesitated. "Is that what you use?"

"No. I have a box that fits into a cavity between my boot soles. It's safer, unless somebody gets suspicious." He laughed. "In which case, a boot is harder to swallow than a bullet."

She glanced at his boots, which lay drying in the sun. Their soles were thick, but not visibly thicker than most.

"I'll show you," he said. "It's where I keep your letter." Nick stood up. He fetched one of his boots and sat down beside her again. With the tip of his knife he pried out the boot's inner sole. From inside, he pulled out a slim metal box.

"That surely isn't big enough to hold my letter."

"You'll be surprised at what it holds." He opened the box, took out the paper that was crammed inside, and began to unfold it. Within the last fold lay a red-gold ring set with garnets and pearls.

"This is for you, if you want it. Of course, you have to take me too."

His hands were jittery as he picked up the ring. "I wanted to ask you properly. I spent three days making up a speech. Now that I'm here, it's gone clear out of my head."

"Every single word?"

"I remember how it ended."

"Tell me that, anyway."

He looked directly into her eyes. "I shall never be happy in my life unless I am with you."

Charlotte gulped hard. "That's how I feel too." She lifted her left hand and Nick put the ring on her finger. For a long time they sat with their arms around each other. Just over Nick's left shoulder she saw two yellow butterflies flutter and tumble above a bush, then rise together into the sky.

Nick let her go. "Read me the letter," he said. "When I was in the bear cave, I tried to imagine your voice saying the words."

She picked up the letter carefully lest it tear along the folds. At the top was the dried splatter of ink drops that her clumsy pen had made. Resting her head on the comfortable spot under his shoulder, she began.

"My dear one, I have heard such news about you, and I rejoice that the obstacles that separated us have disappeared." She read it straight through to the end. Tears were in her eyes by the time she reached, "Someday we shall find another sycamore tree and another green valley. God grant that it be so."

"It will come true," he said in a voice so confident that it left no room for doubt. He kissed her again, and then took the letter from her. Charlotte watched him fold it, replace it in the box, and return the box to his boot.

"I must go back," she said. "My parents worry when I'm away too long. Especially Mama, she imagines horrible accidents."

"Will she think that I'm one?"

"A horrible accident? No, she won't think that. To tell the truth, I don't know what my parents will think." Charlotte stood up. "They will be surprised."

Charlotte helped Nick to gather up his blankets and gear. Everything was dry, or nearly so. Together they packed the canoe.

On the way to Fort Haldimand she knelt in the bow, carefully holding the kettle of raspberries. She felt nervous. Who wouldn't, in this situation? When a girl goes raspberry picking, she doesn't normally return with a long-missing sweetheart and an engagement ring.

Papa was sitting on the log outside the tent, whittling a long spoon from a piece of boxwood, when he saw Charlotte and Nick walking toward him through the Loyalist camp. Setting down his knife and the unfinished spoon, he brushed off his hands and stood up.

"Well, well. So you finally found us," he said, not looking especially surprised. He held out his hand to Nick. "I knew we'd see you sooner or later."

It was Mama who was astounded. Coming out of the tent a minute later, she stared at Nick blankly. For a moment Charlotte wondered whether she even knew who he was.

Nick reddened slightly, as if suspecting that he was unwelcome. He bowed.

"Nick Schyler at your service."

Mama recovered her composure. "Oh, excuse me . . . I didn't expect . . ." She laughed nervously. "I'm really not prepared for guests."

When Papa burst out laughing, even Mama joined in.

After a supper of pea soup, soggy hardtack biscuits from Nick's rucksack, and raspberries, the questions began.

"Where did you go when you rode off on that Rebel's horse?" Papa asked. He picked up his knife and the half-finished spoon that he had been whittling when Nick arrived. The knife bit into the soft wood, scattering tiny shavings as Papa hollowed out the bowl of the spoon.

"Not far. The horse went lame halfway to Albany. I left it in somebody's pasture and headed for New York on foot. Along the way a Loyalist family took me in, but I didn't stay long. By Christmas I was in New York. With no place to live and no money, I was in a bad situation until I met a Quaker who told me that the British needed couriers. He told me to apply to Colonel Robinson, the officer in charge of Guides and Pioneers."

"You never thought to enlist in a regiment?"

"No, sir. I did not."

"You haven't joined the Quakers, have you?"

"No. But I share their hatred of war. As a courier carrying dispatches, I need not take the life of any man. That's a vow I made to myself when this war began."

"But your sympathies lay with the Rebels, as I recall." Papa stopped whittling. He raised his head and looked directly at Nick. "What happened to your Republican ideals?"

Nick flushed. "I haven't lost them completely. I feel no reverence for King George. I still think that taxation without representation is wrong. Nothing could justify the Stamp Act."

"Hold your horses!" Papa said. "Money was needed to pay for the Colonies' defence. Why shouldn't they contribute?"

"That's not the issue. Why should a country on the other side of the Atlantic Ocean run the affairs of the Thirteen Colonies? Even Prime Minister Pitt recognized that we should have a voice in making laws that affect us. There are capable people in America. Brilliant men like Benjamin Franklin, scholars like John Adams, and responsible landowners like Thomas Jefferson." He paused. "I believe in government by the people. Every man should have a vote."

"Why not every woman, too?" Charlotte interrupted.

Nick turned his head and took a look at Charlotte. "Now that *is* a revolutionary idea! But why not?"

"Enough of this radical nonsense!" Papa raised his hand. "Nick, I understand your position. But if you still think like a Republican, what made you decide to help the Loyalist side? I suppose my daughter had something to do with it."

"She did." As Nick said this, his mouth twisted. "Some bad things happened."

What sort of things? Charlotte wondered. A cold feeling ran down her spine. Why did that strange and bitter look cross Nick's face?

Papa cleared his throat. "Bad things happen in war."

"It turns men into beasts," Nick exclaimed. "Look what's happening in the Mohawk Valley. Neighbours fighting neighbours. People's lives turned upside down." He stopped for breath.

"Yes," said Papa, before Nick could continue. "I may not share your goals, but I agree that violence is not the way to make any situation better." He lifted the unfinished wooden spoon that he held in his hand. "Do you see this? There's only one way to work with wood, and that's slowly and carefully until you achieve exactly what you want. You can't use an axe to carve a spoon."

Nick seemed to relax. "That's what I think too, though we may differ about the qualities that make a perfect spoon."

Papa started whittling again. "I can foresee the day when free citizens on this side of the Atlantic will enjoy self-government. But revolution isn't the only way to achieve that goal. You don't need to destroy a way of life in order to make it better." As he pressed his knife blade against the spoon's shallow bowl, another tiny flake of wood dropped to the ground.

Charlotte's eyes moved from the spoon to Nick's face. The tight look around his mouth had relaxed. There was a long pause.

"Nick," Mama said hesitantly, breaking the silence, "I

wonder whether you have been back to the Mohawk Valley?"

"Yes, a fortnight ago. On my way here, I passed through Fort Hunter. I saw your house."

"You mean that it's still standing?" Mama asked.

"It has escaped burning. People are living there."

"Squatters," said Papa bitterly.

Nick nodded. "It's like that everywhere — squatters moving into empty houses that Loyalists have abandoned."

"I'd rather my house burned to the ground," Papa said.

"It wasn't spared by chance," said Nick. "You can be sure a Liberty man wanted it for himself and told his friends to leave it alone. Now that the Continental Congress has banished all Loyalists, their property will be expropriated. If the Rebels win the war, as seems likely, squatters will get clear title."

Charlotte felt sick at the thought of strangers taking over their home, warming themselves by their fireplaces, sleeping in their beds. But she wouldn't go as far as Papa. No matter who lived there, she could not wish her home destroyed.

"Are any Loyalists left in Fort Hunter?" Mama asked.

"Mighty few. I can tell you that the Reverend John Stuart is no longer there. He's in Schenectady."

"What's he doing there?" Papa asked.

"He was arrested. The Board to Detect Conspiracies suspected him of plotting with the enemy. There wasn't enough evidence to charge him, but he isn't allowed to leave Schenectady without the Board's permission. He'll likely be sent up to Canada when there's an exchange of prisoners of war."

Papa frowned. "I hope Mr. Stuart still has my horse. She's a good mare, and I hate the thought of any damn Rebel on her back."

The next morning, Louisa Vrooman came to call, bringing her four children. She hugged Nick and kissed both his cheeks.

"I've been worried about you ever since you stole that Rebel's horse. But here you are, safe and sound."

"It's good to see you and the children out of harm's way," Nick said. "But where's Peter?"

"Off to Fort Niagara with the Royal Greens. Hadn't you heard? So I'm on my own with all these children. We have to wait until the end of the war, then start all over again."

"You mean, produce four more children?"

"Like as not," Louisa laughed, casting a proud glance at her brood, who were sitting on the grass near the tent. The boys were helping their little sisters make daisy chains. They were beautiful children, sunny and blond. Charlotte hoped that Nick's children would look like that.

"Now, what's this I hear about you and Charlotte?" Louisa asked.

"Show her," Nick said to Charlotte.

As Charlotte held out her hand to show Louisa the golden band with its garnets and pearls, she felt almost embarrassed at its beauty amidst the stark hardship all around.

"I won't wear it every day," she said. "We have our valuables buried in a pit under the tent. I'll keep it there."

"Peter and I did the same thing. Peter dug a hole big enough to bury a dog under our tent. We hid everything of value in it — jewelry, documents."

"Documents?" Papa asked.

"You know. Legal papers. We have them sealed in an oilskin pouch: the deed to our land, the bill of sale for a yoke of oxen, my father's last Will and Testament that lists what he left to me."

"Our legal papers are buried back at the farm," said Papa.

Nick sounded surprised. "What good will they do you there?"

"After the war is over, I plan to go back and dig them up, along with our family Bible and some silver that was too bulky to bring with us."

"Maybe they won't still be there."

"They're buried deep."

Nick leaned forward. "Mr. Hooper, if the Rebels win, after the war won't be soon enough. There's a squatter on your land. The farm would be his by the time you went back. He'd shoot you as a trespasser if he spotted you digging. So far, he isn't working the fields. If I were you, I'd find a way to get those papers before he starts ploughing and planting that land."

After waiting a moment to let this sink in, he added: "There's something else you ought to know. The British government has appointed an Inspector of Refugee Claims to catch cheaters. Too many Loyalists have been exaggerating their losses. I heard of a fellow who claimed he'd owned a hundred head of cattle, and it turned out to be one cow."

"That doesn't surprise me," said Papa. "There are bad apples in every barrel."

"True," said Nick. "What's to stop a fellow from lying if he doesn't need to prove what he lost?"

"Honesty," said Papa, "which is often in short supply."

"Exactly. And that's why they've made the new rule: no compensation without proof of loss."

Papa slowly nodded. "You've given me a lot to think about."

Chapter fifteen

Charlotte lay with her arms folded under her head and stared into the dark. Six feet away, on the opposite side of the tent, Nick was sleeping.

Mama and Papa must have thought that she was asleep too, because they were talking in those whispery voices they used when they did not want to waken her.

"You heard what Nick told us," Papa said. "We should have brought our legal papers with us. They would have been no trouble to carry."

"Henry, regret serves no purpose. At that time it seemed safer to bury them. The Sons of Liberty were everywhere."

"I should have known better. I wasn't thinking about compensation. God knows what I was thinking."

"You were thinking about getting Charlotte and me to safety. Don't blame yourself."

Charlotte heard the crunching of the beech leaves in Papa's mattress as he rolled over. He sighed heavily. "Martha, I see everything differently from how I did a year ago."

"Well, it is different."

"Look at me. I hobble along on my crutch like an old man. Three toes missing. I can't clear rocks any longer. I'd wear myself out in half a day if I had to follow a plough. When we left the Mohawk Valley, I was sure I could still do everything I did thirty years ago. But I was wrong. I'm sixty. It may be five years before the Upper Country is surveyed and the land grants assigned. You and I will each receive one hundred acres. What use will it be to us? Two hundred acres of wilderness to clear before we can even start to farm!"

"Sixty-five is not so old," Mama said tactfully. "Wait until we receive our land grants. There's no need to decide now. If you think then that it's too late to start farming again, we can sell our grants."

"Martha, we won't be able to buy a chicken coop with what they will fetch. After the war, there'll be thousands of disbanded soldiers with no interest in farming dumping their grants for whatever they can get. The best thing for us to do will be to hand over our land grants to Charlotte and Nick. They're young and strong. They can make use of them."

"Then what will you do?"

"I'll tell you what I want to do. I'd like to run a general store. As soon as the Upper Country is settled, there'll be a mill on every creek, and a village will grow up around every mill. People will need a store. With fair compensation for our property back home, I'll have the money I need to get started."

"A general store. You'd be good at that, Henry. But as you say, it takes money to set up shop."

"So we must retrieve the papers. The deed to our house and land, bills of sale for the livestock, receipts of payment for furniture. Everything we need is in that strongbox."

"I don't know of any way we can go back there to dig it up." Mama sounded anxious.

"I'll go back myself and dig it up."

"Henry, I don't know how you can."

"I'll find a way." There was a rustling noise as he rolled over again. "We'll talk about this in the morning. Right now, we had better get some sleep."

For Charlotte, sleep was further away than ever. Of course Papa could not make the journey — a crippled man with no means of transportation. And even if he did succeed in reaching Fort Hunter, he might be captured. All Loyalists had been proscribed and banished. If a Whig neighbour recognized Papa and turned him in, he would spend the rest of the war locked up in Schenectady jail. He might even be hanged as a traitor.

On the other side of the tent, Nick sighed in his sleep. It's for our future too, she thought. Nick's and mine. And we're the ones who can make the journey. A plan took shape in her mind. Nick had a swift canoe and a year's experience travelling on secret missions through enemy territory. He didn't know where to dig, but if she went with him, she could show him. In her mind's eye she saw the potato field, the rock pile and the snake fence, the spade marks and boot prints that marked the spot.

If Papa wanted to talk about it in the morning, she would be ready.

Papa said no.

Charlotte had expected that. Looking her father straight in the eye, she could practically read his mind. Too danger-ous for a girl, he was thinking, not proper for a decent girl. But she asked anyway, "Why not?"

"You're a girl."

"But I wouldn't travel as a girl," she explained in a very reasonable tone. "If I wear breeches, a shirt, a broad-brimmed hat, and tie my hair back in a queue, I can easily pass for a boy."

"Huh," said Papa. "You might fool all the world. But you wouldn't fool Nick, and you wouldn't fool yourself."

"Papa, don't you trust us?"

"Alone in the bush for two weeks?" he snorted. "Do you think I was never young?"

Charlotte didn't like to say it, but she wasn't convinced that either parent had ever been young.

"Papa," she answered, "I know what honour is due to me and due to you."

"I am sure you do. But nature has its own laws. In the wilderness, civilization's rules are easy to ignore. Think about it. Given such opportunity, could you and Nick resist desires that are natural and urgent in the young?"

"If we give you our word?"

"What will that be worth in the middle of the night?"

All this time Nick remained silent. He looked from Charlotte to Papa and back again, and when he looked at Charlotte she saw a flicker of interest in his eyes.

At last he spoke up. "Mr. Hooper, I like the idea, and I reckon I can control myself for two weeks, if that's your chief worry. We can't go this summer because my leave is nearly over. In two days I report to the Commander for my next assignment. But in the spring I'll have another leave coming to me. Charlotte and I can go then."

"Won't that be too late?" Charlotte asked.

Nick shook his head. "The squatter isn't farming the land. He has a few sheep in the pasture, but the fields are growing nothing but weeds. He'll wait till the fighting is over before putting in crops."

Papa stroked his chin — a sure sign that he was thinking hard. "You'd be travelling through a hundred miles of disputed territory. There may be Oneidas hiding in the bush."

"No worse dangers than your family went through to get here," said Nick.

"That's true, Henry." Mama broke in. "We need those papers, and we have to weigh need against risk. Besides . . ." She paused and put her hand to her chest. For a moment her breath rasped in her throat, then a deep cough shook her body. Mama pulled a rag from the sleeve of her gown and held it to her mouth. She coughed and coughed. When the fit of coughing passed, she glanced at the rag, folded it carefully, and thrust it back into her sleeve. "As I was about to say, our family Bible and silver tea set are buried there too. Charlotte and Nick must have those, someday."

Charlotte could hardly believe it. Her mother was willing to let her travel with Nick through the wilderness for two weeks with no chaperone. Maybe Mama's body had weakened, but a trace of her old spirit remained. This was the woman who had smiled to see James, Charlie and Isaac in their new uniforms. She had shared their spirit of adventure, their recklessness that was so foreign to Charlotte and Papa, the solid ones.

Papa's resistance collapsed. If Martha was on Charlotte's side, he had no ally. Making a last stand, he argued, "If I drew a map showing the exact spot to dig, Nick could go alone."

Charlotte shook her head. "One rock pile looks much like another."

"Especially at night," Nick agreed. "On my own, I might

not find the right spot at first. With squatters living in the house, there wouldn't be time for digging holes here and there."

"You're probably right," Papa sighed. "I don't like it, but I give my consent."

The time remaining was too short — only two more days for catching up on all the months Charlotte and Nick had been parted.

At sunset, on the eve of Nick's departure, they left the fort and followed a path through the woods to the spot where they had pulled the canoe onto the shore only one week before. There they sat on a limestone ledge and looked across the channel. All that remained of day was a fading pink light above the woods on the far side.

Tree frogs began to peep, and from further down the shore came the loud "harrumph, harrumph" of the bullfrog chorus tuning up. The rising moon appeared like a silver mound above the trees.

Charlotte could not shake off the sadness that had been with her all day. Tomorrow evening at this time Nick would be rolling out his blanket at some lonely campsite on Lake Ontario's south shore.

"Do you think," she asked, "that the war will be over by next summer?"

"No. Washington's forces aren't strong enough to take New York, and the British haven't a chance unless England sends reinforcements. Fighting will drag on for a couple more years."

"At least you'll be back here in the spring."

"Yes, and we'll go to Fort Hunter to dig up those things your father buried. That is, if he doesn't change his mind. We both know that he has doubts. Besides, he doesn't altogether trust me."

"You're a man; I'm his daughter."

"It's not just that. It's partly because I changed sides. Nobody trusts a turncoat."

"Don't call yourself that."

"That's the word for a man who changes sides."

"You haven't told me why." She turned to him. "When are you going to? I've waited all week, and your last chance is tonight."

"I've put it off because I didn't want to hurt you."

"I saw your face when you told Papa that bad things happened. What did you mean?"

Swallows skimmed the surface of the darkening water. A bat swooped overhead. Nick was still looking at the trees on the far side of the channel when he began to speak.

"You'd been gone one week before I found out that your family had left the Mohawk Valley."

"We left without telling anyone."

"I didn't expect you to tell me. I hadn't seen you for five months." Nearby a cricket cheeped. "This is how I heard. Around the end of October, I went with my father to Johnstown to sell some cattle. After we got them into the sales barn, we took a room at the inn. Dad went to bed. I wasn't tired, so I thought I'd go downstairs to the tavern for a beer. I'd just been served when Ben Warren swaggered in with three or four friends."

Ben Warren. A shiver ran down Charlotte's spine.

"As soon as he saw me, he started laughing. He shouted your name. He called you my Tory sweetheart, and other words that I'd never repeat."

"What did you do?"

"I threw my drink in his face."

"And then?" She knew there had to be more.

"He bragged that he and two of his friends had . . . used you."

"Used me how?"

"Like a harlot."

"Harlot!" Charlotte stiffened.

"I couldn't believe it. But when three men attack one woman, what chance does the woman have?" As he spoke, he kept his face turned away.

"That depends on the woman and on how hard she fights. I did more damage to Warren than he did to me. He wanted to kill me. He wanted to kill Mama and Papa too. But another man put a stop to it. That's all that happened."

"Thank God for that. I couldn't stand the thought of any man harming you." Nick let out his breath in a long sigh. "But Warren had one more boast, and this one was true. He bragged about shooting a redcoat in the ravine behind your farm. He said he was deer hunting but bagged bigger game."

"Isaac!" She shivered.

"Yes. It was Isaac. By then I knew that James and Charlie had died at Saratoga and that Isaac was missing. So he might have been in the ravine waiting for a chance to get home. When I got back to Fort Hunter, I went to your house. There was a new grave in the orchard, and your family had gone."

Nick went on to explain how he had quarrelled with his father and left home, but Charlotte heard barely a word of all that. Her thoughts were back in the Mohawk Valley. In her mind's eye she saw Isaac lying on the scuffed carpet of pine needles and dry leaves, his eyes wide open and staring up at the sky.

Charlotte gripped Nick's arm. "Warren will pay for this. He'll get what he deserves."

"You'll need boy's clothes," Nick said in the morning. "I'll be in Montreal before spring. I can buy them there. But you must be measured for them. Come, stand in front of me."

From the corner of her eye, she caught a glimpse of Papa's glum face and the twitch of a smile at the corner of Mama's mouth.

"Closer," said Nick. "We must do this by comparison, since we don't have a measuring tape."

With her body pressed against his and her head tucked under his chin, he measured her, arm against arm, leg against leg. Four hand spans told him the size of her waist. When he had finished, he stood back and grinned. "I enjoyed that, but I'll never get used to your being a boy."

"You'll be amazed at how manly I can be. But Nick, you'll need a disguise as much as I will."

"Maybe more. If they caught me, they could hang me as a traitor or as a horse thief. I'd be dead either way."

She lifted the lock of fine blond hair that fell across his brow. "I'll make a tincture of walnut husks. It dyes wool, so it ought to colour hair. And you must grow a beard. With brown hair and a brown beard, you'll look like a different person."

"Will you still love me?"

"With brotherly love."

Nick laughed and kissed her cheek. "Now I must pack."

"So soon?" She took his hand.

"It's not so soon. If I don't leave now, I won't reach the mouth of the Oswego by nightfall."

Charlotte let go his hand and sat down on her leaf-filled mattress while Nick packed his gear. Into his rucksack he put his steel mirror, his razor and strap, his cup, bowl, knife and spoon. All the while, he said nothing.

She felt miserable. It was so unfair — Nick returning to his life of action, leaving her with nothing to fill the empty months that lay ahead.

"I wish I could go with you," she said. "I would like to be a courier."

Nick looked up. "No. It wouldn't suit you." He rolled up his blankets.

"Why not?"

"Would you like to spend three days in a bear cave?"

"As much as I liked three days in a root cellar."

"Sorry. I take that back. You've lived as rough as most men ever do. But I still don't like the idea."

When he had finished packing, he reached out both hands to pull her to her feet.

"Do you know where you're going?" Charlotte asked.

"The Commander has a mission for me, but I can't tell you anything."

"I'm afraid."

"Don't be. I'll be back."

She touched his face, drew her fingers down his cheek, and then traced his lips. "I'm trying to memorize you, like a poem."

He smiled. "You already know me by heart."

Chapter sixteen

"I'm sorry, Miss Charlotte. No letter for you."

Again, no letter. For three months, no letter. Sergeant Major Clark's moustache drooped in sympathy. His voice was as apologetic as if it were *his* fault that Nick had not written. Or maybe Nick had written, but his letter had strayed, in some courier's pack, to the Ohio Valley or the Carolinas or wherever faraway campaigns were being waged.

"Perhaps the letter you're waiting for will come with the next bateau," said Clark. "There's always a mail packet from Montreal. If your friend . . ."

"His name is Nick."

"If Nick is ever in Montreal, he can leave a letter for you

at Sir John Johnson's house for delivery in care of Fort Haldimand."

"That's what I'm hoping for. When will the next bateau arrive?"

"In about two weeks. It will be the last before winter."

"Just think," Charlotte sighed, "we've been here a whole year. It feels like forever."

"Waiting always feels like forever," Clark said as he measured out the Hoopers' weekly ration of flour. He looked around. No one else stood within earshot. "Never lose hope. I was seven months without word from my dear Fidelia. And now . . . can you keep a secret?"

"Well, I suppose I can."

"You won't have to keep it long." Clark blushed; his cheeks were nearly as red as his scarlet coat.

Charlotte guessed his news, but waited for him to give it.

"Fidelia is with child. A first for us, of course. And, I believe, the first Loyalist child to be born in the Upper Country."

"When may I expect to wish you joy?"

"In April, Fidelia tells me."

Charlotte felt like hugging him, and might have been bold enough to do so if the wide commissary counter had not stood between them.

Every week grew colder. By December Charlotte and her parents were once again wearing all their clothes in layers, and even that was not enough to keep them from shivering through the nights. The pail of hot ashes did little more than take the edge from the chill. Mama was coughing again. She tried to hide the scraps of rag that she held to her mouth, but Charlotte saw one, and it bore the stain of blood.

The last bateau from Montreal brought no letter from Nick. What it did bring, among the tons of winter supplies, were barrels of maggoty salt pork. Charlotte, Papa and Mama watched maggots squirm in the pink flesh and pale fat.

"They're looking healthy," Papa said. "But I can't say that I want to eat them."

"Ugh," said Charlotte. Her stomach lurched at the thought.

"I'll boil up the pork in the camp kettle to render the fat," Mama said. "Then we'll simmer it with wood ash. There's enough fat to make us a few cakes of soap. We may go hungry, but at least we'll be clean."

"By the time we're starving," Papa said, " a bowl of pork and maggot soup won't taste too bad."

Charlotte remembered Mrs. Platto's story of the hungry soldiers' march from Montreal to Lake Champlain — how they had eaten their leather cartridge cases, their boots, and their dog. By the end of winter, she thought, she might appreciate pork and maggot soup. But she was not that hungry yet.

Most nights Mama had to sleep sitting up because she could not breathe lying down. When that happened, Papa sat with his arm around her, and she leaned against his shoulder. Charlotte stayed awake listening to her painful, laboured breath.

"I wish the doctor were still at the fort," Charlotte said. But wishing did no good. The regiment's doctor had accompanied the regiment when the warship *Ontario* sailed in the spring.

"I didn't think highly of his remedies, anyway," Papa said. "Sulphur fumes and blood-letting. What good did they do?"

"The laudanum helped me sleep," Mama gasped. The effort of speaking set her coughing again. When the fit was over, she said, "Please, let me lie down. My breathing is easier now, and I'm so tired."

Charlotte folded her own blanket as a pillow to put under her mother's head. She and Papa went outside. He carried the pail of cold ashes.

With a motion of her head towards the tent, Charlotte asked, "What can we do?"

"Pray," he said gruffly as he dumped the cold ashes. "Keep her warm, dose her with spruce tea, and pray."

"If only I had a magic touch that would cure her," Charlotte said.

"There's no magic touch for what she's got. She's coughing blood."

Charlotte nodded. She knew that coughing blood meant

consumption. It was a death sentence. There was no cure.

There were tears in Papa's eyes as he refilled the pail with hot ashes and limped with it into the tent.

I'd better fetch some firewood, Charlotte said to herself. She picked up the hand axe from where it lay on the ground beside the woodpile. In the forest outside the fort there were always wind-fallen branches that could be dragged back as fuel.

Sleet was falling. Halfway between snow and icy rain, it stung her cheeks. Another winter in the tent lay ahead — but not for Mama. Charlotte wiped the tears from her eyes. No power on earth could keep her mother alive until spring.

When Charlotte returned with the wood that she had gathered, Mama lay trembling in a huddle of blankets. Her breathing-in was a wheeze, and her breathing-out a moan. Except for the hectic pink of her cheeks, her face was as pale as ashes. Papa was holding her hand.

"Martha, is there anything you want?"

"No. I lack . . . nothing." As she spoke, a spasm of coughing took hold. Papa raised her shoulders and held a rag to her mouth. When he took it away, Charlotte saw blood at the corner of Mama's mouth.

"Don't try to talk," he said softly.

All afternoon he held her hand. From time to time he wiped sweat from her forehead, but he seldom spoke. It seemed he had no words to cheer her — not like last winter, when he had talked about a house, a cow and chickens.

With his shoulders slumped and his face lined with grief, Papa looked like a man for whom life held little hope.

Light was fading. Papa gently withdrew his hand from Mama's. "She's sleeping. You stay with her so I can get some wood chopped before dark." He left the tent.

Sitting beside Mama, Charlotte watched her chest rise and fall and listened to the harsh groans of her laboured breath. From outside came the Whack! Whack! of Papa's axe.

Mama stirred. Her eyes blinked open. She turned her head towards Charlotte. "Is that your father chopping wood?"

"Yes. Does the noise disturb you? I can ask him to stop."

"No. I like to listen. When we were first married, I loved to watch him split logs. One blow——" She broke into a fit of coughing. Charlotte raised her shoulders and held the rag to Mama's mouth. When she took the rag away, it was soaked with blood. "One blow, and the two halves flew apart. He was a strong man, your father."

"He still is."

"Not strong enough, I fear, for what lies ahead."

Charlotte didn't know what to say. The rhythmic striking of Papa's axe was the only sound.

"From now on," said Mama, "you'll be all he has."

"Mama! No!" She pressed her mother's limp hand, as if by that she could squeeze her own strength into it. "You mustn't give up."

"Who am I to oppose the will of God? If He wants me now, I'm ready."

But I'm not ready, Charlotte thought furiously. Neither is Papa. We want Mama to stay with us. God spared her once. He can do it again if He wants to. Doesn't God care?

Charlotte felt a rush of fear to see the blue lines of veins at Mama's temples, the dark bruises under her eyes, and the pulse that fluttered in her throat. Sweat had extinguished the fire of her red hair, dampening it into dark tendrils that clung to her cheeks. The bones of her face stood out sharply, the skull beneath the skin reminding her that Mama was going to die. Not some time in the future, as everyone must die. Not next year or next month. What remained of Mama's life could be measured in days or hours. Charlotte's heart ached, as if an unbearable burden pressed upon it.

Outside, the chopping had stopped. Charlotte heard Papa stomping about, throwing sticks onto the woodpile.

"Listen!" Mama said. "There's something I want to tell you . . ." She took a deep wheezing breath, ". . . tell you before I die."

"Mama, you aren't going to die."

"Don't argue, child. Just listen."

Charlotte bowed her head, not bothering to wipe away the tears that ran down her cheeks.

"I was not young when I married," Mama's voice faltered. "Still, I thought I'd live to see you and the boys settled and raising families of your own. I wanted grandchildren." Now she gave Charlotte's hand a feeble squeeze. "Well, I reckon there will be grandchildren, though I shall never see them." Her words became faint. "You and Nick. Be happy."

Mama fell asleep. Gently, Charlotte withdrew her hand. "Be happy." She would remember those words. And, yes, she would be happy, although the time for happiness was a long way off.

Papa entered the tent and knelt beside Charlotte. Together they watched Mama's chest move up and down and listened to the groaning of her breath.

Papa turned towards Charlotte. "Daughter, you should get some rest. I'll keep watch for a couple of hours, and wake you if need be."

She lay down on her mattress, although sure that she would not be able to sleep. But she was tired, so very tired.

It was dark in the tent when Papa woke her. Rubbing her eyes, she got up and joined him at Mama's side. Without a word, Papa put his arm around Charlotte's shoulders. What a quiet night! At first the only sound was the wheeze of Mama's breathing. After a time, she heard wolves howling far away. They were calling to their friends. Why couldn't people do something like that, talk to those they loved across the miles?

"While I was chopping wood," Papa said, "I thought about home — the way things used to be. I always liked winter, when I had hams curing in the smoke house and your mother had her jams and jellies sitting in jars on every shelf. Winter was the time when I took out my books and she busied herself with her knitting and embroidery. She liked me to read to her while she did her fancywork."

"When I was little, I took everything for granted," said Charlotte. "A soft bed, a warm house, three big brothers to spoil me, you and Mama to keep me safe. Why did everything have to change?"

"The world is topsy-turvy," said Papa. "Sometimes I wish I'd signed that document the Rebels kept pushing at me. All I had to do was say that I supported the Revolution. Now look where my stubbornness has landed us!"

"You couldn't have done differently. As soon as my brothers took the King's shilling, everybody knew which side our family was on. Even if you had signed, no one would have believed you."

Mama's eyelids fluttered. She opened her eyes. Her gaze flicked from side to side, sliding in and out of focus.

"I want my sons. Where have they gone?" she cried out.

"Oh, Mama!" Charlotte sobbed.

"The boys are waiting for you," said Papa. "You'll be with them soon."

"They're in Heaven, aren't they? James. Charlie. Isaac." Mama stopped breathing. Then, with a gasp, she took another breath. "Angels in red coats. I see them now. Raise me up. They're calling me. It's time."

Papa lifted her gently. With her head on his shoulder, Mama closed her eyes.

Charlotte cut two sticks to make a cross, just like the cross she had made for Isaac's grave. She felt numb with grief.

Why was all this happening? Back in the Mohawk Valley, before the Revolution began, they had been so happy. Now Mama had joined Isaac, James and Charlie in death. Papa was old. The present was bleak, and the future uncertain.

Papa borrowed a spade and a Bible from Sergeant Major Clark. "I tried to get hold of a Prayer Book," he told Charlotte, "but the Commander's copy is the only one around and he won't lend it to anyone. His aide says he needs it for marriage services. Burials we have to manage ourselves, as best we can."

Charlotte opened the Bible. "Everything we need is here. What do you want to read?"

"There's something in the Old Testament about a good wife: 'Her price is far above rubies.' That's part of it."

"It's in Proverbs. We had to memorize that passage in school, at least the girls did." She flipped through the Bible. "Here it is: The heart of her husband trusteth in her, and he shall have no lack of gain. She doeth him good and not evil all the days of her life. She seeketh wool and flax, and worketh willingly with her hands."

"Every time Mr. Stuart read that in church, I thought of your mother."

Had Mama really been like that? Charlotte remembered Mama's hands kneading bread dough, knitting mittens, braiding rugs, stitching quilts.

Charlotte met Papa's eyes. "Yes. She was that woman."

Louisa Vrooman came to help. She knelt beside Mama's body to say a silent prayer, and then she hugged Papa and Charlotte. The tent felt warmer, just having her there. Louisa cut off a lock of Mama's hair to be saved as a remembrance. As Charlotte held it between her fingers, it reminded her of rust — brittle, dry and dull. How could anything so lifeless help her to remember hair that had been the colour of flame?

"We can dump the leaves from Martha's mattress and use the sacking as a shroud," Louisa said.

"No," said Papa. "Use her blanket."

"Henry," Louisa spoke gently. "It's a good blanket, and no use to Martha now."

"That doesn't matter. My wife deserves a decent burial."

Louisa laid her hand on Papa's arm. "If people see us carry her to the burying ground wrapped in that blanket, by tomorrow somebody will have dug her up to get it."

Papa turned pale. "The hemp sack, then. I would not have her grave disturbed."

Charlotte folded Mama's blanket carefully. Louisa was right about people who looted graves. On cold winter nights a warm woollen blanket was worth its weight in gold. But that wasn't the only reason to keep it. Mama would have wanted Papa and Charlotte to have it. She was never a woman to tolerate waste.

Chapter seventeen

C harlotte lifted the camp kettle from the cooking fire and carried it into the tent. Papa was sitting on his mattress, his face resting on his hands. He had been sitting there all day.

"Time to eat," she said as she set the kettle on the ground. When Papa looked up, she saw that his eyes were moist. Using the spoon that he had so carefully whittled from a piece of boxwood, she filled two bowls with boiled rice and passed one to him.

"Eat it while it's hot."

"Yes." He ate one spoonful, and then another, without seeming to notice what he was doing.

She watched his face as he ate. Only two weeks had passed since Mama's death. It was too soon for the pain to have lessened. But still, Papa should be taking some comfort from her presence, from her love and care. Why could he not? Why must he be so alone in his grief? It feels as if we are no longer a family, she thought. And the thought made her heart as heavy as a stone. After the boys died, they had still been a family. But since Mama's death, Charlotte and Papa lived in their separate worlds, each suspended in a void. It was true for her as well as for him, for she was living for the future, waiting to be with Nick. But Papa, quite the opposite, was living with his heart in the past. For both of them the present meant nothing. They were alive. Their hearts kept beating. They ate and slept. They went through the motions.

After finishing her rice, Charlotte ventured outside to tend the fire, which had died down. She pushed the glowing logs into a heap so that there would be live embers to start the next day's fire. We must always be ready for tomorrow, she thought. Snowflakes fell gently, landing with a soft hiss upon the now smoldering fire.

As Charlotte entered the tent, Papa looked up. "I'm sorry that I'm not better company for you."

"That doesn't matter," she answered. "But we have to keep going, even if it sometimes feels as if we aren't going anywhere."

She was grateful for the routine tasks that kept her busy.

There was wood to gather, food to cook, the fire to tend. Like it or not, she was the one in charge.

The next morning Charlotte went with Louisa to gather wood. Papa stayed behind in the tent, where Charlotte knew he would remain all day if she let him.

"Why doesn't he come with us?" Louisa asked.

"He won't. He won't do anything."

"Don't worry. Time heals all."

"I suppose so. But my father seems to get worse, not better. I talk to him, but it's like having a conversation with a stump."

"He used to be the head of the household," Louisa said. "What is he now?"

A shell, Charlotte thought. Papa is like an empty shell.

When Charlotte and Louisa returned, Charlotte found Papa slumped as usual upon his mattress. She crouched to warm her hands over the pail of ashes. It was cold as a stone.

"Papa," she said reproachfully. "There's no heat in these ashes. How long have you been sitting in the cold?"

"I don't know. I didn't notice."

"It doesn't take much effort to fill the pail with embers."

Papa raised his head. The moment she saw the misery in his eyes, she felt ashamed. "I'm sorry," she murmured. "I shouldn't have said that."

"And I shouldn't have given you cause." He paused. "Daughter, I'm not myself lately. I cannot forgive myself for causing your mother's death."

"But you didn't. Don't blame yourself."

His hands lay weakly in his lap. "I knew that she had a delicate constitution, yet I forced her to leave the Mohawk Valley, walk a hundred miles through the bush, and then live in a tent."

"But it wasn't only that. It was losing the boys. She no longer cared about living."

"True. She didn't care." He flexed his fingers. "My blabbering about cows and chickens went right over her head. And that's what hurts the most. I loved my sons. But after they died, I still had you and your mother." There was bitterness in his voice. "Why weren't you and I enough for her?"

"I don't know. My brothers were so much like her. Maybe that made it harder."

"Everybody called them Martha's boys."

"That was the red hair. But it went deeper than that."

"She didn't care enough," said Papa sadly. "She didn't try."

Winter dragged on. From time to time, couriers arrived at the fort with news. Except for the doorstep war of neighbour against neighbour, there was now very little fighting in New York Province. According to the latest reports, a band of Virginians had captured the British fort of Vincennes, which Charlotte had never heard of, in far-off Indian territory. The English still maintained their hold on New York City, although Rebel forces occupied the Hudson

Valley, where General Washington had made West Point his headquarters.

With so much gloomy news about bloodshed and defeat, Charlotte was beginning to feel it would always be that way. But one day, as she entered the blockhouse to pick up rations, she saw a dozen people standing by the counter laughing. With them was a buckskin-clad stranger, a white man wearing the leather leggings that most couriers preferred for travelling through the bush. She could not remember ever before hearing a courier's report that made people laugh. A victory at last? But the smiles looked more amused than triumphant.

She pressed forward to the counter. "What's happened?" she asked.

Sergeant Major Clark, who was laughing like the others, forced his mouth into a straight line. "According to the latest report . . ."

"Yes?"

"Benedict Arnold has fallen in love."

"That's right," the courier explained. "Our spies report that General Arnold has fallen head-over-heels in love with a seventeen-year-old Tory girl named Margaret Shippen, the daughter of a Philadelphia judge. Arnold met her after George Washington made him Commander of Philadelphia as a reward for his loyalty. You can bet people are talking about it. Apparently he wants to marry her, but he's having some trouble convincing her father."

"General Arnold is too old," Charlotte said.

"Thirty-eight," the courier replied. "Old enough to know better. The girl's a beauty, with expensive tastes. Everybody's waiting to see what happens. Even the Continental Congress has taken note, and the congressmen aren't too happy."

As he handed Charlotte her rations, Clark smiled wryly, "Love conquers all, as they say."

February was bitterly cold, but the days were lengthening. Having no calendar, Charlotte used ration days to mark off the passage of time. The visit to the blockhouse for rations was the highlight of each week, not because there was any excitement in watching Sergeant Major Clark measure out the Hoopers' supply of flour, rice and pork but because there was always the possibility of a letter from Nick.

At last one reached her. One snowy day, when Charlotte pushed open the blockhouse door, the Sergeant Major greeted her with a brighter than usual smile. Reaching under the counter, he brought up a folded paper closed with a red wax seal.

"Miss Charlotte, I have a letter for you. A courier brought it yesterday."

"Thank you." Taking it eagerly from him, she saw the address written in Nick's familiar, scratchy hand: "Miss Charlotte Hooper, In care of Fort Haldimand, Carleton Island."

She snapped the seal between her fingers and began to

read as she carried the letter across the room to a bench by the wall.

February 16, 1779

> *My dear Charlotte,*
>
> *As I write, I am sitting at a farmer's table, warming myself by his kitchen fire. The good wife has fed me roast pork and apple pie. So you see that a courier's life is not all hardship.*
>
> *There is little I can tell you save that I am well. The last six weeks were a trial, for my travels were on foot through rugged country. Friendly people, like my host, have used me well. But spies abound, making me ever careful what I say and write.*
>
> *My host will give this letter to a friend who travels soon to Montreal. He will leave it at Sir John Johnson's house, and from there I trust it will travel safely to your hands.*
>
> *A thousand kisses from your own,*
>
> *Nick*

A warm fire in a farmer's kitchen. Roast pork and apple pie. Yes, the life of a courier provided some compensation for the danger and hardship. It was worth travelling six weeks through rugged country to get a meal like that. Where was he, though? Definitely not in the Mohawk Valley, where there was also plenty of danger but precious little roast pork and apple pie for folks on the Loyalist side.

The letter's closing line promised her a thousand kisses. How long did she have to wait for them? She read the letter again. Not one word to say when Nick would be back.

Sergeant Major Clark had her rations ready on the counter. "Is it good news?" he asked. "From the way your face is glowing, I think it must be."

"As good as I could hope for."

"It's time you got something to smile about." He hesitated. "Your mother's death — that was a dreadful loss."

Charlotte squeezed her eyes shut. Whenever anyone mentioned Mama, she had to fight down tears. "We miss her terribly."

"It's a hard life in the Upper Country for anyone who lacks a strong constitution."

"She never was strong." Charlotte paused, and when she spoke again, changed the subject. "How is Fidelia?"

"Doing well." Clark was all smiles. "Two more months."

His happiness restored Charlotte's good spirits. She picked up the rations. No rice. No dried peas. Supplies must be getting low. But she had a letter, so life was good.

When she left the blockhouse, the red uniforms of the garrison drilling in the parade square were the only brightness to be seen. Such a small garrison — only one hundred men since the regiment had gone. Loyalist fugitives outnumbered them five-to-one. Grey-looking people. Ragged, thin refugees drifting about with nothing to do. Most were women and children, since every man between the ages of thirteen and fifty-nine had been recruited into the Royal Greens and was now fighting in distant fields.

On her way back with the rations, she overheard children quarrelling inside the tents. Women shouted at them to stop their noise. I'd hate to be stuck in a tent with my husband away and three or four children to look after, she thought. But Louisa Vrooman managed to survive, so Charlotte supposed she could too.

Two months passed. In April, Fidelia Clark gave birth to a son, the first white child born in the Upper Country, and from that day the Sergeant Major was a man transformed. His happiness was contagious; it infected everyone with whom he came in contact. To Charlotte, the sun was brighter, the wind gentler, the air warmer. Every day, she looked for Nick's return.

May arrived. On a warm evening, Charlotte was cooking bannock on sticks over the fire — tender bannock made with lard from the latest batch of maggoty pork. She had just taken a bannock roll from the fire, when she raised her head to see a tall man with a bushy beard the colour of straw striding toward her between the rows of tents. On his back was his rucksack, and under one arm he carried a canvas-covered bundle tied with cord. Could that be Nick? A look of surprise must have crossed her face, because the man laughed.

"Didn't you recognize me?"

"Of course I did," she said uncertainly. "But you look . . . well, so different."

He set his bundle on the ground, slipped the rucksack from his shoulders, and wrapped his arms around her. His beard felt warm and scratchy, like fleece, against her cheeks. The sensation when he kissed her was delightful. She nuzzled his beard, exploring its texture with her lips.

"What do you think of it?"

"Kiss me again. I'm still making up my mind."

But she would have to wait, for at that moment Papa came out of the tent.

"Is that Nick?" he asked.

"Whom else would I be kissing?" Charlotte answered.

As Papa and Nick shook hands, Papa studied the beard. "You fair-haired lads always look as if you never needed to shave. I didn't expect you to grow a beard that thick. It makes you look older."

"That's the idea," said Charlotte. "When I've dyed it, he'll look like a regular backwoodsman."

"Do you want to see your disguise?" said Nick. He picked up the canvas-covered bundle.

"Later. Put it in the tent. We'll eat first, while the bannock's warm."

Nick lifted the tent flap and stepped inside. A moment later, he emerged. When Charlotte saw the look of puzzlement on his face, she felt herself shrink back. Nick did not — could not — know about Mama.

"Where——?" Nick began. He had seen that something was wrong. There should have been three mattresses.

"Mama died in December."

Nick looked embarrassed, apologetic, as if not knowing had been his fault. Charlotte felt a hard lump in her throat. The plain fact of Mama's absence hit like a blow. Tears rose to her eyes.

Papa cleared his throat loudly and for a moment did not speak.

"I'm so sorry," Nick said.

They talked little while they ate. After supper, as it grew dark, Charlotte noticed Papa glancing around as if he were looking for someone beyond the circle of firelight.

"Martha is with the boys," he said suddenly. "That's where she wanted to be." He raised his head and gazed far off, as if he saw something not visible to anyone else.

Charlotte moved closer to Nick. His fingers closed upon hers, and he squeezed her hand. Papa broke the silence. Clearing his throat, he turned to Nick. His expression told Charlotte that he had just returned from a journey of his own.

"Well, where have you been since we last saw you?" Papa asked.

"A good few places. After I left here last summer, I travelled through the Ohio Valley to meet with Butler's Rangers, then east over the Catskills to New York."

"It must be bad there," said Papa.

"It's terrible. Thirty thousand soldiers. Ten thousand refugees. The Rebels burned down most of the city before they surrendered it in '76, but Loyalists still keep coming from all over the Thirteen Colonies. I saw two families sharing one room. People tear the paneling from walls to burn in their fireplaces. Scarcely a tree stands in The Bowery. The streets aren't safe. There are cutpurses everywhere."

"I've heard a rumour that France will send a fleet to take New York," Papa said.

"That could happen. There's a report that Lafayette has returned to France to persuade the French government to do exactly that."

"Who's Lafayette?" Charlotte asked. "On Carleton Island, we don't get all the latest news."

"He's a French marquis," Nick said, "and the new hero of the Revolution. Twenty-two years old. He became a captain in the French cavalry at the age of sixteen. Fabulously rich. Two years ago he furnished a ship at his own expense and set sail for America to help the Rebels. George Washington has made him a major general and added him to his staff."

Papa shook his head. "If France sends ships and troops, the Rebels will win this war."

In the morning Nick showed Charlotte the contents of the bundle: a grey hemp shirt, a red neckerchief, black breeches, two pairs of men's stockings, boots, a broad-brimmed hat, a belt, and a knife in a leather sheath. She picked up each item and examined it. Nick had chosen well. Only the breeches and stockings troubled her — would she really have to wear those?

"Try the clothes on," said Nick. "Let's see what you'll look like."

"Not yet."

"Why not? You have to wear them to get used to them. I'll wait outside until you've changed."

How could she object, since travelling as a boy had been her idea? Charlotte unbuttoned her gown and unlaced her petticoat. She put on the shirt and tied the red kerchief about her neck. They felt good. Then came the breeches. She got them on, although they were awfully tight around her bottom, and pulled up the stockings over her calves. With her hair in a queue and the hat upon her head, her disguise was complete.

But how could she leave the tent with the shape of her legs revealed from ankle to knee? Nick should not see her like this, and certainly not Papa. She lingered, dreading the moment when she would have to go outside.

"Charlotte, aren't you dressed yet?" Nick called.

"I'm dressed, but I don't look decent."

"Come out. I'm sure you do."

She stuck her head out of the tent, and in a moment the rest of her followed. The corners of Nick's mouth twitched, but he didn't laugh.

"Will I pass for a boy?"

He studied her for a minute. "Let me see you walk."

"Walk?"

"Yes."

Charlotte marched back and forth in front of the tent. Others outside neighbouring tents were watching. Charlotte pretended they didn't exist.

"You walk like a girl," Nick said.

Charlotte blinked. "For goodness sake, what do you expect?"

"You must learn to walk like a boy. Swing your arms, not your bottom."

"I don't swing my bottom!"

"Yes, you do."

"All right. How's this?" She strode briskly forward, swinging her arms.

"Better, but a bit stiff. You'll need to practise. Try to forget that you're a girl."

"How can I?" She sat down on the log beside the entrance.

"Think how boys act. Little details. Right now you're sitting like a lady. Knees together. Ankles crossed. Boys don't do that. Try crooking one leg over the other."

She tried it. "I feel ridiculous."

"But it's comfortable, isn't it? You couldn't sit that way in a skirt. Now here's your next lesson. Stand up, slouch, and stick your hands in your pockets."

She got to her feet. "Like this?"

"Perfect! Now let's see how far you can spit."

"No! At spitting I draw the line."

"Nick," said Papa. "That's going too far. Martha would turn over in her grave."

"I will not spit," said Charlotte. "I absolutely refuse."

Nick put his arm around her shoulders. "You're excused from spitting if you can whistle."

"Not that either."

Nick laughed. "Charlotte, every boy can——"

Papa interrupted. "You can't call her Charlotte, at least in public."

Well, that was true. Whoever heard of a boy named Charlotte?

"What about Tom, as in tomboy?" she asked.

"Fine," said Nick. "Can you think of a name for me?"

"I'll try," she said. "I'll think of something."

The first day that Charlotte dressed as a boy, she felt everyone staring at her. But on the second day it seemed as though she had wrapped herself in a cloak of invisibility. People whom she knew did not know her. Even Louisa Vrooman walked by without saying hello.

Charlotte devoted the third day to Nick's disguise. In the camp kettle she simmered black walnut husks until the liquid was reduced to an inky black tincture that smelled of rancid nuts. Nick sniffed it suspiciously. "Looks like poison. Smells like poison."

"You're not supposed to drink it," she laughed. "What you should do is soak your head in it overnight. That's how my mother dyed wool."

"You'd better just comb it through."

"Sit down," she said. "We'll get started."

His hair and beard soaked up the dye. One application made them look dirty. After two, they looked streaky. After three, they were dark brown.

"That does it," Charlotte said with satisfaction. "You look like a lumberjack."

"Have you thought of a name for me yet?"

"Joe. May I call you Joe?"

"Tom and Joe. Two brothers travelling together. That's fine."

That evening it rained. They were eating supper in the tent, listening to rain patter on the canvas, when Nick announced: "We're leaving tomorrow."

Papa nodded. "Since it must be done, best do it quickly."

Charlotte looked up. That sounded like her Papa of days gone by. She had sensed this change in him since Nick's return, a look of hope returning to his eyes. It was hope mixed with doubt, but hope nonetheless.

"Do you have enough food for the journey?" Papa asked.

"I bought two weeks' provisions from the Mohawks at Lachine," Nick said. "Dried meat, smoked fish, parched corn and maple sugar. Food that travels well."

Lachine. Wasn't that where Axe Carrier and his warriors

went to spend the first winter? By now Drooping Flower was a married woman, maybe even a mother.

"What else are you taking?" Papa asked.

"A spade. An axe. My rifle. Sacks to carry the strongbox and silver. Apart from our bedrolls, that's all."

"You're wise to travel light," said Papa. "There'll be plenty of portaging. We came down the Oswego River in a long canoe. I don't see how anybody could paddle upstream through those rapids."

"We'll portage when we have to," Nick agreed.

"You're following the route we took, but in reverse," Papa said. "It will be slow paddling up the Oswego, but after you've crossed Oneida Lake and started down the Mohawk River, the current will be with you."

"The journey will take us two weeks, there and back."

"Two weeks," Papa repeated. His gaze shifted from Nick to Charlotte, then settled gloomily upon both. "A lot can happen in two weeks."

"Try not to worry," Charlotte told him. "I'll be safe with Nick."

"You might as well tell a stone not to sink in water," he said gruffly.

"I'll take care of her," Nick promised.

"Remember," said Papa, "she's all I've got."

Chapter eighteen

"There are four actions to every stroke," Nick told her when they set out. "Thrust, pull, lift, and swing. Get a rhythm going, and you won't tire as soon."

Thrust, pull, lift, and swing. After three hours of it, her muscles ached, spurts of pain shot down her arms and across her shoulders, and her knees hurt from kneeling on the bottom of the canoe.

"How much further before we stop for the night?"

"We're about halfway there," Nick said. "If you want to rest, I'll handle the paddling for a while."

"No. If you do it, I will too." She refused to complain, even though her arms felt as if they were being pulled from their sockets.

"Before the mouth of the Oswego, there's a bay where we'll camp for the night. We'll be there in about three hours."

Three hours isn't so long, she thought. The lake was calm, with sunshine sparkling on quiet ripples. If her arms were not so sore, she would be enjoying this. Thrust, pull, lift, and swing. But why couldn't the sun move faster across the sky?

Late in the afternoon Nick said, "Do you see that point straight ahead?"

"Is that where we're stopping?"

"Just beyond."

As they rounded the point, she saw a small bay, not much bigger than a cove, with a beach of light brown sand. Churning the water with his paddle, Nick steered toward it. As the canoe ran up onto the beach, its bow ploughed the soft sand with a scratching sound. Charlotte scrambled out, stretched and looked around.

Along the water's edge ran a piping plover. Beyond the beach stood a line of poplars, shaking their silvery leaves in the breeze.

So this was the place where she and Nick would spend their first night alone together. The thought made her nervous. Restlessly she walked along the beach, right to the end. The sand felt warm under her bare feet. She was comfortable now in breeches. Walking, running, climbing in and out of the canoe — everything was easier than when she had dragged around in long skirts. But under those masculine clothes, Charlotte was still a girl. And it was just as Papa had said; she couldn't fool herself or Nick about that.

Near the water's edge Nick was sitting on a gnarled, old log that the waves had washed in. Charlotte walked across the beach to join him. She sat beside him and laid her hand upon his where it rested on the log. He turned his head and smiled at her.

"Well, here we are."

"Yes, here we are."

"I'm getting hungry," Nick said. "What about you?"

"Not especially, but we ought to eat."

She took a couple of pieces of dried deer meat and two cakes of maple sugar from the rucksack. After a day's paddling, she should have been hungry, yet she barely tasted the food. All she noticed was the toughness of the deer meat — like strips of leather.

While they were eating, a great blue heron flapped across the bay, trailing its long legs, and landed in shallow water beside a patch of reeds. For a time the bird stood motionless. Then suddenly its beak shot forward like a lance, and when the heron raised its head, a frog's limbs waved wildly from either side. A twitch, a shudder, and the frog disappeared down the long gullet. The heron took up its position again, but as dusk fell, it abandoned the hunt and flew away.

Nick stood up. "We'd better make a fire."

Together they wandered down the beach, picking up driftwood. By sunset they had collected enough. Nick got out his tinderbox. While he was lighting the fire, Charlotte fetched their bedrolls from the canoe. She unrolled Nick's blankets on one side of the fire, and then her own on the opposite side. This was being sensible, she told herself. She hoped that Nick would suggest putting the blankets closer together, but he didn't. Nick was being sensible too.

As darkness fell, the beach seemed lonely and desolate. The sky was vast, the lake empty, and Carleton Island far away. Back in the tent, Papa would be thinking about her and wondering what she was doing. If he had a magic lens through which he could see her now, sitting on her blanket watching Nick pile driftwood onto their campfire, would he be reassured? "Don't you trust us?" she had asked Papa. "Alone in the bush for two weeks?" he had answered in a tone that did not sound as if he did. But Papa must have believed them when they gave their word. Otherwise, they wouldn't be here.

When Nick had the fire built up, he sat down beside her and put his arm around her. Gradually the glow of sunset faded from the sky. A loon called. Sparks from their fire flew upwards to join the stars that twinkled far above. Moonlight danced upon the ripples of the bay.

"If we were Indians, this could be our wedding journey," said Charlotte.

"Someday," he said, and pulled her more closely to him.

Charlotte sighed. "Yes. Someday." Why not now? Why were the things she wanted always someday and never now?

When Nick and Charlotte set out the next morning, her arms and shoulders were stiff and sore. But as she paddled, the warm sunshine and the exercise loosened her muscles. Her body was learning the rhythm of paddling: thrust, pull, lift and swing. The further they went, the more natural it seemed.

Their course lay to the south, following the curve of Lake Ontario's shore. Charlotte scarcely recognized the broad marshes at the mouth of the Oswego River. Many months ago, when she had travelled through these wetlands in the long canoe, there had been acres of dead reeds. But now green shoots stuck up through the still water. Redwing blackbirds, clinging to the stalks of last summer's bulrushes, filled the air with their rasping calls. In the water, brown perch and bright sunfish swam leisurely away from the path of the canoe. Once, right off the bow, Charlotte spotted a fish as big as a man lying still as if asleep in the shallows, its pectoral fins slowly fanning the water.

"Look!" she said softly.

"Muskellunge. It could take your hand off." At a nudge from Nick's paddle, the huge fish vanished in a swirl of river-bottom mud.

Late in the afternoon Nick turned the canoe towards shore. The reeds rustled as the bow parted them, like a comb parting hair. When the bow touched land, a dozen frogs leapt into the water.

Charlotte rolled up the legs of her breeches and climbed

out. Up to her ankles in slimy mud that squished between her toes, she hauled the canoe further ashore. The mud made a sucking sound as she lifted each foot.

She did not see the bloodsucker until she sat down to wipe her feet with a handful of grass. Pulsing like a pump, it had fastened itself to her left foot, wedged between her big toe and the next,

"Nick! Help me!"

"What's wrong?"

Shuddering, she pointed to it.

"Oh, a bloodsucker! Don't worry. It will drop off when it's full. It's just a leech, like doctors use to treat bruises."

"I hate leeches." She unsheathed her knife.

"Hey! Don't cut it off. The mouth will keep sucking. Fire's the only thing that will make it let go."

"Then light a fire! Please. Make it let go. I can't stand it."

The creature was swelling, its grey body changing to pink as it filled with her blood.

Nick unpacked his tinderbox. One, two, three times he struck the flint and steel before getting a spark. Usually once was enough, but not this time, while the leech sucked and sucked.

"Hurry!"

"I'm doing the best I can." Squatting beside the smoldering tinder, Nick fed wisps of dry grass to the precious spark.

"Nick! I can't bear it. It's big as a sausage."

Not only as big as a sausage, but the right colour too. A

pink, pulsing sausage attached to Charlotte's foot.

At last Nick held up a stick with a bright, glowing tip. "Hold still."

At the touch of fire, the ruptured membranes spurted blood. The leech let go. Suddenly empty, it was just a small grey bladder lying in a pool of blood. Nick tossed it into the reeds.

"Did it really hurt that much?" he asked.

Charlotte inspected the tiny puncture that the leech's mouth had left. "Not really." As she pulled on her boots, she felt embarrassed because she had acted — yes, she must admit the truth — like a girl.

"The real problem tonight will be mosquitoes," said Nick. "The fire will help keep them away if I throw on some green rushes to make it smoke. And it would be a good idea to smear mud on every bit of your skin that isn't covered by clothes."

But neither smoke nor mud gave much protection. When the mosquitoes arrived, they attacked in hordes, in vicious biting clouds. They were so thick that Charlotte could smack a dozen at a time. It made no difference to their numbers.

Good grief! She thought. First the leech. Now the mosquitoes. I'll have no blood left in me by dawn.

If she hadn't been exhausted, she might not have slept at all. But she did, off and on. At daybreak when she wakened, slapping and scratching, Nick had already loaded the canoe.

"Let's get away from here," he said. "Mosquitoes won't follow us over open water."

They paddled out to the middle of the channel, where they ate their breakfast undisturbed, soothed by the gentle rocking of the canoe.

"I hope there's never another night like that," said Charlotte.

"Not till we're on our way back. By mid-morning we'll be out of the wetlands."

Charlotte dipped her neckerchief in the river. Using it as a washcloth, she scrubbed the dried mud from her face and throat.

"A beard has more uses than I thought," Nick said. "Mosquitoes prefer smooth skin."

"Pity I can't grow a beard," Charlotte said ruefully as she scratched the bites on her cheeks and chin.

"I'm just as glad you can't," Nick replied. He picked up his paddle. "Let's be on our way."

After they had left the wetlands behind and begun their journey up the Oswego River, they were paddling against the current. With every mile it grew stronger, pushing against Charlotte's paddle as if it were a living force, trying to send them back the way they had come. A blister formed in the groove between the thumb and forefinger of her right hand. The sun was hot. Sweat ran down her face. They fought for every inch.

When the sun stood directly overhead, they stopped to eat and rest. Charlotte lay on her back, relaxing on the springy bracken fern that grew along the riverbank. Without turning her head, she glanced at Nick from the corner of her eye. Slumped beside her with his arms wrapped about his knees, he looked exhausted too.

From further upriver came a roaring sound, too steady to be thunder.

"Can you hear the rapids?" Nick asked.

"So that's what it is! It's louder than I remember."

"When you went down the Oswego in the long canoe, it was November. There's a lot more water in the river in May."

She pondered this as she stared up at a drifting white cloud. "Nick, at this rate, we'll never get to Oneida Lake. We could travel faster on foot, even carrying the canoe and our supplies. We must portage."

"There's an easier way."

"Tell me." She continued to watch the cloud. In a minute it would cover the sun.

"The canoe stays in the water, but we walk along the bank and tow it upriver. I can drag the canoe by its bow rope."

"Against the current? Would that be easier than paddling?"

"Yes, because we wouldn't have to unload the canoe, carry everything on our backs, then load the canoe again."

As the cloud covered the sun, the air felt suddenly cooler. With a burst of energy, Charlotte stood up. Taking a few steps to the water's edge, she studied the river. Even close to the riverbank, the greenish-brown water was moving fast.

Sharp-looking rocks jutted from the riverbed so close to the bank that she saw no room for a canoe to pass. Towing the canoe seemed impossible.

But when Charlotte looked further up the river, she noticed that there was a smaller channel flowing from the left into the main channel a few hundred feet from where they were resting,

"Look," she said, pointing to it. "Where do you think that stream comes from?"

Nick turned his head. "From above the rapids. It's a side channel. The spot you're pointing to is where it meets up with the main channel again."

"Could we tow the canoe up that channel? The current looks much weaker. Or would the water be too shallow?"

"Not at this time of year, with the water running high. At worst, we might have to lighten the canoe of part of its load." He hauled himself to his feet and joined Charlotte at the water's edge. "Once we get above the rapids, we won't have far to portage. The closer we get to Oneida Lake, the less current there is to fight."

"But first we'll have to tow the canoe against this current until we reach the side channel."

"There's no great danger if I hold the canoe close to the riverbank, where the current is weaker than in the middle."

"Even at the edge, it looks mighty strong."

"I can handle that." He stretched. "Let's be on our way."

After tossing the paddles into the canoe, he checked the

bowline, giving it a sharp tug. "That should hold."

While Charlotte pushed the canoe into the water, Nick held the bowline with both hands. The rope sprang taut as soon as the current grabbed the canoe. Grasping the rope firmly, Nick walked backwards, knees slightly bent, looking like a fisherman trying to land an enormous fish that was putting up a tremendous fight. The canoe moved jerkily against the current, upright despite a slight wobble. Around the bow, white water foamed.

The cords in Nick's neck stood out as he pulled. His face was red, and his breath came in dull grunts.

"Charlotte . . . uh . . . lend me a hand . . . uh . . ."

She grasped the rope, her hands just below his, and together they towed the canoe the remaining fifty feet to the side channel and eased it into the quieter water.

"Thanks," Nick said. "That current was stronger than I expected."

"Do you want help here?"

"In a channel this narrow, it's easier for me to tow it alone."

Charlotte tramped ahead of him through the knee-deep ferns, feeling guilty because he was doing all the work.

Dense bushes covered the narrow island that separated the side channel from the main channel. Through their foliage, Charlotte caught only glimpses of the rapids, yet their roar drowned out every other noise.

Slowly, carefully, Nick manoeuvered the canoe up the

side channel. About halfway to the main channel, when the canoe scraped bottom, Charlotte lifted out the rucksack, the spade and the rifle. That was enough reduction of weight to allow the canoe to float freely.

As soon as they reached the top of the side channel, Charlotte saw ahead of them, on the main channel, a stretch of rock-free mud where the bank was low.

"That's where we'll start the portage," Nick said.

The mud flat was upriver. To reach it, they would have to tow the canoe through fifty feet of fast moving water at the head of the rapids.

"Shall I help?" Charlotte asked as she set down the rucksack, spade and rifle in the canoe.

"Not for that short distance."

To make the turn from the narrow side channel into the main channel, it would be necessary to nose the bow of the canoe out into the main stream. Charlotte watched as Nick wound the bowline around his wrists and braced his feet, ready for the full force of the current to hit the canoe broadside.

And suddenly the tow rope broke.

Nick staggered backwards and fell while the canoe, rocketing stern first down the river, fled like a runaway horse.

Not waiting for Nick, Charlotte tore after it. Seconds later, he passed her, his long legs unimpeded by the bracken. She kept running as she watched.

The canoe was still upright when Nick came abreast of it

and plunged into the rapids, arms outreached to seize the gunwale. White water eddied and foamed around the canoe. Charlotte could not see through the spray exactly what happened next.

Nick disappeared. The canoe raced on, pitching and wallowing, but she did not try to follow its course.

Where was Nick?

Forty feet downstream, an arm appeared above the white foam. Nick's head and shoulders emerged. For a few moments he clung to a rock, before the water tore him away, and swallowed him again. His body rose, but his face was below the surface. His hand beat feebly at the water.

She raced along the riverbank, stumbling through ferns until she came abreast of him and flung herself into the water. Clinging to rocks wherever she could, swimming like a dog where the river ran clear, she reached him at the bottom of the rapids. When she grabbed his hand, his fingers closed on hers.

Nick was half conscious when she pulled him out. He gasped and choked. A flood of water poured from his mouth. He did not speak, but lay on the crushed ferns with his eyes closed. He had a gash on his forehead from which blood oozed and trickled onto the ground.

She lifted his head and shoulders onto her lap. As she bent her head to kiss his cheek, she heard his heart pounding. For a long time she sat there, cradling Nick and listening to the river. Gradually blood ceased to flow from Nick's gash; it started to congeal. His heart no longer pounding, he breathed quietly, as if he were asleep.

"Where's the canoe?" His voice was low, yet it startled her.

"I don't know."

"We'd better look for it." He lifted his head from her lap, rolled onto his side, and raised himself on one elbow.

"I'll go. You rest here," she said.

She felt the shock of fear as she headed downstream. If the canoe was gone, everything was gone. Had the river swept it away, carried it for miles? Or would she find it smashed upon the rocks? Charlotte prayed, "Please, Lord, spare the canoe!"

And it was spared. She found it upside down but undamaged, with its bow jammed between a fallen tree and a boulder. The rucksack was bobbing in a pool, into which their bedrolls were slowly sinking. The sacks were caught on rocks. The spade, axe and rifle were underwater, resting on the riverbed. Duck-diving through the clear, green water, Charlotte retrieved all three.

It took a long walk downstream before she located both paddles. When she had recovered everything, she stacked their gear and supplies in a pile and returned to Nick. He sat up as she approached.

"I found everything," she said. "When you're rested, we can rescue the canoe. The way it's stuck, it's not going anywhere."

"Tomorrow we'll portage. For today, we've had enough."

The sky clouded over. By the time Nick and Charlotte had dragged the canoe from the river, rain was falling. They made camp on a spot of level ground, where they could turn the canoe over and prop up one side with paddles to make a shelter. Charlotte piled their gear and supplies underneath. Crouching under the canoe, she examined everything to see what damage the water had done. Nick's gunpowder and flax tinder were dry, but the parched corn, dried meat and smoked fish were wet. The maple sugar had simply dissolved — a total loss.

A bolt of lightning ripped the sky, struck somewhere nearby with a bang like an explosion. The thunder was louder than the rapids' roar.

All night they clung to each other, wrapped in their wet blankets, jammed together in the narrow space under the canoe. Rain hammered on the birchbark, inches above their heads. Despite the cold, Nick soon fell asleep. Charlotte lay still, trying to stop shivering. Nick's breath was warm against her cheek, and she felt the warmth of his body through their blankets. She yawned. She was tired too.

When she woke up, the sun was shining, and she peered from under the canoe at water drops sparkling like diamonds on the ferns. She crawled out to have a look around.

Nick was already busy setting out food. They ate deer meat for breakfast. Softened by its dunking in the river, it was easier to chew — more like rubber than leather, and it tasted good.

"The portage will warm us up," said Nick. "Let's get started." He lashed the paddles to the thwarts. "I'll carry the canoe. You take the rest."

He loaded her up with their blankets, the food pack, the spade, axe and rifle while she stood like a patient packhorse.

"It's a heavy load," he said as he tied everything in place, "but the weight is well distributed."

"I can manage." She hoped that this was true.

Nick hoisted the canoe upon his shoulders and started off ahead of her. With wobbly legs she took a first step onto the trail, then a second. For a moment she faltered, but then found her stride.

After the rapids were behind them, they returned to the river. They were deep in Oneida territory now. Each time they came to a bend, Charlotte held her breath, half expecting to see a war party up ahead. But beyond each bend, there was nothing except another stretch of river.

"I'm surprised that we've met no one along the way," she said when they stopped for the night.

"Thank General Sullivan for that. He's made a clean sweep of every Iroquois village in New York Province."

"There used to be a fishing village at the western end of Oneida Lake."

"Tomorrow we'll see if there's anything left of it," Nick said.

Chapter nineteen

Nothing was left of the Oneida fishing village. Grass and wild strawberry plants carpeted the ground between the piles of ashes that once had been bark huts.

Charlotte paid them no attention as she walked by. What she wanted to find was the log where Moses' clothes had been hidden. Nick watched her poking around in the bushes.

"What are you looking for?"

"This." She dropped to her knees.

"A rotting log?"

"Look what's underneath." As she rolled the log over, chunks of decaying wood broke off in her hands. Nick, hands on his thighs, leaned forward to see. Pale fungus threads were growing from the small shirt and breeches.

"A child's clothes. Homespun. How did you know they were here?"

"They belonged to a Canajoharie boy named Moses Cobman. He was with us when we camped beside Oneida Lake. He ran away. Later, we found his clothing under this log."

"So the Oneidas captured him. How old was he?"

"Nine. By now he's eleven if he's still alive."

"If he is, they'll do their best to keep him healthy. He'll be valuable when the bargaining begins."

"What bargaining?" She rolled the log back.

"The Oneidas backed the wrong side. Sullivan's army has burned their villages, and they have nowhere to go. Their best chance is to make peace with the English."

"You think they'll trade Moses for peace?"

"Peace and territory. The English have promised to set aside land in Canada for their Iroquois allies."

"Well, that doesn't include the Oneidas."

"Exactly. If they want to be included, their first step is to bury the hatchet with the other Iroquois nations. When they've done that, some go-between — most likely a Mohawk — will carry a message to an English fort to sue for peace. The Oneidas will hand over their hostage as a token of goodwill, and the negotiations will begin."

"But what if the Oneida have adopted Moses?"

"That would be a different story. If they've adopted him, he is one of their own."

Darkness fell quickly. Just beyond the campfire's circle of light lurked the ghosts of vanished warriors. In every rustling of the grass Charlotte heard the whisper of moccasined feet. When sleep overtook her, it was troubled by dreams. She saw Mrs. Cobman pleading for the return of her lost son. Then the image shifted, and it wasn't Mrs. Cobman, but Mama standing with outstretched hands. Then Moses appeared. Charlotte knew it must be Moses, though older in her dream — a pale youth in fringed buckskin, gripping a scalping knife that dripped blood.

Waking with a start, Charlotte reached instinctively for her own knife. It was still at her belt, safely sheathed. She raised herself on one elbow. On the other side of the fire Nick, rolled in his blanket, slept quietly. She lay back down and folded her arms under her head. The terrors of the night passed as the eastern sky changed from black to indigo.

At sunrise she woke Nick; she was eager to be gone. As they chewed their morning meal of rubbery deer meat, she asked, "Where did the Oneidas go after the soldiers destroyed their villages? They must be somewhere."

"They're living in scattered bands here and there. It takes only a day for Indians to set up a temporary village in a safe place, if they can find one."

When the canoe was packed, they pushed it into the water. As Nick settled in the stern, he said. "The worst part of our journey is behind us. Now that we've left the Oswego

River, we'll have an easy paddle across Oneida Lake."

"The eastern end of the lake was where we camped on our way to Carleton Island," Charlotte said. "We stayed there more than a week, with two Mohawk warriors to protect us."

"You told me about that. One was named Axe Carrier. You seemed to admire him. But you didn't say much about the other man."

"Okwaho? He was younger, about your age." She realized that she had said little about Okwaho. Nick did not need to know that a Mohawk warrior had courted her. "He was very helpful too," she added.

As they paddled eastward, following the south shore of Oneida Lake, thoughts of her Mohawk friends, especially of Okwaho, rose in her mind. Where was he now? Had he found a girl of his own people to love?

When they reached the eastern end of Oneida Lake, Charlotte looked for the landmarks from Papa's map. The pink granite boulder was unchanged, but white lichens shaped like malformed ears now grew from the trunk of the fallen ash tree. Plants had sprouted in the ashes of the cooking fire, and the shelters had collapsed into heaps of bark and broken poles. Yet the abandoned Loyalist campsite felt friendly. If ghosts dwelt here, they would be friendly too.

In the woods nearby, late afternoon sunshine slanted through the trees, bathing with soft light the trilliums, hepaticas and bloodroot that bloomed beside the path.

Wild raspberry canes grew at the edge of the woods. There would be a good crop of berries this year, but they still had a month to go.

Nick unloaded the canoe. While he lit a fire, she started to open the food pack. She sniffed. Something smelled horrible. Even before she had the food pack fully open, the stench made her gag. Charlotte pulled everything out. The parched corn, soaked in river water, had fermented. The smoked fish was rotten, and the deer meat was slimy and green.

She groaned. How could they have been so stupid? They should have dried the food thoroughly after its dunking, not left it sitting in the rucksack on the bottom of the canoe, warmed by the sun.

"Smell this," she said to Nick.

He grimaced. "It stinks."

"What are we going to eat?" Charlotte was almost in tears. "It's too early for berries."

Nick frowned. "Indians eat beech leaves when they're starving."

"We can't live on beech leaves for nine days."

"When we reach some homesteader's field, we'll rob his potato patch at night."

"Nick! You wouldn't!"

"If I were starving . . ."

"We're not starving yet. And even if it weren't stealing, I'd just as soon eat beech leaves as seed potatoes. Ugh! They're

so wizened and soft! Besides, if the homesteader saw tres-
passers scrabbling in his potato patch, he would get out his
gun."

"Then how about frogs? We can catch a couple of dozen
for supper tonight and breakfast tomorrow. By evening
we'll reach the first farms of the Mohawk Valley, where
there's sure to be someone who'll let us work for food."

"Well . . ." Charlotte had practised being a boy, but could
she really fool anyone?

"This time of year, there's plenty of work for farm hands."
He gave Charlotte a quick hug. "Yes. That's what we'll do."

They speared the frogs with sharpened sticks and skew-
ered them to roast over the fire. Most were bullfrogs, but a
few green frogs and leopard frogs were among them. Their
legs had a disagreeable way of jerking as they toasted, as if
the creatures were still trying to jump away. But the result
was delicious.

"A bit like chicken," Charlotte said. "And there are mil-
lions more along the riverbanks all the way to Fort Hunter
and back. As long as we can catch frogs, we don't need to
look for work."

He shook his head. "We can't risk a fire."

"Is there danger from the Sons of Liberty?"

"No. Nothing to do with politics. In the backwoods, some
men would kill to get a rifle and a canoe. There'll be plenty
of frogs to catch, but you'll have to eat them raw."

Now came the Oneida Carry — the long portage that led from Oneida Lake to the Mohawk River's western branch. Beside the portage trail flowed Wood Creek, too shallow for a canoe. But it deepened as other streams flowed into it. By midday it was deep enough to float the canoe. At first they towed it empty, Nick carrying their gear while Charlotte pulled the canoe along by what was left of the bow rope. Bit by bit, they were able to put their gear on board without allowing the canoe to scrape bottom. Late in the afternoon, when the water was deep enough for them to add their own weight, they climbed in. Paddling was easy, now that they were going with the current.

By dusk the creek had joined up with the Mohawk River, and soon they passed the first woodcutters' shanties and scattered backwoods farms. They put ashore in a wooded area.

Nick asked, "Do you want to catch some frogs?"

"Beech leaves will do."

They picked a few handfuls. After they had nibbled their way through two or three leaves, Nick said, "We'd better look for work at one of those farms."

"I agree." She tossed away the rest of her beech leaves. "First, we must decide on our story."

"We're two brothers, Tom and Joe, willing to work for food."

"What's our last name?"

"Smith?"

"Too common."

"Cutler?"

She tried it out. "Joe Cutler. Tom Cutler. Good names. Now, what are we doing in the backwoods?"

"Butler's Rangers burned us out, so we're on our way to Schenectady to join the Rebel army."

"We won't get much sympathy if we happen upon a Loyalist family."

"No chance of that. I know every safe house the length of the Mohawk River, and there are none around here."

Charlotte pulled in her belt. Although she had drunk all the water she could swallow, hoping to convince her stomach that it was full, it growled in protest through most of the night.

At dawn Charlotte and Nick left their canoe hidden in brush near the riverbank and headed along a rough track that was more than a path, but hardly fit to be called a road. They skirted half a dozen woodcutters' shacks before coming to a log cabin that stood beside an acre of unploughed land. Tree stumps still in the ground showed how recently the field had been cleared. A sow with half a dozen piglets rooted around the stumps, while a swaybacked white horse in a paddock fenced with split logs nodded its head over the top rail. At the edge of the woods, a single cow grazed.

The cabin had one window set to the right of the door. The window had real glass — not oiled buckskin like most backwoods shacks. From the cabin came the mouth-watering aroma of baking bread.

Charlotte and Nick sat hunched in bushes where they

could watch the cabin without being seen. A woman in a faded blue gown carried out a basin of water, which she dumped on the ground, and then went back inside. Charlotte heard children laughing. After a time, three small girls came out. The tallest, about five years old, had a grey kitten in her arms. She set it down on the packed earth outside the door. The children dragged a tiny piece of wood the size of a mouse in front of the kitten's nose. They laughed at the kitten's jerky, stiff-legged pounces as it attacked the stick.

"No sign of a man around here," said Charlotte.

"Probably away in the army. That explains why the field hasn't been planted."

"There's a horse," said Charlotte, "so likely there's a plough."

Nick nodded. "That woman could use a couple of farm hands." He stood up. "I'll do the talking. The less you say, the less chance you'll give yourself away."

Walk like a boy, Charlotte reminded herself as she followed Nick to the door. Act like a boy. And don't talk.

At the strangers' approach, the children dashed inside, abandoning the kitten, which mewed piteously to find itself alone. Charlotte ignored it, because that's what a boy would do.

The woman came to the door carrying a rifle.

"What do you want?"

"Work," said Nick. "I reckon you could use some help ploughing and planting. I'm Joe Cutler and this is my brother Tom. We're on our way to Schenectady to join General Washington's army. Our folks had a homestead further up river until Butler's Rangers burned us out."

The woman frowned. "I got no money to pay you."

"We'll work for food. We've eaten nothing since yesterday morning."

"Under the cabin there's five bushels of seed potatoes that should have been planted days ago. I was waiting for my brother to give me a hand. He'll be here by and by, when his own planting's done." She lowered the rifle barrel. "My name is Molly Dow."

"Mrs. Dow, we'll get your potatoes into the ground this very day," said Nick.

"It's a bargain, then." She set the rifle behind the door. "If you haven't eaten since yesterday, you need a slice of bread and a glass of milk to start you off. After you're done planting, I'll feed you a proper meal and pack you something to take along." She started to close the door, and then added, "The plough's in the shed."

The shed was a lean-to against the back wall of the cabin. As Charlotte stepped around the piles of cow, pig and horse manure, she realized that it also served as a barn.

By the time Nick and Charlotte had pulled out the plough and dragged the bushels of seed potatoes from under the cabin, Mrs. Dow had two slabs of buttered bread sprinkled with maple sugar and two glasses of milk set out on the front step.

"One day's work will do it," said Nick between bites. "Then we can rest for a bit and be on our way after dark. From here on, we have to travel at night."

He ploughed; she planted. The seed potatoes were wrinkled and soft, with sprouts like pale, ghostly fingers. Charlotte handled them tenderly, careful not to snap the tender shoots as she set them in the ground.

Now and then Mrs. Dow walked to the edge of the field and watched them work. The little girls brought water, the eldest carrying a jug and each of the younger ones a tin cup.

By mid-afternoon, the job was done. As Nick and Charlotte put away the plough and tools, the smell of boiling turnips drifted through the chinks in the wall between the shed and the house. Charlotte began to worry. Out of doors, it was easy to pretend that she was a boy. Indoors, sitting at a table, would be a different matter. If they asked politely, maybe Mrs. Dow would let them eat outside. It would have to be Nick who asked.

"Nick," she began, "do you suppose . . ."

"Food's ready!" Mrs. Dow opened the door and called them in. It was too late to ask. Charlotte followed Nick inside.

"Sit down."

Charlotte took her place at the trestle table across from Nick. The cabin was simple, with no trace of decoration on the log walls. In the stone fireplace, a slow fire kept the cook pot simmering. "Potato soup," the woman said, "with wild leeks for a bit of flavour." She ladled out two bowlfuls.

"Smells good," said Nick.

Charlotte spooned soup into her mouth as fast as she could, partly because she was ravenous and partly because she wouldn't be expected to talk as long as she was eating.

Mrs. Dow refilled their soup bowls, and then set down a dish of steaming mashed turnips and a platter of sliced ham.

Charlotte piled turnips onto her plate. Now this was real food! As she stuffed herself, she began to relax. By the time the meal was over, she felt right at home.

Nick stood up. "Thank you," he said as he pushed in his chair.

Charlotte stood up too. Automatically she stacked the dirty dishes, placing Nick's plate upon her own, and was about to set the soup bowls on top when she caught the warning look in Nick's eye. He knit his brow; he shook his head.

Too late. Mrs. Dow's eyebrows shot up half an inch. Her piercing eyes studied Charlotte from head to foot, lingering on her bosom.

"Men don't clear the table," she said coldly as she took the dishes from Charlotte's hands. She carried the dishes across the room, set them in the dry sink, and picked up a package that was wrapped in paper and tied with string. Then she turned to face Nick.

"I don't want any trouble. The two of you better get on

your way before her pa comes around searching. Clear out fast, and I'll forget I saw either one of you. Here's the food I promised, packed up and ready."

Nick took the package from Mrs. Dow. "Thank you. We're truly grateful."

On their way back to the canoe, Nick was beaming.

"What in heaven's name was she talking about?" Charlotte asked.

"Why, she thinks that we're runaway lovers. And she's afraid that your father is on his way to shoot me and drag you back."

"I'm sorry, Nick. I did try to act like a boy."

"But it couldn't be better! She's promised to tell no one that she saw us. The truth never entered her head."

At the edge of the woods Nick halted, set down the package of food, and took Charlotte in his arms.

"Stop!" she said. "Mrs. Dow may be watching."

"I hope she is," he said, and kissed Charlotte on the mouth.

They walked back to the canoe with an arm around each other's waist.

"All's well that ends well," said Nick.

"Aren't you saying that a bit too soon?"

"All's well that ends well." But it had not ended yet, Charlotte reflected as she lay on the grass looking up at the tangle of leaves just above her head. In fact, the most important part of their mission lay ahead.

Tonight they would paddle downstream with the current to help them. By dawn they would reach Fort Hunter. All day tomorrow they would hide, waiting for dark. And then they would make their way through the ravine to the path up the hillside that led to the Hoopers' farm.

Tomorrow night was so close! After all the months of waiting and all the days of travelling, it was almost here.

By the day after tomorrow, they would be heading north again with the legal papers, the family Bible and the silver tea set in the bottom of the canoe. Then would be soon enough to say, "All's well that ends well."

Nick lay propped upon his elbows, watching the river.

"What are you staring at?" she asked.

"People going by."

"Is there danger?"

"Not for us."

She sat up and peered through the bushes. A flat-bottomed boat was moving slowly upstream, rowed by two men and two women. An old lady dressed in black — black bonnet, black shawl, black gown — sat on a kitchen chair amidst neatly stacked furniture, looking like a tragic queen upon a rickety throne. She held a small child on her lap. Half a dozen other children perched on tables or leaned over the gunwales with their fingers trailing in the water. In the bow sat a brown dog, facing straight ahead like a prow ornament.

"Loyalists," Charlotte whispered. "They look like two families travelling together. I wonder where they're going."

"Probably Carleton Island," said Nick, "but they'll never make it with all that furniture. Whatever possessed them to bring it?"

"It's hard to leave things behind." She thought of all the things that her family had left. Big things, like the kitchen table, and small things like the sampler she had made when she was twelve. At least she would still have the silver tea set that her grandparents had brought from England. All her life, it had stood on the sideboard at her home in Fort Hunter. Someday it would have a place in the home that she and Nick would build together, and she would treasure it as her link to the past.

"I left everything behind," Nick murmured.

She squeezed his arm. "You still have me."

With his eyes still fixed on the boat as it laboured up the river, he laid his hand on hers. "That I do, and I'll never let you go."

The hills that rimmed the Mohawk Valley loomed against the darkening sky when Nick and Charlotte set out again. They paddled past woods and fields and scattered settlements. The river gleamed with a soft, deep light.

After an hour, they came to a place where stone chimneys silhouetted against the sky showed where houses had been.

"Nick, where are we?"

"Stanwix."

Stanwix. Yes. Mrs. Platto, Mrs. Vankleek, and Mrs. Weegar

had lived there. Perhaps at this very moment the canoe was passing the ruins of their homes.

The river bore them south, past Oriskany, where Brant's Iroquois force and Butler's Rangers had killed hundreds of Rebels in an ambush, and past Canajoharie, where Charlotte and her parents had hidden in the Cobmans' root cellar. The name of every town and village rang a bell in her mind.

By daybreak they were almost home. Charlotte watched for familiar landmarks, but saw few. The gristmill where Papa used to take his grain should have been on the right bank. It wasn't there. Only the huge millwheel remained, turning round and round. Water dripping from its spokes sparkled in the rays of the rising sun.

They passed Herkimer's place — that cheapskate Herkimer, who wouldn't buy Papa's pigs and cattle because he was waiting to pick them up cheap as soon as they were confiscated. Herkimer had refused to take sides, but sitting on the fence had not helped him. His barn was gone and only the chimney remained of his house.

The current bore the canoe smoothly along. Above the trees, she saw the steeple of John Stuart's church — her own parish church where she and her brothers had been baptized and where she had expected to be married, as her parents had been.

She felt like weeping as the canoe glided past the familiar places of her childhood. She had never expected to see them again. The end of this journey would be her final good-bye.

Chapter twenty

They went ashore near the mouth of the little creek that wound its way through the ravine behind the Hoopers' farm. This was as far as they could travel by canoe. The last mile of their journey would be on foot, at night.

After dragging the canoe into a dense thicket near the water's edge, they covered it with leafy boughs. Now the long day stretched before them, and they had nothing to do but wait. Charlotte unwrapped the food that Mrs. Dow had packed. Biscuits and sliced ham.

"Hungry?" she asked.

"Like a horse."

She split open a couple of biscuits, one for each of them, and stuffed a piece of ham inside.

"That's not enough."

"We need to save some for the way back," she protested, but gave him another biscuit.

When he had finished eating, Nick folded his blanket like a pillow, laid his head upon it, and closed his eyes. Within minutes, his regular breathing told her that he was asleep. He was lucky always to fall asleep so easily.

Swallows skimmed the water. Cicadas rasped and trilled. A breeze riffled the leaves overhead. Nick slumbered on. An ant marched across his forehead; Charlotte flicked it off with her fingernail. The skin of Nick's nose was peeling where it had been sunburned. His eyelashes and eyebrows were almost white. Why hadn't she rubbed walnut stain into his eyebrows? She should have thought of that. Nick's eyelids twitched. Probably he was dreaming. She wished he would wake up. It was lonely to be awake all by herself.

Maybe if she lay down and snuggled close and matched her breathing to his, she could relax enough to fall asleep. She might as well try. Inhale, she told herself. Exhale. Don't think about anything. Just breathe like Nick. Steadily, softly she breathed in and breathed out. Gradually her tension melted; drowsiness overcame her, and she slept.

When Charlotte opened her eyes, the angle of the sun told her that it was late afternoon. Nick, already awake, sat with his head cocked to one side as if he were listening to something.

"What do you hear?" she asked.

"Just birds."

She sat up, and he put his arm around her.

"Charlotte, how will you feel when you see your old home?"

"Probably homesick. Definitely angry. I've thought about it many times, and I'm still not sure. I once daydreamed that I walked up to the kitchen door, pressed the latch, and swung the door wide open."

"And then what did you see?"

"A whole family of squatters eating at our kitchen table. The sight made me so furious that I grabbed a broom and swept them out of the house." She laughed. "I wish it could be that easy."

Nick did not laugh.

"Someday," he said, "when the war is over, I want to go back for a visit. It bothers me that I never explained to my father why I changed sides. I want to tell him it wasn't the idea of liberty that I hated. It was the killing."

"My father wondered if you were a Quaker."

"I thought about joining the Quakers, but I don't like the way they control each other's lives. Freedom is important to me."

"So you became a courier . . . for the British."

"Yes, for the British." He paused for a moment. "Do you want to know the whole truth? I was looking for you. Every mission I went on, I asked about you. At every fort that took in Loyalist refugees, I looked for your name in the register."

His arm tightened around her shoulders. "I could think of no better way to search for you."

"If you told your father that, do you think he would understand?"

"I reckon not. I'd still be a turncoat in his eyes."

Charlotte sighed, knowing that in the eyes of some, Nick would carry that stain for the rest of his life.

While the evening shadows lengthened, they lay propped upon their elbows watching minnows slide in and out among the reeds. The smell of mud and decaying vegetation was in her nostrils. She felt the warmth of Nick's shoulder pressing hers.

"Are you nervous?" she asked.

"No. Whenever I'm on a mission, I concentrate on what I have to do one step at a time. I don't let myself worry about the next step until the previous one is completed. That's my method for staying calm." He sat up. "Step one tonight is to eat."

Charlotte brought out the food, but there was not enough saliva in her mouth to moisten a single crumb of biscuit.

"You must eat," he said.

"Afterwards."

"There won't be time afterwards."

She watching him munch his ham and biscuit as if this were a picnic. Then she packed away the food.

After the sun had set, the booming and croaking of the

frogs began. "They're loud tonight," Nick said. "The frogs will cover any noise we make."

"Is it time to start?"

Nick nodded. He fetched his rifle, the spade, and the two hemp sacks from the canoe. They tied the sacks around their waists. He handed the spade to Charlotte and picked up his rifle.

"If all goes well, we'll be back here in less than two hours. But if something goes wrong, you come here and hide."

"By myself?"

"Yes."

"What will you do?"

"If people come after us, I'll make a big noise so they'll follow me. I know how to lead them on a false chase. When it's safe, I'll join you at the canoe."

"I don't want us to be separated."

"We won't be. Nothing's going to go wrong."

"Nick, I'm so afraid of losing you."

"Haven't I told you that I'll never let you go?"

He cupped her face in his hands and kissed her lips.

"Let's get started," he said.

The last time Charlotte had climbed this hill, she and her parents were bringing Isaac home. Mama, her face streaked with tears, had gone first, holding branches out of Papa's way. Papa had carried Isaac's body across his shoulders.

Charlotte remembered the brightness of Isaac's coat and the darkness of his blood, and the way his arm had stuck out stiffly toward her, as if reaching to take her hand.

Tonight it was Nick holding back branches for Charlotte as they climbed. Their boots sent pebbles clattering down the steep slope. How could tiny stones make such a racket? Surely someone would hear!

It was a steep climb, and by the time they reached the top, Charlotte was out of breath. She set down the spade and leaned against the trunk of the great sycamore tree where Nick had carved their initials long ago.

"Listen!" Nick whispered. "Do you hear anything?"

"Only frogs down by the creek."

"I thought I heard rustling in the grass."

"Just a mouse or a vole."

Charlotte's heart was pounding. When Nick put one arm around her and pulled her close, she felt his heart thumping too. Maybe he was more nervous than he wanted to admit. She noticed that he had not put down his rifle.

Nick lowered his mouth to her ear.

"Look here."

She turned her head. Dimly visible on the sycamore's pale bark was the heart with their initials. The carving was raised like a scar. "N.S. loves C. H." She traced the letters with her fingers.

He kissed her cheek, and then took his arm from around her waist.

"You lead the way," he said. She nodded and picked up the spade.

The path from the edge of the ravine to the Hoopers' farm was not as clear as it had been two years ago. It seemed rough and narrow. Perhaps no one used it now. If there had not been a full moon, she might have lost her way.

Ahead of her, the grey wood of the snake fence had a silvery sheen in the moonlight. The fence had not changed: three cedar rails, the top one waist high.

When they reached the fence, they lowered themselves to their hands and knees to peer between the rails. The rock pile was forty feet away. Charlotte pointed to it.

"There," she whispered.

He handed her his rifle and climbed over the fence. When he reached the other side, she passed him his rifle and the spade, and then climbed over to join him.

They headed for the rock pile in a crouching run. After reaching it, they stayed low, listening for danger. All they heard was their own breathing and the sighing of the wind.

Charlotte cautiously raised her head and looked over the top of the rock pile. She saw that weeds and grasses were taking over the back acre where Papa had grown potatoes. That was a relief; it meant that no plough had so far disturbed the earth.

Across the field, near the far corner of the pasture, lay a couple of dozen white mounds. Sheep, not cows. Their cropping would wreck the pasture. But why should she care?

Beyond the pasture was the apple orchard. It was blossom time, filling the air with sweet perfume. Looking between the rows of trees, Charlotte had a clear view all the way to the house. It had not changed.

Every window was dark except one. Near the back of the house, the kitchen window glowed faintly, a dusky rose rectangle divided into tiny squares.

"They've banked the fire," she whispered. "I don't see any candles lit. I think they've gone to bed."

They. How many? And who were these people that cooked their food in the Hoopers' fireplace and slept in their beds? A married couple? A family with children? She supposed that she would never know.

Nick stepped from behind the rock pile. He touched the head of the spade to the ground.

"Here?"

She nodded. The spade bit into the earth with a scratchy sound. A few times she heard the grating of metal scraping stone. Then a clang rang out. Charlotte's heart stood still. "You hit the tea set. Come back."

Nick returned to cover. They crouched side by side, waiting to see whether the noise had raised an alarm. But all remained quiet.

"I'll dig it out," Charlotte said. She crept over to the hole. Working carefully with her fingernails and the knife, she unearthed the tea set piece by piece. The canvas in which it had been wrapped was rotted away. She lifted the tray, the creamer, the sugar bowl and the teapot and shook off the earth. There was a dent in the teapot. Nick's spade must have done that. Charlotte sheathed her knife, put everything into the sack and lugged it behind the rock pile.

Nick returned to the digging, quickly tossing spadefuls of earth from the deepening hole. Apart from his breathing and the rasp of the spade, all was quiet.

Suddenly a second clang rang out as loud as a schoolyard bell. Charlotte held her breath. This time Nick stayed where he was. He laid the spade on the ground, knelt down, and began to dig with his knife and hands. All was quiet again, except for the scratching sounds of Nick scrabbling in the earth. He grunted while lifting the strongbox from the hole and stooped as he carried it behind the rock pile.

"What's it filled with? Rocks?"

"Our family Bible."

"It must weigh fifty pounds."

Charlotte held the second sack open for him to slip it in. She took a deep breath. The worst was over.

Then a dog barked.

Slowly Charlotte stuck her head around the side of the rock pile. Looking towards the house, she saw a man's shape appear at the kitchen window. His bulk blocked half the light. She would never forget those big sloping shoulders and bull neck. A chill ran up her spine.

"Look who it is." She grabbed Nick's arm.

"Ben Warren! Oh, God! I was afraid of that."

The dog kept on barking — the deep woof, woof of a large

dog. Warren stepped away from the window. A minute passed. Nothing happened.

"Maybe he'll go back to bed," Charlotte whispered.

"I don't think so."

The pink glow of the window flared as bright as sunrise.

"He's built up the fire," Nick said.

The door opened. Warren came out, a long rifle cradled against his shoulder.

"What's the trouble? Them damn wolves again?" His voice carried clearly — a harsh voice, too high-pitched for a man. "Well, Scout, let's have a look."

Scout was a farm dog, black and white — a sheep dog mixed with some larger breed. It trotted ahead, glancing back every few steps to make sure that its master followed, straight through the orchard and up to the fence that Papa had built to keep pasturing cattle from getting at the apples.

Warren stopped at the fence, but the dog squeezed under the bottom rail and took a few steps towards the rock pile. When it saw that Warren was not following, it whined and turned back. It jumped up on the fence, placing its front paws on the top rail.

Go back! Charlotte silently urged. Warren hesitated. Obviously he had no wish to go further. But the dog insisted. It barked again. Woof. Woof. Woof.

"All right, all right," he grumbled. "Show me what it is." And he climbed over the fence.

Straight ahead of him, across the open pasture and the

untended field, was the rock pile. To Warren's left, a couple of hundred feet away, the sheep lay on the grass. Warren, his rifle held ready, turned left.

Good. If the sheep were all he cared about, he would go back to the house as soon as he saw that the flock was safe.

But the dog would not let him approach the sheep. It ran back and forth, whimpering.

"What's got into you, Scout? Are you afraid to meet a wolf?" Warren kept on walking.

The dog grew frantic. It ran circles around its master, herding him away from the sheep and towards the rock pile. Warren stopped and looked about. Three or four sheep stood up. They bleated peevishly, as if annoyed but not afraid.

"Scout, I don't know what you're trying to tell me, but I hope there ain't no savages behind that rock pile."

Charlotte held her breath.

Warren looked at the rock pile, then toward the house. He looked at the rock pile again. If he feared marauding Indians, common sense should send him back. The dog, still barking, made quick, short runs, returning each time to its master, determined that he should investigate.

"Oh, all right," Warren said.

Charlotte ducked for cover. Turning to Nick, she saw that he held the spade gripped in both hands.

"Where's your rifle?" she hissed.

"By the hole. I can't get to it."

The dog growled. Warren's footsteps were drawing near. Charlotte picked up a stone. Nick shifted his stance, planted one foot firmly, and prepared to spring.

The dog charged. It came around the side of the rock pile, snarling with bared teeth. Charlotte hurled the stone. She missed. The dog's jaws closed upon her ankle, and she felt its teeth bite to the bone.

There was a crack of sound and a puff of flame and smoke. At the same instant a shattering blow hit the rock pile, sending a chip of stone whizzing by Charlotte's head. The dog let go.

Until he reloaded, Warren could not fire again. Nick's chance was now. He launched himself at Warren, swinging the spade like a battle-axe. Warren threw up his rifle barrel to fend off the spade. Sparks flashed. Metal rang against metal. Nick spun around, swung the spade again with his whole weight behind it. This time Charlotte heard a thud, and then a grunt.

Ben Warren dropped his rifle. As he sank to his knees, he reached out both hands as if trying to grab something, and then fell upon his face. Charlotte saw the shine of fresh blood on the side of his head.

Barking frantically, the dog ran to its master. It crouched beside him, licked his hand, and whimpered.

In the glowing rectangle of the kitchen window, another man appeared. Behind him, other figures moved about. The room was crowded with men. Half a dozen at least.

"Nick! Look!"

He did not hear her. He stood motionless, leaning heavily on the spade.

"I killed him," Nick mumbled. "See what I have done." He seemed unable to move.

When she grabbed his arms, she felt how slack his muscles were. Charlotte snatched the spade from his hands and threw it to the ground.

"Forget about Warren! Get the strongbox. Hurry!"

Charlotte slung the sack holding the tea set over one shoulder and raced toward the snake fence. When she reached it, she glanced back. Nick was right behind her. He was carrying his rifle, nothing else, and he looked dazed.

"Where's the strongbox?"

"Still back there."

"Then get it!"

Charlotte dropped her sack over the fence. Shouts came from the house; dogs barked. Between the house and the barn, scurrying figures rushed in no particular direction. Nick seemed to wake up. He looked over his shoulder. There was still time.

"I'll get it," he said. "See you at the canoe. Hurry. Go!"

Charlotte scrambled over the fence. When she had reached the other side, she looked back. Nick was running toward her with the strongbox clutched to his chest. He was halfway to the fence.

By the rock pile, Ben Warren was sitting up, one hand

clapped to his head. So he wasn't dead. Did Nick know that? She'd tell him later.

Charlotte hoisted her sack and ran.

The sack bumped against her back. The silver clashed and clanged. Behind her, a man's voice shouted, "Fire! Fire! Fire!" She stopped and turned around. The sky over the farm was filled with flaring light. For a moment Charlotte stood still, unable to move. Flames rose high above the trees in the orchard, and the smoke glowed rosy gold.

She choked back a sob and started running again, plunging blindly ahead. Her breath came in panting gasps, her heart thudded against her ribs, and her knees felt weak with fear.

Something tripped her. She stumbled, scrambled to her feet, kept on running. She felt the pain of a stitch in her side but dared not stop to ease it. With every step, the sack banged and bumped against her back. Maybe she should drop it. But she must not lose the tea set.

Where was she now? This was not the path. She looked back over her shoulder. The sky was aglow, but Nick was nowhere in sight. The edge of the ravine must be close, but she could not see it. Bushes shadowed everything.

Brambles caught at her clothes, scratched her face. She stumbled again, recovered her balance. When she put her foot forward for the next step, it met empty air.

Charlotte fell. Clutching desperately at bushes, roots — anything to stop her fall — she grabbed a handful of twigs that broke off in her hands. Like a stone in a rock fall, her body skidded, bounced, and rolled. She dropped the sack. The clanging of the hollow silver was the last thing she heard. When the noise stopped, everything stopped.

Chapter twenty-one

Charlotte lay very still. Her body felt numb, dull and heavy, and she was utterly tired. She knew that she must get back to the canoe, but had no desire to move. Her head ached. Her right ankle hurt. That must be from the dog bite. When she tried to sit up, she felt dizzy, and a burning pain shot through her left shoulder. Charlotte lay down again.

She was lying at the foot of a birch tree halfway down the hill. The tree must have stopped her fall. Inches from Charlotte's face, a green caterpillar climbed the white bark. Overhead, sunlight splattered on green leaves that shifted dizzily. So now it was day. How long had she lain here? Last thing

she knew, it had been night. The farmhouse had been burning. Men had been shouting, dogs barking, shadows rushing back and forth.

At least I'm alive, she thought, and nobody is chasing me.
Even if I can't return to the canoe on my own, Nick will
find me. As soon as it's safe, he'll search for me, unless. . . .

Unless! Oh, dear God! She wasn't going to think about
that. Surely Nick had escaped. Those men and dogs would
be no match for him. He had said that he would lead them
on a false chase if anything went wrong, and obviously
that's what he did. At this very moment he was back at the
canoe, with the strongbox, waiting. Or maybe he was already searching for her. Keep calm, she told herself.

Nick was sure to find her. The sack holding the tea set
must have landed nearby. When he found her, he would
recover it too. And she was lucky to have fallen into this
place that was completely hidden. If she had not fallen
when she did, she might have been captured. Who knows
what would have happened to her then? Did the Sons of
Liberty hang girls? But she was not visibly a girl. Would that
make a difference?

What if they discovered that she was a girl? She shuddered at the memory of Ben Warren's hands upon her
body, his stinking breath in her face.

So Warren and his friends were the squatters. They had
turned the Hoopers' home into a nest of Liberty men. Last
year, when Papa had said he would rather his house burned

to the ground than have Rebels take it over, she had not
shared his feelings. But now she did. Those men, all rushing into the yard, should have had more sense than to leave
a roaring fire untended.

She was glad that the fire had cheated the Sons of Liberty
of their spoils. It showed that there was some justice even in
this topsy-turvy world. As for Ben Warren, he did not de-
serve to live. But for Nick's sake she was glad he had not
died. Let Heaven be Warren's judge. His fate was in God's
hands.

And so was her fate. Helpless as a baby, she certainly
lacked the strength to save herself.

From where she lay, she could hear the murmur of the
creek a hundred feet below, its cool water rushing over the
little brown pebbles. Suddenly she realized how thirsty she
was. If she could drag herself to the creek, she could put her
face into the water and lap like a dog. And if she could get
as far as the creek, she might be able to follow it downstream to the canoe.

But her pain was growing worse. At the slightest movement, her shoulder felt as if it were being speared with a
red-hot poker. Her ankle had swollen to double its normal
size. Charlotte stared up at the birch leaves dancing in the
sunshine. I reckon I'm not going anywhere, she thought.

As she lay thinking about this, the skin at the back of her
neck began to prickle. She heard no one, saw no one, yet
some instinct warned that she was being watched.

Slowly she slid her hand towards the sheath on her belt. Her knife was her only weapon — not much use to her when she was flat on her back. But she had to try.

Before she could grip the handle, her arm was seized and wrenched back. She turned her head to see a pair of black eyes looking straight into hers. A warrior gripped her arm with one hand while his other hand deftly drew her knife from its sheath. His cheeks were painted with yellow stripes like lightning bolts, and his scalp lock rose in a bristling crest with trailing feathers.

Charlotte fixed her eyes on his, determined to show no fear. Don't plead, she told herself. Be defiant. Whatever you do, don't cry. One sign of cowardice, and he'll take your scalp.

The warrior let go of her arm. Raising his head, he gave a call that sounded like the warble of a bird. A few minutes passed. Then two other warriors came gliding from the underbrush. Both were dressed like him, in buckskin leggings, loincloth and moccasins. Their faces were also painted with yellow lightning bolts, and they wore trophy feathers in their scalp locks.

The three warriors inspected her ankle and then spoke to each other in a language that sounded a lot like Mohawk. The man who had taken her knife lifted her in his arms. At the movement, her shoulder felt as if it were being struck with an axe. She moaned. The pain was so terrible that she welcomed the blackness that swept over her, blotting out all feeling and all fear.

She awoke to find herself in a twilight world, drifting between sleep and waking. Somehow, she was high in that birch tree on the slope of the ravine, rocking gently in the topmost branches. But it might have been a canoe. She smelled river mud and heard the sound of lapping water.

When the mists cleared at last from her mind, she was lying on her back in a bark-covered hut that had a sappy smell like new wood. The inner side of the bark slabs was pale yellow, and the poles that formed the frame of the hut looked freshly peeled.

Under Charlotte's body was something cushiony and warm. Prodding it with her fingers, she felt the coarse, dense pelt of what might have been a bear. Covering her was a fur blanket woven from narrow strips of rabbit skin, as soft and light as silk. The blanket was the only thing that covered her. Under it, Charlotte was naked. Someone had taken away her clothes.

She moved her leg and could feel that her right ankle was bound. Then with her hand she touched her left shoulder and realized it was tied up in a kind of bandage. Her right arm stung as if she had thrust it into a bed of nettles. When she raised it, she saw dozens of long welts and scratches, which had been rubbed with ointment.

Turning her head, Charlotte noticed that she was not alone. Across from her, amidst a jumble of hides and baskets, sat a young girl watching her with keen, bright eyes. The girl's skin was dusky rose, her eyelashes long and silky, and her eyebrows delicately arched. She wore two long, jet braids, and the parting of her hair was painted red.

"Where am I?" Charlotte asked.

The girl's answer was a shrug.

"Do you speak English?"

Another shrug.

If the girl didn't speak English, Charlotte could learn nothing from her, not even where she was. Had she been carried in a canoe? She remembered a rocking sensation, the sound of lapping water, the smell of river mud.

The girl stood up and with light steps left the hut. A minute later she returned carrying a cone-shaped birch-bark cup. Putting her arm around Charlotte's shoulders, she raised her and held the cup to her lips. Charlotte gulped the water. "*Nya weh*," she said. No response. It seemed that the girl did not recognize the Mohawk word for thank-you. If she wasn't a Mohawk, what was she? With her braids and fringed doeskin dress, she could belong to any tribe.

After taking the cup away, the girl lifted her eyebrows inquiringly and mimed the action of eating. Charlotte nodded. At the suggestion of food, she realized that she was hungry. When had she last eaten? A day ago? Two days?

Again the girl left the hut, returning a few minutes later with a wooden bowl of something that resembled boiled potatoes. She arranged a stack of pelts for Charlotte to rest against, then held out the bowl. Charlotte picked up a piece of the food with her fingers and popped it into her mouth. It tasted a bit like potatoes, but nuttier and slightly crisp.

The more she chewed, the more she liked it. After Charlotte had eaten, the girl gave her a handful of dry grass to wipe her fingers.

Charlotte leaned back against the pelts. It felt good to have something in her stomach, even though the rest of her body still ached, stung and throbbed.

The bright-eyed girl was still watching. She was younger than Charlotte, probably about thirteen. A pity they could not talk to each other. Charlotte tapped herself on the chest with her free hand and announced her name.

"Char-let," the girl repeated with a smile. She had a lovely smile, though her two front teeth were a trifle large. "Charlet." She tapped her own chest. "Chi-gwi-lat."

Charlotte repeated the unfamiliar syllables. She didn't know what they meant. But then, she didn't know what her own name meant, except that she was named after the queen.

An old woman, bent and withered, now entered the hut. She had small, deep-set eyes, sunken cheeks, and a chin that jutted so far beyond her toothless mouth that her face looked as if it had collapsed upon itself. Chi-gwi-lat spoke to the woman in a respectful tone. She must be Chi-gwi-lat's grandmother, or even her great-grandmother. The old woman glanced at Charlotte, mumbled a series of indecipherable syllables, and then hobbled outside.

Chi-gwi-lat brought a covered basket from the other side of the hut, rummaged inside, and pulled out an assortment of leather garments. There was a fringed poncho shirt, a wide panel of doeskin, a belt, and moccasins. She held them up for Charlotte to see. Naked under the rabbit skin blanket, Charlotte nodded her approval.

Chi-gwi-lat tugged a moccasin onto Charlotte's uninjured foot and then helped her to her feet. She wrapped the doeskin panel around her hips to form a skirt, which she secured in place by means of a leather belt tied with buckskin laces, and then slipped the poncho over her head. The poncho was soft as velvet, and roomy enough to accommodate Charlotte's bound shoulder.

Now that she was dressed, Charlotte felt less helpless, though her head was still light and her body terribly heavy. She would have been happy to lie down again. But Chi-gwi-lat took her firmly by the arm and led her out of the hut into the sunshine.

Charlotte blinked and looked around. In front of the hut lay a large log, and in front of the log a clay pot filled with water. The old woman whom Charlotte had seen in the hut was poking at a small fire burning a few yards away. Using two sticks as pincers, she picked up a stone the size of potato from a pile of similar stones heaped in the middle of the fire. She hobbled to the pot and dropped in the stone. The water hissed.

Chi-gwi-lat helped Charlotte to sit down on the log, where she watched the old woman carry stone after stone from the fire until the water in the pot was steaming.

In the meantime, Chi-gwi-lat unwound the strips of leather binding Charlotte's right ankle, which throbbed with pain. What a mess of pus! Charlotte had seen enough abscesses on injured animals to know how bad it was. When Chi-gwi-lat lifted her swollen foot and plunged it into the hot water, she did not flinch.

From where she sat, Charlotte could see green forest, a sparkling river, and eleven bark huts. The huts were neither in rows nor in a circle, but seemed to have sprung up randomly from the earth. In the centre — so far as the camp had a centre — was an open space, and in the centre of that a smoldering fire burned.

Again Charlotte wondered where she was. And where was Nick? She remembered her last glimpse of him, running with the strongbox in his arms, halfway to the fence. He must have escaped. Her mind admitted no other possibility. And he must be searching for her. But how could he find her? How far away from Fort Hunter was this camp? The sparkling river that ran by was smaller than the Mohawk. Maybe it was a tributary. If she could follow it, she might find her way back to the Mohawk River. But how could that help her? Even if she reached it, she had no way to get back to Carleton Island, where Papa was waiting.

The thought of him rose unbidden in her mind. She pictured him standing outside the palisade gate, leaning on his crutch, scanning the horizon for the return of the canoe. "Remember, she's all I've got," had been his parting words to Nick. People could die of a broken heart; Mama had proved that.

For days, Charlotte did nothing but eat, rest and soak her foot. The welts and scratches on her right arm healed. The infected dog bite on her ankle slowly began to respond to the soaking in hot water. But her right shoulder remained encased in rawhide as hard as wood.

Through the endless hours, she had nothing to do but think. And the more she thought, the surer she became that she was the prisoner of an Oneida band. The newness of the huts showed that these people had only recently arrived, probably as refugees whom General Sullivan's soldiers had driven from their homes. Unless they were Oneidas, they would have sought the safety of an English fort. Everything pointed to them being Oneidas.

The thought did not frighten her. Nick had explained the value of a healthy hostage. She supposed that her captors wanted her to be in good condition when the time came to negotiate her freedom. They certainly were treating her with tender care.

But what if they wanted to adopt her? They couldn't turn her into an Oneida against her will, could they? When Axe Carrier had explained about the Oneidas adopting Moses Cobman, he had not dealt with that point.

Often, as the days passed, Charlotte had a strong feeling that Nick was close by, perhaps lurking in the forest to keep watch over her. And so she was only half surprised when one morning, as she sat with her foot immersed, a pebble landed with a plop in her lap.

Charlotte jumped. The pebble seemed to have dropped from the sky.

The old woman had hobbled off to one of the other huts. Chi-gwi-lat was at the river fetching water. No one saw Charlotte pick up the pebble from the fold of her skirt.

The pebble was smooth and round, about two inches across and half an inch thick, and brown like the little stones in the creek behind the Hoopers' farm. On one side was scratched the outline of a heart. Turning the pebble over, she read the initials "N.S." and "C.H." As she curled her fingers tenderly around it, she could not suppress a smile. One minute ago, this pebble had been in Nick's hand. Now it was in hers. Nick, at this moment, was near enough to have tossed it into her lap.

She looked about at the bushes that ringed the camp. Birds twittered and fluttered in every thicket save one. So that was the thicket where Nick had concealed himself, disturbing the birds.

It would be wise to follow the example of the birds. Sit quiet and still. Don't try to see Nick through the thick foliage. Reluctantly she dropped the pebble and pushed it under the log with her heel. The pebble had served its purpose.

After a while, the birds started twittering again. For a long time she watched the thicket, yet could not tell when Nick left his hiding place.

For the rest of the day Charlotte felt jittery. The old woman looked at her suspiciously. Late in the afternoon three warriors came by — the same three who had found Charlotte in the ravine. As they talked with the old woman, they glanced frequently at Charlotte. Then the warriors glided into the bushes.

She heard a shout from beneath the trees outside the camp, and then a sharp call from further away. Charlotte glanced up casually, as if this did not concern her. For a long time she remained as still as the log on which she was sitting.

A rifle cracked, but far enough away that the sound was muffled by countless trees and bushes. Then two shots were fired in quick succession.

She waited, numb with dread, terrified to think what or whom the warriors were pursuing, or what kind of prey they would drag back to camp.

When the warriors returned empty-handed, one gave her an angry look. He's disappointed, she thought. So it was Nick whom they had hunted. And he had got away.

All the next day she waited for another signal, thinking that Nick might have lingered in the forest, waiting for her injuries to heal so that they could run away together. When by evening there was no further sign, her regret was mingled with relief. She hoped that Nick had gone back to Carleton Island to tell Papa what had happened. Better for him to know that his daughter was a captive than to think that she was dead.

Chi-gwi-lat's friends — three girls, all about thirteen — came to call. They had tawny skin and bright inquisitive eyes, and they giggled constantly. Charlotte's hair amused them. Fascinated by its curliness, they braided it into two smooth plaits that hung over her shoulders. As a finishing touch, they painted a bright red stripe down the centre part, just like theirs.

The passing days blurred together. Charlotte's ankle healed completely. On sunny mornings Chi-gwi-lat and her friends disappeared into the woods with baskets on their arms. When they emerged, the baskets were heaped with raspberries and blackberries. Charlotte wanted to go with them, but that was not allowed. Her captors may have feared that she would try to run away. Or perhaps they simply thought that she would be useless as a berry picker, having the use of only one arm.

After many days, when it began to feel as though nothing was ever going to happen, a hunting party of men and boys arrived in camp with fresh deer meat. One of the boys had brown hair and blue eyes. He wore a leather breechcloth, leggings and moccasins, and he carried a birchbark quiver on his shoulder. Although he was taller than two years ago, and as brown as any Indian, she knew Moses Cobman at once.

The moment he saw her, sitting in her usual spot on the log outside the old woman's hut, he stopped and stared. Leaving his companions, he walked directly to her.

"I remember you. You're Charlotte."

"And you are Moses Cobman."

His features stiffened. "No longer. My name is Broken Trail."

"But you're Moses Cobman, all the same."

His face darkened. As he turned away, she recognized the flash of anger in his eyes. Moses stalked off with dignity, or at least as much dignity as an eleven-year-old could muster. Charlotte had offended him, but she didn't care. Did Moses really think that he could get rid of his identity so easily, shed it like his old clothes that the Oneidas had hidden under a log? When she got a chance, she must talk to him about his mother and Elijah and Hope. Surely he still had some affection for them.

The next day, Moses was back, accompanied by two older warriors.

"This is Black Elk," he said, indicating a broad-cheeked man with greying hair. "The other is Swift Fox." From the bulge of belly over the top of his breechcloth, Swift Fox looked as if swiftness had deserted him long ago. "Black Elk and Swift Fox speak for the elders of our band. They were waiting for my return in order to question you."

The two men squatted on the ground facing her. Each had a blanket draped about his bare shoulders, though the day was warm. Moses stood to one side.

Black Elk asked the first question.

"He wants to know why you were wearing men's clothing," Moses said.

"Tell him I dressed as a man because it was dangerous to

travel as a woman. I came from the Upper Country to Fort Hunter to find things that my father had buried to hide from the Rebels."

The two elders exchanged a few words. Moses translated. "What were those things?"

"Legal papers, a silver tea set and our family Bible."

Moses looked confused. How would he manage to translate that into Oneida? Charlotte reckoned that he knew precious little about the Bible, less about tea sets, and nothing about legal papers.

He told the warriors something, at any rate. When Moses had finished speaking, the two men nodded solemnly and conversed in hushed tones, glancing frequently in Charlotte's direction.

"What are they talking about?" she asked.

"How many presents you are worth."

"Presents!"

"We need rifles and blankets. We fled with nothing from our old homes. In summer we can live off the land from day to day. But when winter comes, we shall be hungry and cold. We have no stored-up food. No corn."

Charlotte nodded. She knew all about cold and hunger. But these Oneidas needed more than guns and blankets. They needed a new home, a place where they could plant their crops of corn, squash and beans. A place where they could live without fear. They asked too little. Presents would not save them.

As the elders conversed, a plan came to Charlotte's mind.

She saw that it was in her power to give the Oneidas something better than blankets and guns. As a go-between, she could help to restore their old relationship with the Mohawk nation, a beginning from which peace with the English would follow. No longer fugitives, the Oneidas could join their brother Iroquois in the Upper Country, where there would be land to replace what they had lost.

She would need Axe Carrier's help, and she knew that he would give it freely. She remembered all that he and his warriors had done for her family and the other Loyalists. And she remembered his sadness — the sorrow with which he had stared into the fire one rainy night during the journey to Carleton Island. "The breaking of nations is a terrible thing," he had said. "We were United People, but today we are no longer united."

Now she had a chance to repay Axe Carrier. By bringing the Mohawk and Oneida nations together in peace, she could help to restore what had been lost. ·

There was work to be done. Why should she sit here on a log day after day, waiting and waiting for someone to rescue her? If negotiations were necessary, she would start them herself.

Black Elk and Swift Fox stood up and adjusted their blankets over their shoulders.

"Wait!" Charlotte said. "Moses, tell them that I have—"

"Don't call me by that name," he snarled.

"All right. Broken Trail, if you prefer. Just tell them I have something important to say. Ask them whether they know my father's friend, Axe Carrier of the Mohawk nation."

That question worked magic. The elders' eyebrows rose. Sitting down again, they spoke a few words to Moses.

"They know Axe Carrier," Moses explained. "He is famous for his influence with the Mohawks and the English."

"Tell them that I will write a letter to Axe Carrier. When he knows where I am, he will come here to take me away. He will come with Mohawk elders to smoke the pipe of peace. He will help the Oneida people end their quarrel with the English."

When Moses translated this, Black Elk frowned and Swift Fox sneered. As they answered, Charlotte heard mockery in their voices.

"What's wrong?" she asked Moses.

"They say you are only a woman. How can you promise such things?"

"Oh, is that what they say!" Lifting her chin, Charlotte tried to look as haughty as a queen. "Tell them they will see for themselves what I can do. I ask only that they send a messenger to Axe Carrier with a letter from me."

Again, they spoke to each other for several minutes, glancing often in Charlotte's direction. Moses translated what they had said.

"They have wanted for a long time to bury the tomahawk with their brothers. Even if they had nothing to fear from soldiers, they would not want to stay here. They say that this land is no good. The soil is thin, like a skin stretched over hard rocks. No crops will grow in this place. They say that we must find a new home."

"Then tell them that I shall write my letter. It will have power with Axe Carrier. I promise that. If I am wrong, then they can trade me for blankets and guns."

Once again, Black Elk and Swift Fox adjusted their blankets upon their shoulders. This time they walked away, their heads bent together as they continued their conversation. Moses started to follow.

"Wait!" Charlotte called to him.

"What do you want?"

"A sheet of birchbark that I can use for paper, a feather to make a pen, and some kind of berry juice for ink."

"I'll find you a feather and cut you a sheet of birchbark. But dyes are women's work. I'll tell Chi-gwi-lat what you need."

Moses cut the birchbark neatly to the shape and size of a sheet of writing paper and flattened it by passing a flame over the inner side. Borrowing his knife, Charlotte trimmed a wild goose feather into a serviceable pen. Chi-gwi-lat's contribution was not berry juice, but dark brown dye made by boiling hemlock root.

The only flat, smooth surface for writing a letter was the floor of the hut. Since she did not have a free hand to hold the birchbark in place, Charlotte placed a stone as a paperweight on each of its four corners. Crouching on the earth floor, she dipped her quill into the tiny clay pot of dye. The birchbark was not as smooth as real paper, nor was her quill as well trimmed as the one that Sergeant Major Clark had lent her for her letter to Nick. "This will have to be a very short letter," she muttered. "The fewer the words, the fewer the blots."

Moses returned with Black Elk and Swift Fox. When Charlotte handed over the letter to Black Elk, both elders eyed it mistrustfully. Perhaps they had been betrayed before by the marks that white men made on paper. Black Elk thrust the letter into Moses' hands, uttering what sounded like a command.

"What did he say?" Charlotte asked.

"He wants me to tell him what the marks mean."

"You can read it, can't you?"

"It starts out, 'Dear Axe Carrier.' He flushed. "That's as far as I can go."

She took the letter back. "This is what it says."

Dear Axe Carrier,

Please come at once. I am a captive of the Oneidas. They want to bury the tomahawk with the Mohawk people. They will free me if you will help them to make peace with the English. I know how much you want the Six Nations to be united again.

"That's all. I signed it, *Your friend, Charlotte Hooper.*"

"I'll tell them that it's a good letter. They're asking if you know where to find Axe Carrier."

"Their messenger should try Lachine. That's where he spends the winters. If he isn't there, someone will know where he has gone."

As Black Elk and Swift Fox got up to leave, Charlotte said to Moses, "Please don't go yet. I have something to ask you."

He waited.

"Moses, what happened the day you ran away?"

"Why should I tell you?"

"Because I was your friend."

"I will if you stop calling me Moses. That was my name in a different life. Call me Broken Trail."

"I'll try. But it's hard to remember."

He sat down on the log beside her. "I didn't mean to run away. I just wanted to scare Ma and Elijah so that Ma would tell Polly Platto to leave me alone and Elijah would take me hunting. But I got tired and it started to rain. I made a leaf pile and crawled in. The warriors found me asleep, with my head sticking out of the leaves. After they pulled me out, they stood laughing at me and talking to each other. One warrior gave me a chunk of maple sugar. He pointed along the trail and tugged my arm to show me that I had to go with them. I wasn't afraid. I'd rather be captured by Indians than tormented by Polly Platto."

"So they took you to their fishing village?"

"Yes. And the next day everybody packed up, loaded the canoes, and we left for the band's main village, where people lived in longhouses. I had to run the gauntlet."

"They made a child run the gauntlet?"

"It was nothing — just two rows of women and children swatting me with corn stalks while I raced between them. After that, a warrior who spoke English told me that a man and woman whose son had died wanted to adopt me. The woman's brother would teach me how to hunt. I told them I'd like that. So they gave me a little cut to let out my white blood. They washed me and gave me new moccasins and named me Broken Trail. They said my old life was dead and I'd been born again."

"And now you don't want to leave?"

"I'll never leave. I told my parents — my new parents — that if I was sent away, I would escape and come back to them."

"But you have a mother and a little sister at Carleton Island. You have a father and two brothers fighting for the King."

He hesitated. When he spoke again, his voice was husky. "Are they well? It is my duty to forget them, but I would like to know that they are well."

"Your mother and sister are well. I don't know about the others. But Moses, how can you——?"

He slammed his clenched fist on the log. "My name is Broken Trail."

Chapter twenty-two

Charlotte and Chi-gwi-lat sat on the log outside the old woman's hut. Chi-gwi-lat was sewing coloured porcupine quills onto a new, doeskin dress, which had a pattern of triangles, crosses and squares pricked out across the yoke. Charlotte's job was to flatten each quill by drawing it between her teeth, then hand it to Chi-gwi-lat, who attached it to the dress with a sinew thread.

Charlotte had a quill between her teeth when Moses approached the hut.

"*Se-go-li*," he said to Chi-gwi-lat. To Charlotte he said, "Hello."

"Hello," Charlotte said, after taking the quill out of her mouth.

He stood in front of her, shuffling his feet. She studied him: the brown hair, the blue eyes. On his skinny chest he wore a bear-claw necklace. Apart from moccasins, a belt and breechcloth were his only garments.

"I've come to say good-bye."

"You're leaving?"

"It's better for me to be away when Axe Carrier comes. Today my uncle takes me on a long trail." He fidgeted as if he had something serious on his mind but could not bring himself to say it. After an awkward pause, he turned to Chi-gwi-lat and, with a laugh, said something in Oneida. Chi-gwi-lat giggled.

"What did you say to her?" asked Charlotte.

"I asked who was going to fill her tree with nuts."

"You asked her *what*?"

"Well, she's old enough to marry. As soon as she leaves Wolf Woman's house, she'll have her ceremony of maidenhood.

"Wolf Woman? So the old woman isn't Chi-gwi-lat's granny?"

"Of course not. Wolf Woman is her teacher. Every girl has to spend six months serving a wise woman so she can learn medicines and other wisdom. After that, she goes back to her mother and father's lodge until she chooses a husband."

"What does this have to do with nuts?"

"It was a joke. Chi-gwi-lat means squirrel."

"It does? Her name is Squirrel?" Bright eyes, front teeth

a bit too large. Lively, always busy. Charlotte laughed. "It suits her."

"Names should suit people. Yours suits you."

"Charlotte suits me?"

"I meant your Oneida name."

"I didn't know I had one."

"You are Woman-who-dresses-like-a-man."

"Oh, I don't like it."

He shrugged. "That doesn't matter. As long as your story is told around the campfire, Woman-who-dresses-like-a-man will be your name." He paused, and his expression became serious. "Before I go, I want to thank you."

"For what?"

"For rescuing me. Some Elders wanted to send me back to the English, even though I'd been adopted."

"To buy peace?"

He nodded.

"So I appeared at the right moment to take your place." Things certainly did work out in strange ways, as if everything were part of a plan.

"Would it be so bad to go back?" Charlotte searched his face for any sign that he might weaken.

His mouth twisted into an odd smile. "My new mother never makes me gather wood and nuts like a girl. I fish and trap and paddle my own canoe. My uncle teaches me to hunt. Training to be a warrior is better than going to school, where you have to sit at a desk and learn stupid stuff like spelling."

With part of her mind, Charlotte sympathized. She knew of other stories like his. Not all white captives wanted to be freed.

She sighed. "When I go back, what shall I tell your mother?"

"My first mother? I have nothing to tell her."

"No message at all?"

He shook his head.

The boy's coldness stunned her. Not one word of love or remembrance for the woman who had given him life.

"Don't you ever want to see her again?" Charlotte pleaded. "Or Elijah? Or your baby sister?"

For a moment his eyes wavered. Then his face became rigid as a mask — the face of a warrior. "No. It is finished."

Charlotte held out her hand, but he did not take it. "Then I shall never see you again."

Next morning the whole camp was busy with preparations. The best hut was cleared and swept. Venison simmered in the cooking pots. Dancers practised their steps. Charlotte guessed what it meant: the Mohawk delegation would soon arrive.

Chi-gwi-lat's friends paid another visit. This time they brought with them a collection of different coloured paints: red, white, yellow, blue and green, each in a separate horn container. They set out the paint horns on the log, and then knelt, two on each side facing each other.

The girls worked in pairs, dipping the flattened ends of

their twig brushes into the paint horns to scoop up greasy daubs of colour. Chi-gwi-lat's partner received a large red spot on each cheek and another on her forehead. Chi-gwi-lat was decorated with green wavy lines across her brow and rings of blue dots on her cheeks and chin. The girls did not hurry. To create the perfect arrangement of lines, dots, circles and spots took half the afternoon.

When they had finished with each other, the Oneida girls descended upon Charlotte with grins, giggles and a flourish of paintbrushes. They took turns, their eyes sparkling gleefully as they worked on their designs.

After packing away their paints, they took Charlotte with them to the river that flowed by the camp to see her reflection in the water. There were red circles on her cheeks, a broad blue line down the length of her nose, green parallel stripes across her forehead, and fresh red paint in the parting of her hair. Even to herself, she didn't look different from the other girls: the same dark braids, the same fringed leather clothing, the same dazzling face paint. "Woman of Two Worlds," she murmured.

When she looked up, Charlotte saw a canoe appear from around a bend in the river. A second canoe, a third, and a fourth came into view, and then a fifth, lagging behind the others.

There were three men in each of the first four canoes: two paddlers and a passenger. But the fifth canoe held only two people: a man and a girl.

As the canoes came nearer, Charlotte recognized Axe Carrier in the bow of the lead canoe. The rear paddler was a warrior she had not seen before. Their passenger was an elderly man who sat very still, with an air of great dignity. The second, third and fourth canoes were also paddled by warriors of middle years, and in each of them the passenger was an older man.

But the fifth canoe! Who was that young warrior with trophy feathers trailing from his bristling scalp lock? Okwaho? It couldn't be! But it was. And who was the girl?

Why did Okwaho have a girl in his canoe?

As the canoe touched the creek bank, the girl sprang out with the grace of a wildcat. She steadied the canoe for Okwaho, giving him her hand as he stepped onto the riverbank. The girl was as tall as Charlotte and about the same age. Her hair was braided in a single plait, which was looped up and tied with a lace at the back of her neck, as was the custom for Iroquois married women. From the way Okwaho smiled and held her hand in his, Charlotte knew that the young warrior had found a wife.

As the warriors from the first four canoes formed up in procession, Charlotte saw Axe Carrier's eyes scanning the crowd. He looked right past her, and then looked again. His eyes brightened. After a nod that acknowledged her presence, he took his place, second in the line.

The man who appeared to be the oldest walked ahead, holding upon his outstretched hands a beaded belt that shone in the sun. The beads, purple and white, were woven into a pattern of squares and diamonds. In the centre were the figures of two men clasping hands.

"Wampum?" Charlotte asked.

Chi-gwi-lat nodded: "*Ga-swe-da.*"

When the Oneida elders and warriors had greeted the Mohawk delegation, the bearer of the wampum belt gave it to Black Elk. Then the men of both nations sat down in a circle. Several made speeches, each holding an eagle feather as he spoke.

After the speeches, Axe Carrier took a stone pipe and stem from a pouch carried at his side. He fitted the bowl and stem together, filled the bowl with tobacco, and lit it from a burning stick.

That must be the peace pipe, Charlotte thought. The silence told her that this was the most sacred part of the ceremony. Axe Carrier handed the pipe to the wampum bearer, who took a few puffs and passed it on. The pipe travelled around and around the circle, each man taking a few puffs until it was burned out.

As soon as the last man had dumped the ashes from the pipe bowl into the fire, everyone stood up. The Mohawk and Oneida warriors walked about, chatting like friends who had not met for a long time. Axe Carrier was deep in conversation with Black Elk and Swift Fox. After a few minutes, he raised his head and looked around. When he saw Charlotte, he pointed to her. Black Elk and Swift Fox nodded, then all three began to walk in her direction.

As they approached, Charlotte was very conscious of her painted face. To have her face coloured red, blue and green had certainly been unplanned, but when she had seen her reflection in the river, she had liked the look. Dressed like an Oneida woman, she felt herself to be part of the celebration.

"Ho! Woman of Two Worlds," Axe Carrier greeted her.

"I didn't think you would recognize me."

"I didn't, at first."

Black Elk and Swift Fox stepped forward. They were looking at her with respect, as if she had performed a brave and noble act. Each said a few words, their faces grave.

Axe Carrier interpreted. "The band elders wish to thank you for writing the letter, and so do I. They say that you are wise for one so young."

She looked at each of them in turn, meeting their level gaze. "Give them my thanks, and tell them that I shall always think of the Oneidas as my friends."

When Black Elk and Swift Fox had strolled away to speak with other warriors, Axe Carrier said, "I have brought my daughter to meet you."

He beckoned to Okwaho and the Mohawk girl.

"Drooping Flower?" Charlotte asked as the girl approached.

The girl nodded.

"My wife," said Okwaho.

Charlotte looked at Drooping Flower. Tall and big-framed, she looked as if she could paddle a canoe all day without breaking a sweat. How did this robust young woman receive the unlikely name, Drooping Flower?

"I hear about you," said Drooping Flower. "My father call you his white daughter. Okwaho call you his friend."

"Good friend," said Charlotte.

She was happy for Okwaho, yet here was a puzzle that she did not understand. According to Axe Carrier, Drooping Flower had chosen a husband nearly two years ago. Yet it could not have been Okwaho — not when Okwaho was courting Charlotte right under Axe Carrier's nose.

"Have you been married long?" she asked, hoping for enlightenment.

"Long?" Okwaho asked.

Axe Carrier explained in Mohawk.

"Ho!" Drooping Flower smiled. "We marry short. One moon."

"My daughter and Okwaho were about to leave on their wedding journey," said Axe Carrier, "when the Oneida messenger arrived at Lachine. As soon as I told them about my mission, they wanted to come along. They will travel with us as far as Carleton Island, and then go on by themselves to the Bay of Quinte, where Thayendanegea has asked the English to reserve land for the Mohawk nation."

"We go to look," said Drooping Flower. "Maybe we live there."

When Okwaho and Drooping Flower had wandered off, Charlotte said, "I didn't think Okwaho was the man Drooping Flower wanted to marry."

"He wasn't. Her first sweetheart died when smallpox wiped out his village. Drooping Flower mourned for a year; then Okwaho dried her tears."

"Did she hang a basket of biscuits outside his lodge?"

"Ha! You remember."

"Well? Did she?"

"She made twenty-four double ball biscuit loaves, and he ate every one."

"She should teach me how to make them." Charlotte paused. "Except I don't even know where my sweetheart is."

"Before leaving Lachine, I sent a messenger to Carleton Island to tell your father that I myself will bring you back. By now he has received this good news. He waits for you. Perhaps your sweetheart waits too."

She felt herself blush under the paint. "Perhaps."

"Tonight we feast and dance. Tomorrow we set off. In five days, you will see."

First came the feasting. Women raked the hot embers from around the cooking pots and removed the flat stones that served as lids, releasing the delicious smell of venison stew. There were bowls of boiled water lily bulbs, as well as wooden platters of fish, game birds and rabbit baked in clay. At the end of the feast, children passed around baskets filled with berries.

After the women had removed the remnants of feasting, an open space was cleared around the fire. A few thumps on a drum announced that the dancing was about to begin. Rattles joined in. Singers began their chant: "*Hey-ga hey a heh, hey a heh."* Axe Carrier and Okwaho left the girls and joined the other men.

The first dancers were warriors. They shuffled and stamped in a wide circle as they moved to the beat of the drum. *"Hey-ga hey a heh, hey a heh."* The chant went on and on. Around and around the dancers went. When one man left the circle, another took his place. How long was this going to last? It seemed to be never-ending. But from the intent expression on other faces, Charlotte suspected that she was the only person who found it monotonous. After a long, long time the pounding of the drums faltered and died. The warriors sat down to watch the next dancers.

A group of women stepped into the circle of light. Chi-gwi-lat and her friends were among them. This dance was different from that of the men. The women did not dance in single file, but walked around each other, swaying as they moved, twining their hands together over their heads as they met. The song that accompanied this dance had words, not just thumping syllables, though Charlotte had no key to what they meant.

"What dance is it?" she asked Drooping Flower.

"We call it Sisters of the Fields. Your body sway like the corn. Your hands make the bean vine grow up the corn."

Charlotte liked this dance. The women's graceful movements seemed to have a spiritual meaning, like the enactment of a prayer.

At the end of the women's dance, when the drumming

and singing had stopped, a hushed silence fell. Then the drum started up again, but with a different rhythm. It was louder and stronger, making the heart beat faster and the air itself pulse with the beat. Drooping Flower, her fingers drumming rhythmically on the ground, stared off into the darkness with an expectant look.

Suddenly a figure burst in upon the dancing circle with a wild yell, brandishing a war club. There was another yell, and another warrior shot forth into the firelight, his tomahawk upraised. Another followed, brandishing a spear. Then another, and another. Okwaho was among them, shouting and leaping. Above his head he waved something that looked like an embroidery hoop mounted on a pole. The piece of leather stretched on the hoop was painted half red and half black on one side. The other side was brown and bore a crest of stiff black hair with trophy feathers still attached. Charlotte shuddered. She had never seen a scalp before. Looking at it made the top of her head prickle. She glanced at Drooping Flower, whose dark eyes glittered with excitement.

It was a wild dance, with its display of charging, striking and slashing. Eight warriors, naked except for breechcloth and moccasins, circled the fire, their bodies gleaming in the firelight, their feet thumping on the hard earth. The pounding of the drums set Charlotte's blood racing.

Suddenly it was over. The drumming stopped. The warriors lowered their weapons and their trophies and returned to their places around the fire. Okwaho, glistening with sweat, joined Charlotte and Drooping Flower.

"Tonight you saw real dancing," he said.

"Yes. That was real dancing." She was glad that she had seen it, knowing that she would never see it again.

She returned to the hut moments before the old woman and Chi-gwi-lat. Lying on the bearskin with the rabbit fur blanket pulled up to her chin, Charlotte put her fingers to her face and rubbed at the greasy paint. Tomorrow she would scrub her face clean. But she knew that this day would remain in her memory long after the last trace of paint was gone.

Chapter twenty-three

C harlotte had awakened before dawn, and now she sat
on the log outside the hut watching the sunrise. Beside her, tied into a bundle, were the boy's clothes that she
had been wearing when the Oneida warriors found her. The
old woman had returned them to her. Charlotte knew that
she would never wear them again, just as she knew that she
would never again have her face painted red, green and blue.
She had had a taste of being a boy and a taste of being an
Iroquois maiden. Perhaps a little from both experiences
would cling to her. She hoped that it would. But now she
was ready to be Charlotte Hooper again.

Wolf Woman had sponged the rawhide bands that bound

Charlotte's shoulder, wetting them over and over again until they became pliable enough to unwind. While they softened, she scrubbed the paint from Charlotte's face.

When at last her arm was free, Charlotte cautiously stretched it, rotated it, shook it, and raised it high. The arm still worked, though the skin was pale and pasty and the muscles had no strength. There would be no paddling for her on the journey to Carleton Island. She could relax while others did the work.

Down by the river, Axe Carrier and another Mohawk warrior were loading the canoes. After a few minutes, Okwaho and Drooping Flower joined them. It was time to leave.

Charlotte picked up the bundle of clothes. Some youth back at the Loyalist camp would be glad to have them. But was there anything in the bundle that Chi-gwi-lat and the old woman might like? Quickly Charlotte untied it. Her knife was there in its sheath. She was surprised to see it, for she had taken for granted that the warrior who disarmed her would have kept it. Wolf Woman would be sure to value a good knife. Now what about a gift for Chi-gwi-lat? The red neckerchief? That would please her, for it matched the paint that Chi-gwi-lat used to colour the part in her hair.

Down at the river, the two canoes were already in the water.

Charlotte handed the knife to the old woman. "*Atatawi*," she said, hoping that she would understand the Mohawk word. Then Charlotte ran into the hut carrying the red neckerchief. Chi-gwi-lat still was not stirring. Charlotte lifted the girl's sleeping head to pull the neckerchief around her neck, a surprise for when she wakened. But as Charlotte was tying the ends, Chi-gwi-lat's eyes blinked open.

"Good-bye," Charlotte said. "I'll miss you."

The Oneida girl reached out her slender brown arm, touched Charlotte's cheek and murmured something that probably meant good-bye.

Sitting on a folded blanket in the bottom of the canoe, Charlotte leaned back against the centre thwart and watched the fields and towns of the Mohawk Valley roll by. It was safe to travel in broad daylight, for there was nothing suspicious about a pair of Indian canoes heading north.

Although paddling against the current, they made good progress. On the second day they passed the place where Nick's canoe had been hidden while Tom and Joe planted Mrs. Dow's potatoes. The third day was spent paddling west up the tributary of the Mohawk that would carry them toward Oneida Lake. In two more days they completed the portage to Oneida Lake, crossed the lake, and reached the Oswego River. They lost one day to rain, huddling in the shelter of the canoes while lightning flashed and thunder rolled. But the skies cleared before morning, and the river ran in sunshine again.

On the final day of her journey, the morning song of the birds wakened Charlotte. For a few minutes, she lay rolled in her blanket, listening to trills and twitters from the trees. From the camp kettle came the sweet smell of corn meal mush. Drooping Flower was already preparing breakfast. Charlotte climbed out of her blanket and joined her. Drooping Flower filled a bowl for each of them, and the two girls sat down beside the fire.

"Tonight you see father," said Drooping Flower. "You be home."

"Yes," said Charlotte doubtfully. "I'll be home."

She knew it was not true. The army tent in the Loyalist refugee camp was not home. Her old home was forever lost; her new one existed only in her mind. Yet she could picture it clearly: neatly chinked log walls, a window set with four little panes of glass, a big stone fireplace. There would be a long wooden table in the kitchen, and a cradle for the baby in a corner where it was warm but not too close to the fire. Nick would come in from the fields. Who could ask more?

"Drooping Flower, do you have a home?"

Drooping Flower pointed to Okwaho, who was still rolled up in his blanket, asleep near the canoes. "My husband. He make any place my home."

"Yes," said Charlotte, with a bit of envy. She had a further question that she had wanted to ask for days. "How did you get married? I know about the basket of biscuits. But after Okwaho ate the biscuits, did you have a ceremony, or just start living together?"

"We have marriage council."

"Please tell me about it."

Drooping Flower frowned. "I try to." She paused for a minute. "At marriage council we sit around fire. Okwaho sit one side, me other side. Man speak for Okwaho. Woman speak for me. Woman speak first. She say Drooping Flower is daughter of Turtle Clan. She say good things about me. I beautiful. I good cook. I make nice clothes. I faithful to ceremonies of our people. She tell me, be true and kind.

"Man speak for Okwaho. He say Okwaho is son of Bear Clan. He is good hunter and brave warrior. He follow teachings of elders. He know sacred dances and songs. Man tell Okwaho, be true and kind.

"Then we stand up. I have two braids that time. I throw my braids over my husband's shoulders. He give me bunch of flowers. Everybody smile. We make big feast."

"That's beautiful," said Charlotte.

Charlotte, kneeling in the bottom of the canoe, peered over the broad shoulder of the paddler in the bow. Carleton Island lay ahead. She could see the red, white and blue of the English flag. Then the tower and the top of the blockhouse came into view, and after that the Indians' huts outside the fort's walls. When she put up her hand to shadow her eyes, she saw two men standing on the shore, looking west, straight at her, or so it seemed. One appeared to be leaning on a crutch.

Why couldn't the warriors paddle faster? If she had a

paddle in her hands, the canoe would be racing like the wind. She turned around, intending to urge Axe Carrier to pick up the pace, but changed her mind. Axe Carrier was not the kind of man one told to hurry up. He even paddled with dignity.

Slowly, slowly the canoe neared the limestone landing stage. When it touched, Nick reached out, taking both her hands in his, and pulled her out of the canoe. She wrapped her arms around his neck and kissed him. It did not trouble her that Papa was watching. She would have kissed Nick in front of the King of England and the Archbishop of Canterbury too, if they had been here.

When Nick released her, she turned to her father. His face glowed as if it were lit up from within by happiness. He put his hand on her shoulder and kissed her cheek.

"Well, here you are!" He beamed, looking her up and down. "Last time I saw you, you looked like a boy, and now you're decked out like an Iroquois maiden, all beaded and fringed. When am I going to get my daughter back again?"

"You've got her, Papa."

But what about the strongbox? Did he have that back? She was afraid to ask, but Papa must have read her mind.

"Nick brought everything. The strongbox and the tea service too."

The tea service? Then Nick must have found it on the slope of the ravine.

Charlotte smiled. "Then we did not fail."

Dusk turned the lake to the colour of clouds before a storm. Charlotte sat on a rock near the water's edge, watching Nick clean a pickerel. Loose scales glistened on his fingers.

A pair of herring gulls, bobbing offshore, watched in anticipation. They looked like mates, companionable and at ease. Nick set the pickerel on a rock, slit its belly and pulled out the entrails. Then he threw the entrails to the gulls. Such a screech from both birds! The larger grabbed everything and flew away; the other pursued with squawks and screams.

Nick turned toward Charlotte. "Married life!" he laughed.

"Let it be a warning."

"I shall keep it in mind." He knelt to wash his hands. "I'll always save the guts for you."

A big fish broke the surface in a flash of silver.

"Did you see that?" said Charlotte.

After the fish had sunk beneath the surface again, the ripples moved outward in a widening circle.

"Ripples." Nick rocked back on his haunches and gazed thoughtfully. "I wonder if they go on and on forever."

"I think they do. Like memories."

The moon rose. Charlotte, Nick and Papa sat by the fire outside the tent. Papa sat on one side, Charlotte and Nick on the other, their hands touching.

After so many weeks of solitude, it seemed that Papa needed to talk. He told them about clearing his fields when he was young, trading a day's work for the loan of an ox to pull stumps. He told them about courting Mama, and about his happiness when his children were born.

"I thought that my sons . . ." A bleak look passed over his face. He turned his head sharply away. "Charlotte, I never expected that you would have to start out all over again." He got heavily to his feet. "Well, I better get some sleep and leave you young people alone." He limped into the tent.

"He's had a hard life, for so much to come to naught," said Nick. He put his arm around Charlotte, and she snuggled close, feeling how nicely her body fit against his. All day she had waited for this. She looked at his face, half veiled by darkness. He had shaved off his beard and cut his hair. Now it was only about an inch long, a blond halo in the firelight.

Nick asked, "Do you want to talk about that night?"

She understood which night he meant, and she did not want to talk about it. But there were things she needed to know.

"Just tell me what you did after I headed for the ravine."

"I climbed over the snake fence and followed you. As soon as I figured nobody could see me from the farm, I ran back and forth to confuse the trail. Everything was chaos — the house burning, dogs barking, men shouting. For a few minutes I hoped they'd have their hands too full to bother chasing me. But they did come after me — at least some of them did. I couldn't run fast carrying the strongbox. I knew they'd be right on my heels as soon as they puzzled out my trail. The only way to escape was to reach the creek and walk in the water so the dogs would lose my scent. I scrambled down the hill at the same place you and I climbed up. When I reached the creek, I waded upstream, away from the canoe. After sloshing along for about half a mile, I climbed out and hid. For a couple of hours I listened to the shouting and barking. The search never came near me. When I figured they'd given up, I went downstream to meet you at the canoe."

"But I wasn't there."

"No, you weren't there." He paused. "I didn't know where you were. You might be hurt. You might be dead. When it started to get light, I said to myself: Don't lose hope; she's hiding somewhere. Soon she'll be back. But you didn't come back. After sunrise, the search was on again. Men were crashing around in the ravine, but it didn't sound as if they'd found you."

"I don't know how long I lay unconscious. When I woke up, the sun was shining."

"The Liberty men gave up hunting for me about noon. Then I started searching again. After I'd covered the bottom of the ravine, I climbed up and walked along the rim. About half a mile from our sycamore tree, I came to some broken bushes where it looked as if someone had gone over the edge. I climbed down to investigate. It was easy to see where you'd landed. Plants crushed. The ground scuffed up. But no boot marks, so I knew the Sons of Liberty hadn't found you."

"How did you know it was me?"

"I didn't know until I found the sack with the tea set. I took it to the canoe and hid it with the strongbox. It was starting to get dark, so I stayed by the canoe all night, still hoping that you'd make your way there.

"In the morning I decided to try something different. I have friends in Johnstown, Loyalists, although they hide their politics. If you had been captured, the news would have spread fast. Trusting my disguise, I walked right into town. It was a market day, with a good crowd of people in the street. As I passed the tavern, you wouldn't believe the sight that met my eyes."

"After all that's happened, I can believe anything."

"It was Ben Warren, his head wrapped in bandages, sitting on the bench outside. Even with a tankard in his hand, he looked mighty unhappy. Three of his friends were there too, lounging about and looking sorry for themselves. They paid me no heed as I strode along the opposite side of the street, being careful not to vary my pace or look their way. But I tell you, darling, I was bursting with gratitude to see Warren alive. Thanks be to God, I had not broken my vow."

"Thanks be to God," Charlotte agreed, and she meant it. She reached up to touch Nick's cheek. "Did you speak to your friends?"

"I did. It was the talk of the town, they said, how a mob of Tories had attacked a farm near Fort Hunter, assaulted one man, and set fire to the house."

"You and I were a mob?"

"That's the word they used."

"Those Liberty men caused the fire themselves when they built up the kitchen fire, and then left it unattended."

"I reckon that's exactly what happened. But a Tory mob firing the house makes a better story." His mouth twisted in a bitter smile. "Now that I knew you hadn't been caught, I went back to the canoe and searched for the rest of the day. By nightfall, I suspected that Indians had carried you off."

"Did you think it was Oneidas?"

"An Oneida raiding party seemed the likeliest explanation. So I set out to find you."

"How did you begin? I could have been anywhere."

"Indians always camp beside water. So I set out to trace every creek and river, working my way north. My plan was to rescue you. But as soon as I saw you in that Oneida camp, sitting on a log with your shoulder bound up and your foot in a pot of water, I knew you were in no condition to run away."

"It's hard to run if you can't even walk."

"Or paddle with one shoulder tied up in rawhide. But I could see they were taking good care of you. I shadowed the camp for a couple of days, waiting for a chance to give you a sign."

"The pebble?"

"That's right. I sat in that thicket watching you. You turned the pebble over in your hand and gave such a smile I could hardly resist running to you and throwing my arms around you. Like this . . ."

He pulled her close and kissed her mouth. His warm lips

made her remember how long it had been since he last held her in his arms. The kiss lingered. Several minutes passed before she pulled away.

"Just as well you did resist," she said. "You'd be of little use to me, after they lifted your scalp."

"They nearly did catch me," Nick admitted. "I hated to leave you behind, but there was no way to rescue you. The sensible course was to return to Carleton Island and report what had happened. I didn't expect Commander Fraser to order out the garrison. The important thing was to let your father know that that you were safe."

Nick paused. His voice was husky when he spoke again. "You can imagine how I dreaded telling your father that I'd recovered his strongbox and silver but lost his daughter." Another pause. "I didn't know how to deliver that news. And then I didn't have to. By the time I reached Carleton Island, Axe Carrier's messenger had arrived."

The fire was burning low. Charlotte thought about adding more wood, but she did not want to leave Nick's side.

He continued, "What puzzles me is how you got word to Axe Carrier."

"I wrote him a letter."

Nick laughed. "You make it sound so simple."

"It was, as a matter of fact. Moses Cobman, the runaway boy I told you about, belongs to that Oneida band. He acted as interpreter when their elders questioned me. They looked mighty pleased to learn that Axe Carrier was Papa's friend.

When I had my letter written, they sent a runner to take it to Axe Carrier."

"When you told me about that boy, I thought that the Oneidas would offer him in exchange for peace."

"That nearly happened. Some of the elders were prepared to hand him over, even though he had been adopted. He didn't want to leave the band, so he's as happy as I am with the way things turned out."

He tightened his arm around her. "There's something else I want to say. When Commander Fraser learned that I was at the fort, he had an express message he wanted me to take to headquarters in Montreal."

Several seconds passed. Charlotte glanced up. "Yes?"

"While I was there . . ." He hesitated again. "I thought I might as well buy a wedding ring. You see, darling, you and I are going to be married before either of us goes anywhere again."

Chapter twenty-four

"Now? Get married now?" Papa turned to Nick. "When did you say you have to leave again?"

"In one week."

Papa shook his head. "That's no way to start a marriage, to go away in one week and leave your wife waiting in a tent."

"I'll be waiting in a tent anyway," Charlotte said. "What difference will it make whether we're married or not?"

Before Papa had a chance to answer, Nick broke in. "Sir, all we can be sure of is one week. I don't know when I'll be back. I don't know how long the war will go on. Suppose it lasts five more years. Would you expect us to wait that long?"

Papa cleared his throat. "I waited seven years for Charlotte's mother, and it's more than I would wish on anyone. You have my blessing. You must ask Commander Fraser if he'll perform the service."

"I already have," said Nick. "He'll do it tomorrow."

One day to prepare for a wedding. What should she wear? Her fringed poncho and leather skirt were new, but not right for a wedding.

The choice really came down to the two gowns she had worn on the trek from the Mohawk Valley nearly two years ago. The one gown was grey, the other blue and white. Both were the worse for wear. But the grey gown had the remains of lace at the throat. So that's the one she would wear, and with it, Mama's cameo brooch.

A pity that there could be no wedding breakfast. All that she had to share with others was her own happiness, but that she had in abundance. She and Nick and Drooping Flower also planned a small surprise, which no one else knew about.

In the morning, Louisa Vrooman, who had begged to serve as Charlotte's lady's maid, arrived at the Hoopers' tent with a silver-mounted mirror in her hand.

"Where did you get that?" Charlotte asked.

"I borrowed it from the Sergeant Major's wife."

Louisa had fine ideas for arranging Charlotte's hair. "I'll put curls about your face, then smooth your tress into a roll at the nape of your neck. That's a pretty fashion for a bride."

"Please," Charlotte said, "just braid my hair. Two simple braids is all I want."

"Are you serious?"

"Yes. I mean it."

"Well, it's your wedding." Louisa sounded disappointed but did as Charlotte asked. As soon as the two long, glossy braids lay upon Charlotte's shoulders, Louisa had a new idea. "Suppose we wind the braids around your head the way Dutch girls do."

"So I'll look like a Dutch girl?" Charlotte considered the idea. It would please Nick. "Yes. Let's do that."

"Then I'll weave in some sprigs of flowers, and you'll look like the Queen of the May."

"A Queen of the May in July?" Charlotte smiled. "It sounds lovely."

When Louisa finished and held up the looking glass, Charlotte saw in it a young lady whom she scarcely recognized.

"Well?" said Louisa. "Do you like what you see?"

Charlotte turned her head from side to side, examining from various angles the molding of her cheekbones, the curve of her lips, the line of her throat and shoulders, and the crown of hair that shone like jet sprigged with blue lobelias and red cardinal flowers. Where was the country girl with round cheeks and flyaway curls?

"I am greatly changed," Charlotte murmured. Prettier, but it wasn't just that. In her brown eyes she saw maturity.

That's me, she thought: Charlotte Hooper, who in two hours will be Mrs. Nicholas Schyler. The idea overwhelmed her. In two hours she would be a wife.

She handed the looking glass back to Louisa. "Thank you."

"Then let's be off," said Louisa as she set down the looking glass. "Your father is outside the tent ready to walk with you to the blockhouse. We must not keep the Commander waiting."

Louisa kissed Charlotte on both cheeks and started to sniffle. "Sorry," she said. "Weddings always make me cry."

It was a beautiful day for a wedding, sunny after a night of scattered showers. Holding her skirt out of the mud, Charlotte walked through the Loyalist camp with Louisa on one side and Papa on the other. Papa had brushed his clothes and powdered his hair, which added a nice touch of formality.

As they approached the blockhouse, they received a few curious stares, but not many. Although it was difficult to believe, for most people this was an ordinary day.

When the blockhouse door opened, however, the sight that greeted Charlotte was far from ordinary. The big, square room was crowded with people, not lined up waiting for rations but standing in a half circle, applauding as she entered on her father's arm.

There was Mrs. Cobman with Hope at her side, one hand clutching her mother's skirt and the thumb of the other thrust into her mouth. The two sisters, Mrs. Weegar and Mrs. Vankleek, stood surrounded by their mingled brood. Beside them were Mrs. Platto and her children, with Polly restraining a small, wriggling brother by his shirt collar. Sergeant Major Clark was at the commissary counter, but on the near side for a change. Beside him stood his wife Fidelia, holding their shawl-wrapped baby in her arms. Next, standing together, were Axe Carrier, Okwaho, and Drooping Flower, wearing not their everyday leather clothes, but the finest doeskin garments, beaded and deeply fringed. Drooping Flower held a small bunch of buttercups mixed with wild asters.

The blockhouse did not in the least resemble a church. No altar. No cross. No choir gallery. But the Hooper family Bible sat on the commissary counter, and in front of the counter stood Commander Alexander Fraser with the *Book of Common Prayer* in his hands.

What a fine figure he cut, with his red jacket, gold braid and white wig! But no one was more gallant than Nick, arrayed in a ruffled shirt and blue velvet trousers with silver buckles at the knee. (Where had he managed to borrow those?)

The Commander cleared his throat: "Dearly beloved we are gathered here together in the sight of God, and in the face of this Congregation, to join together this man and this woman in holy Matrimony..."

Charlotte heard Louisa sniffling, but that did not distract

her. Charlotte had been to other weddings, had listened to these words before. But this was her own wedding, and they held her spellbound.

The caution came next. Charlotte knew no reason why anyone would leap up to stop her from marrying Nick, but she held her breath while the Commander read, "If any man can shew just cause, why they may not be lawfully joined together, let him now speak, or else hereafter for ever hold his peace."

When nobody did, she let out a faint sigh of relief, and the Commander read on: "Nicholas, wilt thou have this woman to thy wedded wife, to live together after God's ordinance in the holy estate of matrimony. Wilt thou love her, comfort her, honour and keep her, in sickness and in health; and, forsaking all other, keep thee only unto her, so long as ye both shall live?"

Nick's answer was prompt and firm, "I will."

Now it was Charlotte's turn. Would she have this man to her wedded husband? Would she obey and serve him, love honour and keep him? At "obey" she winced, knowing herself Nick's equal in heart and mind. But he would not ask that of her. For them there would be no "give orders" or "obey," but rather a consensus of loving minds. In a voice as firm as Nick's she made her promise, "I will."

When Nick placed the simple gold band upon her finger, his eyes met hers, and she saw that he, like her, was close to tears. From this day forth, she thought, Nick is my wedded husband, and I am his wedded wife."

Then the Commander joined their hands and addressed the crowd:

"Those whom God hath joined together let no man put asunder."

All in a blur Nick and Charlotte signed their names in the register, then Louisa and Sergeant Major Clark signed as witnesses.

"Do you feel married?" Nick asked.

"Not quite."

He gave her a wink and, as they turned to face the crowd, raised his hand to make sure of everyone's attention. "There's one thing left to do," he said, and he beckoned to Drooping Flower.

With a smile, the Mohawk girl stepped forward and put her bunch of wild flowers into Nick's hands. Seeing that smile, Charlotte felt sure that Drooping Flower was remembering her own wedding council and the words spoken there. Simple words: "Be true and kind."

With a silent promise to follow those words, Charlotte pulled the pins from her hair so that the crown of braids tumbled down, and she threw her two braids over Nick's shoulders. Then he gave her the flowers. Most people looked puzzled, but everybody cheered.

Axe Carrier said to Charlotte. "Truly you are a woman of two worlds."

"Do you feel married now?" Nick asked with a smile.

She kissed him, "I believe I do."

Now Papa placed his hand upon the Hoopers' family Bible, which sat on the commissary counter. He opened it to the page that bore the heading:

FAMILY REGISTER

At the top of the page in spidery letters were the names of Daniel Hooper and Margaret Ann Henderson, married in 1694. Then came the names of all their children with the dates when they were born and when they had died. The marriage of Papa's parents was recorded, and Papa's own birth: Henry John Hooper, born 1721. Then came the births of his brothers and sisters, and for some the dates when they had died. The marriage of Henry John Hooper to Martha Ruth Riley was in the record: June 1753, followed by the births of James, Charles, Isaac and Charlotte. The last entries were all deaths. James, Charles and Isaac in October 1777. Martha in December 1778.

Charlotte, standing with Papa's hands on her shoulders, silently read all the names. These people were her family — all those people who had come before her, who had been born, been married, raised children of their own, and died.

"What do those marks on paper mean?" asked Okwaho.

"Those are names," Axe Carrier said. "This is the way white people carry the past into the future, so that the power of names is not lost."

Papa opened a jar of writing fluid and picked up the quill

from its holder on the commissary counter. Carefully he made a new entry:

Charlotte Jane Hooper and
Nicholas John Schyler married July 25, 1779.

He sprinkled sand to dry the writing fluid, and in a moment blew it away.

Charlotte turned the page, and then another page, and another.

"Look at how many pages are still blank," she said. "It will take a hundred years to fill them all."

She felt Nick's arm around her waist, pulling her towards him.

"At least a hundred years," said Nick. "We'd better get started."

Charlotte looked around. About her were friendly faces: some coppery brown and some white, some smiling and some solemn. They all parted to make way for the newlyweds as they walked towards the door.

When Charlotte stepped outside, she felt the sunshine on her face. Even the sky smiled upon her wedding day. Beyond the palisade lay green forests and great lakes.

She tucked her arm in Nick's and realized suddenly that she was home.

ABOUT THE AUTHOR

 Jean Rae Baxter grew up in Hamilton, but "down home" was the region of Essex and Kent Counties on the shores of Lake Erie where her ancestors had settled, some following the American Revolution and some a century earlier, in the days of New France. There were many family stories to awaken her interest in Canada's past, and frequently the lives of settlers were interwoven with those of many different First Nation peoples. Following university, she worked in radio before becoming a teacher. She has written a variety of short stories. *The Way Lies North* is her first novel. For many years she lived in Eastern Ontario, but has now returned to Hamilton, where she devotes herself to writing and to a charming Scottish terrier named Robbie.

MEMBER OF SCABRINI GROUP

Québec, Canada
2007